ALSO BY DON MANN WITH RALPH PEZZULLO

Seal Team Six: Hunt the Wolf

Seal Team Six: Hunt the Scorpion

Inside SEAL Team Six

SEAL TEAM SIX

HUNT THE FALCON

DON MANN
WITH RALPH PEZZULLO

MULHOLLAND
BOOKS
HODDER

First published in Great Britain in 2013 by Mulholland Books
An imprint of Hodder & Stoughton
An Hachette UK company

1

A CIP catalogue record for this title is available from the British Library

Trade Paperback ISBN 978 1 444 76906 7
eBook ISBN 978 1 444 76907 4

Printed and bound by CPI Group (UK) Ltd, Croydon, CR0 4YY

Hodder & Stoughton policy is to use papers that are natural,
renewable and recyclable products and made from wood grown in sustainable
forests. The logging and manufacturing processes are expected to conform
to the environmental regulations of the country of origin.

Hodder & Stoughton Ltd
338 Euston Road
London NW1 3BH

www.hodder.co.uk

"We make war that we may live in peace."

—Aristotle

*To all servicemen, servicewomen, CIA employees,
and diplomats who have shed their blood
so the rest of us can live in peace*

SEAL TEAM SIX: HUNT THE FALCON

CHAPTER ONE

*Let me not pray to be sheltered from dangers, but to be
fearless in facing them.*
                                    —Rabindranath Tagore

JOHN AND Lenora Rinehart had just watched their thirteen-
year-old son Alex dress himself for the first time. It was a
special morning. Usually days at the Rinehart house started
with a delicate dance, determined by their son's moods.

Just because his son Alex was autistic didn't mean he
wasn't smart, John Rinehart reminded himself as his shoes
met the uneven surface of the slate walk and he punched
the electronic button that opened the door to his dark blue
Saab 900. His son was exceptional in the IQ department.
But his brain's ability to control the warp-speed flow of information, and his emotional impulses, was out of whack.
When it didn't work the way Alex wanted it to, the boy got
frustrated. And when he got frustrated, he got mad as hell.
Screaming, beat-the-shit-out-of-whatever-he-could-get-his-
hands-on angry sometimes.

Ask him to find the positive difference of the fourth power

of two consecutive positive integers that must be divisible by one more than twice the larger integer? No problem. But little things like buttoning a shirt or fastening a zipper often tripped him up.

"Little things…little victories," forty-two-year-old John Rinehart said as he reached across the console between the front seats and squeezed his wife Lena's hand.

She smiled past the straight black bangs that almost brushed her eyes and said, "I credit Alex's new school. It's been a major positive."

"Yes," John whispered back. His heart felt like it might leap out of his chest with delight.

John felt things strongly. Like his son. Sometimes so strongly that it scared him and he, too, had to fight hard to control himself.

His half-Asian wife was the more emotionally balanced of the two. She understood that tomorrow morning might be completely different; that life with a child like Alex was unpredictable at best.

John found it much harder to let go of the hope that his son would one day lead a normal life. He kept looking for a path, or an unopened doorway in his son's psyche, that would lead to that result. Which made sense, because part of what he did for a living as the economic counselor at the U.S. embassy was to look for patterns of activity and use them to try to predict future events—Chinese-Thai trade, baht volatility, Thai-U.S. trading algorithms.

He was a brilliant man who studied the world and saw tendencies, vectors, roads traveled, like the one he steered the highly polished car onto now, into the knot of cars, trucks, motorcycles, and bicycles on what the Thais called Thanon Phetchaburi.

He'd learned to expect the eight-mile ride to the embassy to take forty minutes because of the traffic, but he didn't mind. It gave him and his wife a chance to listen to music and spend some quiet time together.

This morning he didn't want to think about the embassy where she also worked, as an administrative assistant in the CIA station. Nor did he want to consider the problems he'd deal with when he got there.

Instead he listened as Stan Getz played a smooth, moving "Body and Soul" over the stereo, and he hummed along, feeling unusually optimistic and calm. He even entertained the possibility that when his tour in Thailand ended in a year, he would return to teaching. Maybe even accept the position on the faculty of University of California, Berkeley that had been offered him a little while back. Lena would like that.

The sky above was a murky, almost iridescent yellow. Bangkok was a surreal blend of staggeringly beautiful and disgusting, rich and poor, spiritual and depraved, all living pressed together. He found the yin-yang dynamic of the city fascinating.

Adjusting the air-conditioning, he turned to his wife. "I'm proud of you, darling," he said.

"I'm proud of *you*. And Alex, too."

"Our Alex," he added.

Through the windshield John noticed a battered blue truck squeezing into the little space between his front bumper and the Nissan taxi four feet to the right. He applied the brake, hit the horn, then turned to his wife.

He noticed the way the light accentuated her cheekbones, then out of the corner of his right eye glimpsed a motorcycle near the back bumper. Two helmets, both black with mirrored visors. The driver and rider looked like aliens.

Past the soaring saxophone solo and through the soundproof door panels, he heard a metal click. Seconds later the motorcycle roared past, narrowly avoiding a bus.

He was thinking about the first time he had seen Lena, standing near the entrance to the Georgetown University library. She was a sophomore; he was pursuing a master's degree in economics.

He remembered how he had stopped to ask her for directions to White-Gravenor Hall even though he knew where it was. And how when she turned, he was struck by her beauty, and the strength and intelligence in her eyes.

John Rinehart opened his mouth to tell Lena how he had felt at that moment, how certain he had been that something important was happening. But before he could get the words out, the small but powerful explosive device that had been magnetically attached to the car's rear fender exploded, tearing through the chassis, igniting the high-octane fuel in the gas tank and causing the car to burst into flames.

John and Lenora Rinehart were dead within seconds. Another eight poor souls riding bicycles and motorbikes in the vicinity also died. Twenty-three were seriously injured.

Before Thai police officials had finished their inspection of the site and carted away the wreckage of the Saab 900, a similar magnetic device had killed a U.S. military attaché and his assistant in their car a half mile away. That same day bombs placed by riders on motorcycles killed fifteen more U.S. and Israeli officials in Rome, Athens, Mumbai, and Cairo.

The pain the bombings caused was incalculable—children denied fathers, wives turned into widows, friends and colleagues left questioning their faith in God.

Alex Rinehart, on hearing the news that his parents had been killed, retreated inside himself and refused to talk.

That night, 2,410 miles northwest of Bangkok, Navy SEAL Team Six leader Thomas Crocker wiped the snow from the goggles fastened to his FAST Ballistic Helmet and adjusted the seventy-five-pound pack on his back.

"This remind you of anything, boss?" his blond commo man, Davis, asked in a gravelly voice behind him, little icicles clinging to the half-inch reddish growth on his jaw and chin.

"*The Nightmare Before Christmas*?" Crocker replied as he retaped the straps on his backpack so they wouldn't make noise as he approached the target. His left hand burned from a frigid wind that whistled through the craggy rocks along the ridge in southeastern Afghanistan.

"K2," Davis said, referring to a training climb Crocker had taken the team on, during which a female friend of his had died in an avalanche. Then, noticing that his chief's left hand was bare, he asked, "What happened to your glove?"

"Lost it attending to Dog." Dog, a.k.a. Timothy L. Douglas, was the new guy who had just completed Green Team. He trudged ahead of them favoring his left leg and carrying "the pig"—SEALspeak for the MK43 Mod 0 machine gun, which Crocker preferred to call "the nasty."

Dog, a former middle linebacker at the University of Tennessee, had slipped about a half mile back as they were climbing and ripped a foot-long gash in his right thigh, which Crocker had bandaged up.

"I got a spare pair," Davis said, white fog shooting from his mouth and mixing with the condensation around them. He removed a pair of black cold-weather gloves from his drop leg pouch and handed them to Crocker.

"Colder than a witch's tit," the team leader groaned, shaking his exposed hand to keep the blood moving, then slipping them on. "Thanks."

He was leading twelve men, all SEALs from Team Six, who had been at Jalalabad Airfield chilling, listening to music, playing video games, reading, sleeping, shooting the shit, when the urgent message came over the radio that Observation Post Memphis (OPM) was under attack. Two things made this significant and alarming: One, the difficulty of the terrain in the middle of the Hindu Kush range combined with the blizzard made it impossible to reinforce the post by air or provide it with any sort of air support. People who had been to OPM referred to it as being "on the dark side of the moon." And two, five operators from Six had been dispatched to the post a week earlier and were now trapped and fighting for their lives, along with a dozen marines, several national guardsmen from Pennsylvania, and a platoon of soldiers from the U.S. Army's 17th Infantry Alpha Company.

As a general rule, when teammates are under attack, you don't sit back at base with your thumb up your ass.

Adding to Crocker's sense of duty was the fact that one of the Team Six operators fighting for his life in OPM was his running partner Neal Stafford—a former cowboy from

Waco, Texas, with two wild young boys and a lovely wife named Alyssa, who was the best friend of Crocker's wife, Holly. Crocker's teenage daughter Jenny babysat for their kids.

All of this explained why Crocker had sought out the one helicopter pilot from the 160th Special Operations Aviation Regiment (SOAR) who was crazy enough to brave the fifty-mile-an-hour gusts and drop them off as high up the mountain as possible, and why they had slowly been picking their way through the snow, ice, and rocks like goats. The 160th SOAR was also known as the Night Stalkers. Their motto: Night Stalkers don't quit.

Coming up the other side—the east side—was out of the question, since the whole Kunar Valley, and most of Nuristan Province, was firmly under Taliban control, and had been for over a year. Most Americans weren't aware that this part of Afghanistan was called the Islamic Emirate of Afghanistan and flew a white flag with a mujahideen call-to-arms slogan scrawled on it.

Which begged the question Crocker had been asking himself for hours: what the fuck was OPM doing there in the first place? Someone in Jalalabad had told him that a general had it built to monitor traffic along one of the most important access roads to Kabul. Another person had told him that Iranians had been seen in the area.

Was OPM monitoring the movement of arms, heroin, Taliban fighters? Where was that general now? Sitting in some warm room with his feet up watching college football?

Crocker stopped himself. It didn't matter now. All he cared about were the lives of the SEALs and other soldiers trapped at OPM, and helping to fight back the Taliban assault until the storm abated and rescue helicopters could pull them out.

Judging from the unrelenting ferocity of the storm, that might be a while.

Crocker held up his right fist, indicating to the men that he wanted them to huddle around him. Facing him were twelve grizzled faces caked with ice and snow. Aside from his core five, which included Davis (commo), Ritchie (demolitions), Mancini (equipment and weapons), Cal (sniper), and Akil (maps and logistics), there were machine gunners Dog and Yale, Gabe, Langer, Jake, Chauncey, and Phillips.

"How you doing, Dog?" Crocker asked over the muffled sounds of warfare echoing up from the other side of the mountain.

"Hurtin' a little and embarrassed, but ready to kick some ass."

"I like that attitude."

As long as Dog was physically and mentally strong enough to set up and operate the twenty-pound, gas-operated, belt-fed, air-cooled killing machine (capable of firing as many as fourteen 7.62 caliber rounds per second) he cradled in his arms, Crocker didn't care how much discomfort he was in. To his mind, pain was weakness leaving the body.

"Refuel. Rehydrate," Crocker barked. "In a few minutes we're gonna reach the top of this ice cube and enter the shit. I want us all to stick together until I say otherwise. Maintain three-sixty security. Visibility is terrible. I don't want us shooting at one another. Any questions? Any problems?"

Several of the SEALs shook their heads.

Cal, the sniper, spoke up. "This peashooter ain't gonna do a whole lot of good in this weather, boss," he said, slapping the MK11 Mod 0 sniper weapons system he carried slung across his back.

"Manny's got an extra MP7. He'll lend it to you. Right, Manny?"

"A round of beers at the Guadalajara when we get back," Mancini said. The Guadalajara was a popular watering hole close to the SEAL base in Virginia Beach.

"With nachos," Ritchie added.

Crocker said, "Davis, call the post commander. Tell him we're approaching from the northwest ridge."

A marine corporal back at Jalalabad had explained to him that the only possible land approach to OPM was along the northwest ridge, then down rope ladders that had been rigged along the rocks that formed the back wall of the base.

"Roger, boss," Davis responded.

Guys squeezed energy gel into their mouths, wolfed down energy bars, and gulped water from their CamelBaks. Crocker checked his Garmin 450t GPS with a preloaded 3-D map of the area and confirmed that they were within four hundred yards of the observation post. Visibility was so bad he couldn't see more than four feet ahead.

Davis pointed at him, and seconds later a transmission from the marine major in charge of OPM blared through the F3 radio transmitter in Crocker's helmet.

"Tango-six-two, this is Memphis-five-central. I thank the Holy Father for your assistance. Condition double-red here. Need medevac, immediate support. Taking heavy casualties. Two of our guard stations have already been overrun!"

Crocker thought it was both strange and alarming that

Neal Stafford was at the post. Last time he had seen him he was halfway around the world, tossing a miniature football to his two young sons on the front lawn of his house in Virginia. Now, as he considered how Neal's safety might affect Neal's family and the tender network of relationships and emotions that connected Neal's life to his own, he felt a responsibility to get him out of OPM unharmed.

"Memphis-five-central, we'll soon be approaching along the northwest ridge," Crocker responded. "Alert your perimeter. Is the path clear? Over." He'd been trained to compartmentalize his feelings in order to effectively do this job.

"Tango-six-two, we're under attack from the east and the south. Keep following the ridge. I'll send two men out to meet you. They'll disarm the alarms and show you the way down. Do you copy?"

"Copy, Memphis. Have them whistle. Three short blasts in succession, so we know it's them."

"Three short whistles. Copy, Tango. Welcome and Godspeed. Over and out."

Crocker saw the wary look on some of the men's faces and barked, "Be sure to stay alert and stick together!"

"And don't feed the trolls," Akil added.

"You've got the wrong continent," Mancini growled back. "Trolls are mythological beings from Scandinavian folklore."

Akil shook his head. "Are you serious?"

"Yes, I'm serious. When you say shit, get it right."

Crocker had taken a mere twenty steps along the snow-covered trail at the top of the ridge when the first rounds of automatic fire whizzed by, and he shouted to his men to hold fire and take cover behind nearby rocks and boulders. Then the firing picked up and was augmented by a barrage of missiles, mortars, and propelled grenades.

Pieces of hot metal hissed into the snow and ice. Explosions lit up the craggy landscape nearby, but visibility was still limited.

Crocker was high on adrenaline. His mind worked at warp speed, measuring distance, speed, the sequence of information, and making calculations. Something was very wrong.

"Should we return fire, boss?" asked Davis, crouched to his right.

"Negative!" Crocker shouted.

From somewhere behind him Dog muttered, "This situation is double fucked."

"Double fucked or not, we'll accomplish the mission." Then Crocker spoke into his headset: "Hold your fire. We don't want to give away our position. Pull back to the other side of the ridge."

He was referring to the one they had recently climbed. On their way up they had followed a snow-covered trail, and now they literally clung to ice-covered rocks as they moved parallel to the ridge. The muscles in their arms and legs burned as they struggled to maintain balance while carrying roughly a hundred pounds of equipment on their backs. Akil led the way, carefully stepping from one toehold to another, in a generally southeastern direction, keeping his head down to avoid the rocks, snow, ice, and hot metal flying past.

"Tango-six-two this is Memphis-five-central. Report your position!" screamed the voice in Crocker's headset. "Tango-six-two, report!" The fear in it was palpable.

He wished he could tell the major to hold his shit together.

Instead he said sternly, "We're proceeding, Memphis-five-central. Over and out."

A large explosion shook the top of the mountain, dislodging an icy boulder that tumbled and hit another outcropping of rock with a large smash, splitting the boulder in two. A refrigerator-sized piece spun toward the spot where Dog, Phillips, and Jake were standing.

"Watch out!" Crocker screamed.

The men had little room to maneuver, and there was nothing the other SEALs could do but watch the massive hunk of rock glance off the backs of their three teammates, who had pressed themselves against the snow and ice.

Time slowed down. Jake froze, his legs went limp, and he fell backward. Phillips stretched his arms out and caught him. Dog's whole body twisted violently to the left. Crocker saw the acute agony on his face, then watched as the MK43 Mod 0 machine gun flew out of his arms and disappeared into the shower of falling snow. He didn't even hear it land. Could have ended up hundreds or even thousands of feet below.

Gone. Not that Crocker was worried about the weapon as he squeezed past Mancini, Davis, and Chauncey, reaching for the emergency medical pack at the back of his waist and looking down at Jake lying on the narrow ledge, his blue eyes frozen and staring into space as Phillips tried to remove Jake's backpack.

"Don't!" Crocker said.

"But—"

"Don't touch him!"

"Sir, he's breathing but can't speak."

"He's in shock," Crocker replied, feeling along Jake's neck

for a pulse and finding it higher than normal. He knelt in the snow and carefully reached under Jake's backpack to the place below his neck where the rock had struck. There was swelling and loose, dislocated bone under the skin. Damage to some of the vertebrae.

"Tango-six-two this is Memphis-five-central. Report your position!" the army major from OPM screamed in Crocker's headset.

Ignoring him, Crocker turned to Phillips. "Help me lay Jake on his side and wrap him in some Kevlar blankets," he said. "He can't be moved. You hear me? Don't move him!"

"Yes, sir. You want me to stay with him?"

The major from OPM screeched again, "Tango-six-two this is Memphis-five-central. Do you copy? Report!"

"Yeah, I copy!" Crocker barked into his helmet mike.

Panic was dangerous. Phillips touched Crocker's arm and whispered, "Sir, you want me to remain with Jake?"

The sounds of combat had moved farther down the mountain to the approximate location of OPM. The Taliban had stopped directing fire at the ridge.

Crocker waved Mancini over and said, "Manny, go back the way we came. First reconnoiter the ridge. If it's clear, retake it. If there are a number of Taliban there, call and inform me. We can't let the enemy hold that position."

"No, boss, we can't. If we do, I believe the base will be surrounded."

"Which will make it real tough for us to fight our way in."

"Roger that."

"Take three men with you, and let me know."

"Got it."

He looked down at Jake again, then watched Phillips carefully slipping a Kevlar blanket under him. A gust of wind rushed up the side of the mountain, creating what sounded like a wolf's howl.

A voice in his head reminded him that Phillips had previously asked him a question. He squeezed Phillips's arm and said, "Yes, I want you to stay with him." Phillips's long, narrow face reminded Crocker of a marine he had served with in Okinawa, who fell in love with and married a Filipino prostitute—something straight-arrow Phillips would never do.

Phillips looked up with calm, intelligent, light-brown eyes. "You want me to try to monitor his vital signs, sir?"

"Every ten minutes or so, try at least to check his pulse. If it gets below sixty or over a hundred beats a minute, let me know."

"Will do, chief."

Crocker scooted over to Dog. Dog was leaning against the side of the mountain holding his left shoulder, which was hanging at an odd angle. A rocket whizzed overhead and Crocker instinctively ducked. For a second he forgot he was in Nuristan Province, Afghanistan—the setting of one of his favorite movies, *The Man Who Would Be King*, and throughout history a very dangerous place to be.

Who wants to be king now? he asked himself, looking at Dog, whose head was turned away from Crocker. The Tennessean's stocky body trembled. Crocker whispered his name, and when Dog turned, Crocker saw tears streaming down his freckled face.

"Fucking new-guy bad luck," Dog snarled through small, gritted teeth. "I'm sorry."

"For what?" Crocker asked, inspecting Dog's shoulder.

"Letting go of the pig."

"Fuck the pig. Bite into this," Crocker said, handing Dog a thick square of rubber he kept in a plastic bag in his emergency medical kit.

"Why?"

"Bite on it and tell me something: Who was quarterback at UT when you played there?"

"What—" Dog's answer was interrupted by an unbelievable jolt of pain as Crocker pulled Dog's right arm away from his shoulder, then forcefully pushed it up and into the socket with a pop.

"*ELI-FUCKING-MANNING!*"

Happier tears streamed from Dog's blue eyes as he lifted his arm and realized that his shoulder worked again and was almost pain free.

"You're a lucky man," Crocker said in a low voice.

"Thank you," Dog responded, removing the piece of rubber from his mouth, wiping it on his sleeve, then handing it back.

"Grab an extra weapon from someone."

"Right away."

"Let's go kill some fucking Taliban."

Crocker joined Akil at the front of the column. The barrel-chested Egyptian American former marine raised his arm and pointed out a route he had just explored, which he said would take them along the top of the mountain up to the ridge.

That's when Mancini's voice came over his headset. "Boss, Mancini. We've taken the position. All secure. Advise."

"Hold, Manny. As well as you can, try to protect the north-west access."

"Roger."

"Holler if you see any enemy activity."

"What's your location?" Mancini asked.

"We're proceeding south."

Crocker and the remaining six crossed three hundred yards until they were directly above OPM. There they assembled behind a low wall blanketed with snow. Since visibility was still terrible, Crocker blew three times into the whistle he kept on a chain around his neck.

Someone to his right whistled back. He rose with his HK416 ready and tried peering through the swirling mass of snow. In a crouch he proceeded another five feet, until he saw a blurry dark shape standing beside a collapsed stone wall.

"You Chief Crocker?" the voice asked through wind.

"That's right, who are you?"

"Lance Corporal Novak, sir, of Alpha Company. Welcome to OP Memphis, otherwise known as the House of Blues."

CHAPTER TWO

If you're going through hell, keep going.
                                        —Winston Churchill

SEVERAL TENSE, difficult minutes later, minutes spent climbing down a rope ladder and sliding down the face of slippery rocks, the seven SEALs arrived in Station Presley, the post's main building and observation point, built on a narrow finger of rock that jutted over the Kunar Valley. The structure was roughly twenty-five by fifteen feet, built of rough-hewn logs, stone, and concrete, reinforced with metal Conex panels and sandbags.

The room itself was a chaotic mess strewn with the debris of battle. Twin M2HGs and an M240 .50 caliber machine gun fired at Taliban attackers below and to the right, spitting hot casings onto the concrete floor, which was slick with blood, spilled oil, and water. About a dozen soldiers crouched before slits in the forward wall, firing M4s, M5s, M27s, MP7s, and HK416s. Others, including an Afghan, screamed over the pounding of weapons into radios. Two army medics attended to the wounded, which included a young African American who had been hit in the face.

The noise was deafening. The cordite in the air made it hard to breathe. The desperation of the men fighting was real and contagious.

Crocker was relieved to learn from Captain Jason Battier that Presley's location made it extremely difficult to assault from above or below. The SEALs had just spent six hours climbing a mountain, then sliding down a rock slope to reach it from the west. Its east side, which faced the valley, fell off into two thousand feet of sheer cliff. About a hundred feet below and two hundred feet south of Presley sat another small grassy plateau that housed two barracks, known as King and Wolf.

At the foremost tip of that plateau another rocky cliff descended an additional hundred feet to a U-shaped band of land that swept around the entire east, north, and south faces of the promontory.

"Where's the officer in charge?" Crocker asked.

Battier pointed to a body at the back of the room covered with a sheet of blue plastic.

"But I just spoke to him."

"About two minutes 'fore you got here," he said in a thick Cajun accent, "he caught a round in the head."

Captain Battier continued, explaining that the narrow U-shaped band of land below was the location of the post's four guard stations, named A, B, C, and D. Stations A and B—directly below Presley and to the left—had taken the brunt of the initial Taliban attack, which had been launched approximately seven hours ago. Both A and B had recently been overrun, resulting in the death of six Pennsylvania national guardsmen, five marines, six members of the army's Alpha Company, and an undetermined number of Afghan National Army (ANA) soldiers.

"Where's the hottest action now?" Crocker asked.

"The Taliban are directing everything at Stations C and D. Once they fall, they'll have easy access to King and Wolf, to our right," Battier said, pointing to a chart on the wall. "Once King and Wolf go, we're fucked."

He was a wiry, tall fellow with a prominent nose and several days' worth of light brown growth on his face. His camouflage-covered FAST Ballistic Helmet was pulled low over long, narrow eyes.

"They're not going to fall," Crocker said.

"Why?"

"We won't let 'em."

"Okay."

"How many men do you have fighting at Stations C and D, and what are you planning to do to reinforce them?"

An RPG round glanced off the roof and exploded, stinging their ears.

Captain Battier shook his head as if to get it to restart and pointed to his right. "How many men we got out there? Fifteen maybe. Another five or six injured. Three dead. But as you can see, chief, we're spread so thin. I only got eight men guarding King and Wolf. That's where our supplies are. Maybe we should think of pulling back."

"We're not pulling back. Who's in charge down there?"

"Marine Staff Sergeant Perez. A tough Chicano, former gangbanger from East L.A. Crazy motherfucker."

Crocker said, "I need you to send a medic and a couple of soldiers to retrieve an injured teammate of mine."

"Where?"

"I'll draw a map."

As they conversed, an Afghan officer in a crisp green uniform spoke into a push-pull radio. "Who's he?" Crocker asked.

"He's our ANA coordinator. His name is Major Jawid Mohammed. We call him Weed."

"How many men does he have here?" Crocker asked, noting that Weed was a handsome man of about five feet seven, with a short black beard and, like most Afghans, compelling eyes.

"Weed? Shit, I don't know. Yo, Weed, how many men you got?"

The Afghan frowned when he heard Battier's question, clutched the radio under his arm, and held up eight fingers.

"That all?" Crocker asked.

"About fifteen of 'em ran soon as the battle started," Battier answered.

"What's Jalalabad telling you about the storm?" Crocker asked.

Another rocket-launched grenade exploded into the south wall, throwing back two marines who had been firing through the closest port window and sending smoke and shards of rock and wood flying inside.

Crocker helped one of the marines to his feet. He had several long splinters of wood stuck in his face, which made him look like a character from a slasher movie. "You know where you are, son?" Crocker asked.

"Does it matter?" the marine grunted back. He retrieved his weapon, returned to his position, and resumed firing.

The second marine was sitting up and shaking his head. He asked no one in particular, "Don't these people ever fucking stop?" An army medic knelt beside him and gave him water.

"The weather's bad, chief," Battier said. "Not looking good at all. Jalalabad is saying another four hours minimum before they can launch a single drone. Six, seven maybe before a bird can make it up here. Four more hours, we'll all be dead."

Crocker grabbed the front of his camouflage jacket. "Don't talk like that. You hear me?"

"Chief?"

Technically the captain outranked him. In spite of that Crocker growled, "Man up, Captain. Your men are counting on you."

"Yes."

Crocker motioned to Akil to join them. Then, nodding toward Weed, who continued talking into the radio, he asked, "Who's he talking to?"

Akil listened and answered, "He's speaking in some strange local dialect, boss. I don't know."

"Any idea what he's saying?"

Crocker imagined for a moment that he heard the blades of an approaching helicopter, but it was the *pop-pop-pop* of one of the big guns.

"I think he's talking about us," Akil answered. "You know, the arrival of seven more Americans."

Crocker nodded, then turned to Battier and said, "My men

and I are going down below to relieve Stations C and D. I'm counting on you to keep order up here. Concentrate your fire on the enemy attacking C and D."

Battier said, "Okay, chief. But how are you planning to get there?"

"The fastest way possible," Crocker responded, pulling on his pack and grabbing his HK416.

Battier said, "Jonesy's our best climber. He'll show you. Jonesy, yo!"

A tall African American kid with a shaved head stopped firing his MK19 automatic grenade launcher, walked over, and removed the purple plastic plugs from his ears. "What's up, Captain?"

"I need you to take Chief Crocker and his men down the chute to Station C."

"The chute, for sure. You bad boys ready?"

"Hell, yes!"

The SEALs reentered the wet and bitter cold weather. Snow continued to blow in all directions. Blasts and automatic arms fire echoed from the valley below.

"Follow me," Jonesy said, walking with an M27 resting on his shoulder as if he was taking a stroll in the woods.

"I like this guy," Akil commented to Crocker, who was thinking ahead, trying to cobble a plan together.

Jonesy spoke as he walked. "Mofos musta been planning this assault for some time, waiting for the first big winter storm. The major, he thought he'd been building up good relations with the elders in the village. All the time, they been aiding the Taliban. Now he's dead. Mofos must have been assembling in that damn village, man, storing weapons and supplies, 'cause that's where they attacked us from."

Beyond two large pine trees they arrived at the edge of the cliff and a narrow gully in the rock. In warmer weather, it probably carried water, Crocker thought. He couldn't see where the natural gully ended; fog and snow had reduced visibility to less than three yards.

"How far does it descend?" he asked Jonesy.

The skinny soldier hitched up his camouflage pants and answered, "Over a hundred yards. Most of the way down to Station C."

Jonesy shook the snow off a plastic cover, lifted it off, then picked up a large coil of rope, which he heaved into the gully. The end of it was tied to a U-shaped pipe that had been cemented into the rock.

"You guys are SEALs, right?" he asked. "Then this kinda shit is probably like pissing in a pot to you. You want me to lead the way?"

"Sure," Crocker answered. "We'll be right behind you."

As he pulled on a pair of worn leather gloves, Jonesy said, "Somebody's gotta stay behind and pull this sucker up so the Tal-i-bads can't use it."

Crocker turned to Dog and barked, "You're not gonna be able to do this with your shoulder, so on my signal, pull up the rope."

"Yes, chief."

Jonesy spit into his gloves, made sure the M27 was strapped securely across his back and shoulder, grabbed the rope, and started to shimmy down. Crocker went second, followed by Akil, Davis, Ritchie, Cal, and Yale.

Twelve feet down they entered a cloud of mist so thick Crocker couldn't see Jonesy in front of him. All he heard was the hiss of snow and dull percussions in the distance. The scene reminded him of dreams he'd had as a kid, and similarly thrilling experiences skydiving through clouds. There was something exhilarating about not knowing what was coming next.

At twenty feet he heard the explosion. *Wham!* It hurt his ears and sent pieces of rock flying, crashing into him. Still, he managed to hold on to the rope.

Jonesy screamed, "Mofos! Stupid mofos! Why you gotta be pissing me off?"

A voice overlapped in Crocker's headset. "Boss. Boss!"

Secondary explosions followed, thankfully none of them as close. Bullets flew their way, loose rock falling on top of them, hitting their shoulders, backs, and helmets.

"Boss! Boss, what the fuck?"

"Down!" he shouted at Jonesy. "Fast-rope down!"

His feet and hands eased up on the rope and he started flying down fast, still surrounded by fog, trying to count the distance in his head. Twenty feet, thirty, forty, fifty, sixty, seventy. At eighty he started to tighten his grip around the line.

Into the mike in his headset, he shouted, "Slow down at eighty feet. Remember to slow down!"

The rope burned through his gloves. The heat and pain was intense by the time he emerged from the mist and saw ground, and Jonesy rolling onto a patch of moss-covered dirt.

"Hit the ground and roll!" he exclaimed into the mike before he hit, lowering his head and shoulder, and executing a modified parachute landing fall, popping up into a crouch. He spotted Jonesy waving him over to a group of boulders that formed a natural wall.

The enemy were still directing their fire above them into the gully. Crocker suspected that the Afghan major with the push-pull radio might have something to do with it.

He helped the remaining five and directed them to where Jonesy waited. Over the radio he ordered Dog to pull up the fast-rope, then joined the group huddled behind the rock. The sounds of battle were crisper and closer—so close he could make out men shouting in a foreign language.

Jonesy said, "The Taliban's about a hundred yards in front of us. Station C stands over there to the right."

Crocker turned and looked in the direction of a smooth rock that rose like the back of a blue whale. Beyond it sat a higher patch of land that was barely visible. Through wisps of fog and a patch of low shrubs, he thought he saw the top of a flat, fortlike structure.

"That it?"

"You got it, boss. We're kinda behind the freakin' Tal-i-bad lines."

The fresh, piney smell reminded Crocker of happier times, in the White Mountains of New Hampshire where he spent summer vacations as a kid. He turned to Davis. "Get Sergeant Perez on the horn and tell him we're approaching north-northwest."

"Roger."

"Follow me." This wasn't the first time he'd rushed into something blind. He hoped it wouldn't be the last.

He ran in a low crouch until he reached the slick, smooth surface of the rock, and holding on to it, started to scurry upward on all fours. Tough going. Every foot gained was a struggle. He was out of breath by the time he reached the top and spotted the shrubs ahead. Beyond them and to the right he saw the backs of three men wearing black turbans. One was kneeling on the ground setting up a machine gun.

Crocker aimed his HK416 and raked fire across their backs, left to right, then left again into the slumping, twitching bodies. One shouted an oath to Allah that echoed past him.

Akil, Jonesy, and Cal hurried up behind him.

"What the fuck was that?" one of them exclaimed, interrupted by the clank and clatter of metal against rock. Crocker located the grenade and pointed at it. Together they sprinted, then dove to the opposite side of a berm and hit the ground.

Crocker felt his chin crash into the ground as snow entered his nose and mouth. The explosion lifted his chest and belly into the air. Shards of metal fell around him as he hit earth again and saw stars.

A big gun was pounding. It seemed to be firing from a position closer to the cliff. His head spinning, he tried to lift himself up as voices called, "Chief! Chief!" Couldn't tell who it was, but he realized it had to be coming over his headset. When he reached for the mike, he realized his helmet had been pushed back off his head. He was trying to adjust it when he noticed Akil pointing at him. A third man Crocker didn't know was standing with him. Jonesy hurried over and helped him up.

The stranger said, "You can't rest now, sir. You'll miss all the fun."

Some fun.

The man looked Hispanic—high cheekbones, a tribal tattoo on his neck. He said, "Chief Crocker, Sergeant Chino Perez." His two gold front teeth gleamed in the muted light.

"You with us?"

"Fuck, yeah."

Crocker still felt woozy, but he managed to run with them toward the guard station. The next thing he remembered, he was sitting on a sandbag. Someone handed him a bottle of water. When he swallowed, he tasted blood.

"Boss, you okay?"

Davis looked down at him with a face smudged with dirt. Crocker used his tongue to feel along the ridge of his mouth and realized that a piece of one of his front teeth was missing.

"You see the rest of my tooth?" he asked.

"Did I see what?"

"Never mind."

The noise in the cramped, smoke-filled room was hellacious. He saw bodies thrown into a corner and covered with a blue tarp. Blood and entrails peeked out from under it.

Perez, kneeling beside him, said that including himself he was down to four men.

"Four men? How many behind us in D?"

"Another five, sir."

"Any of them Afghans?"

"No."

"No?"

Then who the fuck was that Weed guy talking to?

One of the gunners in front of them called out, "We're running low on ammo for the fifty-cal!"

Perez shouted back, "Conserve, guys. Select fire."

The gunner growled, "Then we better start collecting rocks."

Crocker tried to think clearly and consider their options. He asked, "How many enemy?"

"Unclear, sir," Perez answered. "They just keep coming."

"Best estimate?" Davis asked.

"I don't know. Fifty, a hundred, a million. Maybe there's a hole and they're coming up from Middle Earth."

Crocker turned to Davis and yelled, "Call Captain Battier. Tell him we're gonna need ammo and reinforcements."

"Okay, boss."

Twin .50 caliber machine guns continued to pound away in front of him. He saw Ritchie firing a MK19 grenade launcher. Remembering something, he stopped Perez, who was dragging a box of ammo over to the M2HG. "What about the six SEALs who were dropped in last week?" he asked.

"Two of 'em are behind us in D."

Davis broke his train of thought, which had drifted to his friend Neal Stafford. "Boss! Yo, boss! The captain says no can do."

"No what?"

"No reinforcements."

"Let me talk to him." He grabbed the receiver and spoke in an urgent but authoritative voice. "Hey, Captain, we're a hair away from being overrun here. We got a lot of men down and are in dire need of support and ammo, fifty-cal rounds especially. What can you do?"

A mortar round tore into the sandbag-reinforced wall on the right side of the station and exploded, sending the gunner of one of the M2HGs sliding across the floor. He scurried back, wiped a stream of blood from his nose, righted the machine gun, and continued firing.

"Captain, do you hear me?" The gunner in front of him shouted a stream of curses. Apparently he'd burned his hand on the hot barrel of his weapon.

"I hear you, chief. I hear you loud and clear. Where are you, exactly?"

"Station C."

"Have you considered pulling out of there?"

"For a whole lotta reasons that I don't have time to explain now, it's not an option."

"But I'm unable to send reinforcements," Battier responded via the radio receiver.

"What about ammo?"

"Negative on that, too."

"Why the fuck not?"

"Chief, I'm looking at the big picture. Presley, King, and Wolf are my priorities," Battier responded.

"You've got men dying down here, Captain. The position is eminently defendable with help!"

"Sorry, chief."

"I'm sorry, too. Fuck you!"

He threw down the radio and peered through a slit in the reinforced wall, guns pounding all around him, casings spilling onto the floor. Saw the sparks of guns firing from Taliban positions behind rocks, trees, and other natural barriers.

Perez, beside him, was peering through binoculars. Crocker asked, "Where are the bastards coming from?"

"You can't see from here, but there are a couple of trails up from the valley that are in the vicinity of Station B, which was the first to fall."

Snow continued to drop, and the light seemed to be fading. Crocker glanced at his Suunto GPS watch, which read 1642 hours. In another hour the sky would turn dark and they'd be even more vulnerable. Screwed, most likely.

"What'd the captain say?" Perez asked, putting down the glasses and grabbing his MP7 4.6x30mm submachine gun.

"We're on our own."

"I thought so."

Crocker hated the thought of giving up the station. His instincts told him to make a stand. "What have you got in terms of supplies?" he shouted to Perez over the tremendous racket.

"Bottled water, MREs, boxes of energy bars, heaters, lamps."

"Ammo?"

"There's a storage bunker behind Station D that contains some explosives, but no mags or fifty-cal rounds."

"What kind of explosives?"

"C-four and claymores."

"Okay." He started to turn to Ritchie on his right and stopped. "You told me two of the Team Six guys were behind us in Station D. What happened to the other four?"

Perez lowered his brown eyes. "Taken out resisting the initial charge."

Crocker was afraid to ask, but had to. "Neal Stafford?"

Perez nodded and pointed over his shoulder to the tarp-covered bodies in the back corner. Crocker pictured Neal's pretty, blond-haired wife and young sons. He wanted to beat the shit out of something, or scream so loud that time stopped and rewound. But he swallowed hard and summoned Ritchie instead. With his arm around the tall man's shoulder, he led him to the back of the bunker so the two men could hear themselves speak.

Crocker said, "Take Jonesy with you and go back to Station D. There's a…" Neal's smiling face flashed in his head. He gathered himself and started again, "There's a storage bunker there, back of D. I want you to grab all the explosives you can find and bring them here. Ask the SEALs there to help you."

Ritchie, his eyes burning with intensity, pointed to his backpack stacked against the back wall. "I've got blasting caps and detonators. You okay, boss?"

"I'm fine. I want to do something bold. Imaginative. Insane. Get the stuff."

"You want bold? You tapped the right man," Ritchie said, grinning. "Depending on what we find in D, I'll give you cataclysmic."

"I like the way you're thinking. Now go."

CHAPTER THREE

What we need are more people who specialize in the im-
possible.

—Theodore Roethke

CHECK THIS mother out!" Jonesy shouted as he burst
through the back door carrying a GAU-17/A 7.62x51mm
minigun, which featured six rotating barrels capable of delivering a whopping 4,000 rounds per minute.

He got grunts of approval from some of the men crowded
inside the dark, smoke-filled room, and one shout of "Sweet!"
Otherwise the eight soldiers were occupied with trying to
hold back an enemy that wouldn't let up.

With a sheer cliff to the right of Guard Station C, and con-
siderably higher terrain behind them and to the left, which is
where Station D was located, the Taliban had only one way of
overrunning the guard post, and that was head-on, which they
seemed determined to do, no matter how many new martyrs
they created in the process.

One M2HG heavy machine gun covered the Taliban assault from the right; a second was trained on the left, which

posed more of a challenge. The six soldiers in between fired a combination of MK19s, M4A1s, MK13s, HK416s, and one MK11 medium sniper rifle.

Crocker's head, right arm, and shoulder were numb. His ears and knees ached. After adjusting the five-position butt stock of the HK416, he looked through the diopter sight, located the torso of a Taliban fighter crouching and shouldering an RPG-2 in the crosshairs, and pulled the trigger, releasing a stream of 5.56x45mm bullets that tore into the enemy's torso, neck, and head. The weapon was a marvel of modern engineering that offered power, maneuverability, and reliability.

The Americans were outnumbered, perhaps as much as thirty to one, and due to that and the approaching darkness, Crocker could tell that the Taliban sensed victory. He saw it in the confident way they moved forward and maintained their position despite everything the Americans were throwing at them.

He glanced at his Suunto, then turned to Jonesy, who was busily setting up the minigun with Sergeant Perez's help.

"Where's Rich?"

"Ritchie, man, he's doing his bad thing."

"Where?" Crocker asked.

"Outside."

He stepped over the thick stream of blood oozing from the tarp-covered bodies, said a quick prayer for his neighbor Neal Stafford, and ducked through the low door as if leaving one chamber of hell and entering another. Outside, the fresh air smelled good and revived him. On higher ground behind him and to his right, the men at Station D were firing at Taliban targets on the rocks in front of the cliff. Tracers wove through the darkening mist like angry, lethal insects. The top of the mountain and the main structures of the post remained shrouded in white.

A thick, freckle-faced soldier from Alpha Company was taking a piss against the back wall. Crocker took one, too, and in the brief moment of calm thought about snowboarding in similar weather in Vermont.

For a second he remembered Neal standing on a slope beside him. He started to compose the expletive-filled tirade he planned to direct at Captain Battier and stopped. He had to focus. Hearing footsteps crunch the snow, he turned and saw Ritchie walking with a bearded soldier who was pointing out fissures in the rock.

"Ritchie?" he called. "What the hell's going on?"

"This is Corporal Henne. In real life, he's a geological something or other," Ritchie said enthusiastically, seemingly oblivious to the danger around them.

"I'm a geological engineer, sir," the serious-looking Henne explained. "I should be working for a big oil company."

"You will be someday, if we get out of here alive," Crocker said.

"Maybe."

"You find what you need?" Crocker asked Ritchie.

"More than enough. We're planning something extra special, aren't we, corporal?"

"Yes, sir."

"Good," Crocker said, blowing into his gloved hands. "You need to move fast."

Crocker returned to Station C to get Akil, and the four of them spent the next forty minutes placing explosive charges and running fuse wire. His back was complaining and his face was burning from the cold and wind when he returned to C and spoke to Perez.

"Here's the plan," he said. "Me and my men are gonna take over the big guns while you and your guys in Stations C and D go up to Wolf and King. Take as many weapons and bodies as you can. When you arrive on the next plateau, call me and let me know."

"I will."

"How much time you think you'll need?"

"Fifteen minutes max."

"Good. Get going."

Perez immediately started shouting orders, and the grim-faced, exhausted collection of Alpha Company soldiers, national guardsmen, and marines packed their gear, collected their weapons, and rigged the bodies in makeshift plastic stretchers. After wishing the SEALs good luck, they took off.

The light was fading fast, so the SEALs donned their PS-15 night-vision goggles and laid down as intense and relentless a volley of fire as they could squeeze out of the big weapons. Crocker manned the GAU-17/A minigun, which spit out a bolt of white tracers that obliterated targets. He raked fire right to left, left to right, until his arms were almost completely numb, then reloaded.

He was so focused on what he was doing that he didn't hear the voice over his helmet headset. Davis reached over and slapped him on the back.

"What?"

"It's Perez! He's trying to tell you something."

His hearing was messed up. He shouted, "What's he saying?"

"They've arrived!"

"Already? They're up on the higher plateau?" Crocker asked, looking at his watch and realizing that almost twenty minutes had passed.

"Yeah. They're up at Wolf and on their way to Presley."

"Good." He carefully straightened his back, cracked his neck, then shouted, "Grab what you can and pull back to Station D. Akil and I will meet you there in five."

"Roger."

Crocker blew through the last three belts of 7.62x51mm shells, pulled the gun from its mount, and screamed at Akil, "Let's go!"

"You sure, boss? I'm having too much fun!"

"It ain't over yet. Follow me!"

They ran out the back door, scrambling and slipping up the path to Station D. The SEALs had pretty much cleaned the place out, except for the twin mounted M2HG machine guns, which were currently being fired by Davis and Yale. "Where're the others?" Crocker asked, excitedly and out of breath.

"They're waiting by the chain ladder up to the next plateau," Davis answered, sweat dripping from the tip of his nose.

"Grab the radio and come with me. Akil, you and Yale lay down three more minutes of fire and join us."

"We can't do four?"

"Three, baby, three!"

They ran out through the falling snow, up a steep incline

to the dark wall of the cliff. Ritchie stood there clutching an MP7. "Twelve more minutes," he shouted to Crocker, "before the shit blows!"

"The rest of the men are already up the ladder?"

"Roger!"

Crocker pushed him and said, "You go. You and Davis. I'll wait for Akil and Yale."

"Chief—"

He took Davis by the shoulders. "Listen, this is important. Before you go, I want you to call Battier. Tell him we ran out of ammunition and are abandoning Stations C and D. Tell him we're sorry, but we didn't have time to rig any booby traps. And tell him to make sure to repeat all this to that ANA guy he calls Weed."

"Okay."

"The last part is the most important."

Davis was already readying the radio. "Okay, boss. I'm calling him now."

"Remember Weed."

"Yeah. I got it."

Ritchie had started up the chain ladder. Crocker checked his watch. Two minutes had passed since he had arrived at the base of the cliff. That meant there were roughly ten minutes left.

Davis said, "Message delivered, loud and clear, boss."

Crocker pointed to the ladder. "Good. You're next."

Another minute had passed. He heard the Taliban hoot and cheer as they reached Station C. Thirty seconds later he made out the sound of footsteps approaching. Past the trees, he saw Yale and Akil lugging one of the big M2HG guns.

"Drop that mother. Leave it! Let's go," he shouted.

He helped Yale onto the ladder, then Akil, then started up himself, wondering how much weight the ladder could hold. He climbed and looked at his watch. Six more minutes until the charges went off!

The chain creaked and twisted with the weight, and visibility was bad. He continued blindly, the muscles in his calves, arms, and back burning. Three minutes. Two.

He clung tightly to the ladder and took a deep breath. As he exhaled, a huge ball of light lit up the sky, then he heard the explosion and felt the force push him forward into the rock wall, smashing his hands. He struggled to hold on.

The ladder bucked. Secondary explosions rocked the mountain. Something hit him hard in the upper back near his right shoulder. Good thing he was wearing Dragon Skin silicon carbide ceramic body armor under his uniform, otherwise whatever it was might have gone right through him.

Hot air churned around him. He heard screams from below. His lungs wanted oxygen but could find little in the mountain air. Feeling light-headed, and with debris raining down around him, he kept climbing as well as he could and somehow neared the top, where arms reached out and helped him up.

"Thanks."

He sat on a rock, caught his breath, and checked to see if his shoulder was still working. It was. To his left he saw the barracks King and Wolf behind him. The snow continued to fall in a steady hiss in the otherwise quiet valley.

Davis handed him a bottle of water. "Boss, you okay?" he asked.

He nodded. "Everybody good? They all make it up?"

"Yeah."

The sounds of combat were gone. "The enemy's stopped firing," he said, looking up at Davis.

"That's correct. Ritchie thinks a good part of the land Stations C and D were sitting on slid down the hill."

"No shit."

"Talk to Ritchie."

He did, as they climbed together up to Presley. Ritchie and Corporal Henne—the guardsman from Reading, Pennsylvania—explained how the charges they had strategically placed had opened enough fissures in the rock that it could no longer support the weight of the plateau, thus causing the whole damn thing to tumble down the mountain.

"Stations C and D, too?" Crocker asked.

"The whole kit and caboodle," Henne answered. "Including the Taliban attackers."

"Sweet."

The first thing Crocker did when he reached Presley was grab ANA Major Jawid Shahar Mohammed and hold him at gunpoint while Davis disarmed him and Akil used tie-ties to secure his wrists behind his back.

Captain Battier, seeing what was going on, got in Crocker's face. "What the hell do you think you're doing?"

"I'm detaining this man."

"On whose authority?"

Crocker had to stop himself from punching Battier in the throat. He growled, "I strongly suspect that Major Mohammed was communicating with the enemy the whole time, right under your nose, Captain."

"No way. Impossible!"

"I think you are a criminal!" Major Mohammed shouted.

"I really don't care what either of you think," Crocker explained. "When we return to Jalalabad, I'll inform your CO, Captain. He'll order an investigation. We'll find out if I'm right."

"Go to hell!" the Afghan shouted.

Next he called Mancini, who was still guarding the ridge above the post, and told him to climb down to Presley. Then he did a quick inventory of his men and their injuries. Aside from some minor scrapes, burns, bruises, hunger, thirst, and exhaustion, they were all okay.

Jake slipped in and out of consciousness. Also, his blood pressure was low, his pulse rapid and weak—symptoms of neurogenic shock. Crocker administered a shot of dopamine to help elevate his blood pressure and ordered Phillips to continue keeping him warm and monitoring his IV.

He was halfway through his dinner of hot green tea, an energy bar, and a cup of noodles when he fell asleep. He dreamt he was alone in Station C, firing the GAU-17/A minigun at men in black turbans who kept charging from all directions.

In the morning when he awoke, the muscles in his arms and hands were clenched tight. His attention quickly shifted to the sun shining through intermittent clouds. By 0930 hours, medevac and relief helicopters had arrived. By noon he and his men were back at Jalalabad.

Humping toward his tent, he remembered something his former SEAL buddy and workout partner Neal Stafford always used to say: If it don't suck, we don't do it.

It did suck that his friend had to die defending a mountain-top in southeastern Afghanistan. They had shared a strong belief in the cause of defending freedom, a love of friends and family, and an unconquerable will to win.

As long as men like Neal fight on our side, Crocker said to himself, *we'll be okay.*

CHAPTER FOUR

*If you're going to try, go all the way. Otherwise, don't
even start.*

— Charles Bukowski

TWO DAYS later Crocker pulled his pickup into the driveway
of his home in Virginia Beach. He parked on the graveled
drive and looked at his watch: 0214 Thursday morning,
November twenty-second.

Exhausted and happy to be home, he entered through the
garage past Holly's silver Subaru and climbed the concrete
steps to his combined rec room/home office, which was
crowded with stuff—weights, a desk piled with mail he had
to either answer or throw out, an elliptical training machine
he had partially assembled. Photos on the wall—one of him
in his white uniform the day he received his SEAL trident,
various platoon and skydiving photos, others of him crossing
the finish line at the Hawaii Ironman competition, and kissing
Holly on their wedding day.

He opened the door to the hallway and saw their German
shepherd Brando curled up on the floor asleep. The dog

looked up at Crocker as if to ask, "Where the hell have *you* been?"

You don't want to know.

Seductive smells emanated from the kitchen, but he wasn't hungry, so he set down his kit bag next to a potted ficus and climbed the steps to the second floor. Moonlight streamed through the skylight. The grandfather clock chimed once, marking the quarter hour.

He wanted to look into Jenny's room at the end of the hall, but she wasn't a little girl anymore. She was seventeen and hypersensitive to people entering her private space unannounced. So Crocker walked in the opposite direction along the carpeted floor toward the master bedroom, turned the brass knob, and pushed the door inward.

He stopped and inhaled the sweet smells of jasmine and rosewater—two scents his wife favored. She slept on her side on the far side of the bed with her back facing him. Setting his backpack on the floor, he entered the bathroom on his right. Splashed water on his face, which looked like it belonged to someone else, brushed his teeth, and undressed.

Reentering the bedroom, he lifted the soft white duvet and sheet and slipped into the big bed. The warmth of Holly's body surrounded him.

He lay on the bed taking it all in—the sound of Holly breathing, the shadows on the ceiling, the LED TV screen on the opposite wall—thinking it was hard to believe that he was really here and not in a tent in some far-off land. He realized that he felt even closer to and more protective of Holly since her kidnapping in Libya. Her colleague had been tortured and killed before her eyes. She had been tied up for days and told she was going to die. Yet she still had the strength and grace to pull herself together and continue to be the loving, generous person she had been before.

Silently, he thanked God as the trees outside swayed in the breeze. An owl hooted. Holly sighed, turned, and opened one eye. "Tom?" she asked half asleep. "Tom, is that really you?" as if she was still dreaming.

"It's me, sweetheart. I'm back, but I didn't want to wake you."

"Wake me? Don't be silly." She reached out, wrapped her arms around him and held on as if she didn't want to let go. "Oh, Tom. I missed you so much. Welcome home."

He said, "I'm sorry about Neal."

She flinched slightly, then rolled over and kissed him on the lips. "Don't be sorry," she whispered. "It's awful, yes, but it's the price he knew he might pay."

"How are Alyssa and the boys?"

"They're grieving and trying to cope. But let's not talk about that now."

He kissed her back, and held her, and they gently made love.

The next thing he knew it was morning, and Holly was walking toward him through the dappled light carrying a glass of orange juice. She caressed his forehead and informed him that the first guests would be arriving in an hour.

"What guests?" Crocker asked, glancing at the clock and seeing that it was almost eleven.

"Your sister and her family. My brother."

"Why?"

"It's Thanksgiving, Tom. Jenny and I are making dinner."

"I didn't realize."

He carved the turkey, sat at the head of the table and said grace, ate, talked to Jenny about school, and conversed with everyone about everything, including the approaching end of the Mayan calendar, the recent presidential election, Hurricane Sandy, and the resignation of General Petraeus. He even retired with the men and boys to watch the Redskins-Cowboys game on TV.

He did everything that was expected of him, but he wasn't completely present. Part of him was still on the mountain in Nuristan Province, fighting the enemy, making split-second decisions, arguing with Captain Battier about the need to reinforce Station C.

The adjustment from combat to civilian life was always difficult. This time it was especially hard because of the four SEAL teammates who had returned in flag-covered coffins. He carried his memories of them like an extra weight on his shoulders.

The first three funerals took place the following day in Virginia Beach as a cold rain fell from a cement-colored sky. The chapels and funeral homes were interchangeable and the routine was the same—people dressed in black, bouquets of roses, eulogies, and grieving families. One ran into another. By the end of the day he felt numb, hollowed out. If life had a purpose, he'd forgotten what it was.

By the time Saturday arrived and he and Holly drove up to Arlington National Cemetery for Neal Stafford's burial, Crocker thought he was inured to sadness. But when Alyssa spoke about her husband as a soul mate, lover, and companion, not sparing the intimate details of their life together as a married couple—including the way Neal liked to tease her and call her his bunny when they made love—Crocker broke down and wept.

Holly squeezed his hand. He looked at her and saw that she was thinking it could have been him.

Life was tough and precious. It contained unbelievably beautiful, gentle moments, and hard, ugly, difficult ones. Then it ended. The bodies piled up, and the struggles continued. Love and friendship made life worth living.

Crocker considered himself part of a proud tradition of warriors—including his grandfather, uncle, and father—dedicated to defending people's freedom, which to his mind was an unalienable right. The enemies might have changed over the years—from fascists, to communists, to Muslim radicals—but their goals were the same: to subject people to a monolithic set of rules and beliefs.

As long as he was alive, he would fight to the death to defend what he believed. To his mind it was almost a spiritual quest.

Crocker didn't pretend to be a philosopher or an intellectual, and he didn't belong to a church or political party, but he believed that the principle of self-determination was critical to human progress and survival. People had to make their own decisions and their own mistakes if they were going to learn and evolve—which to Crocker's way of thinking is what we have been put on this earth to do.

By the time Monday morning rolled around, he still wasn't himself and was having trouble sleeping at night. Even when he was awake, he found himself drifting back to Afghanistan—the cold, snow, smells, faces, and close scrapes with death.

Running in the woods was the only thing that seemed to clear his head. He ran for over an hour with Brando past still marshes, Broad Bay, and Lake Susan Constant. He then showered, dressed, breakfasted, and climbed into his beat-up Ford pickup and drove to the SEAL Team Six compound. He was seated in front of his cage inventorying his gear when an aide arrived to tell him that the CO, Captain Alan Sutter, wanted to see him in his office.

"Now?" Crocker asked.

"Yes, he's waiting."

He put down the six-inch suppressed-air silencer he'd been cleaning and trudged across the concrete assembly area where some SEALs were rehearsing unarmed defensive tactics, thinking that he was probably going to be asked about what had transpired at OPM, and especially his arrest of ANA Major Jawid Shahar Mohammed. If Captain Battier had filed a formal complaint, he knew there was a possibility he could be called before the Naval Special Warfare Incident Determination Committee.

He was preparing answers in his head as he entered the CO's office. Sutter put his hand over the receiver he was talking into and said, "Welcome back, Warrant. Grab yourself a cup of coffee. Jim Anders from CIA will be here in a minute."

Anders is here? Why? he asked himself, filling a cup with water, then gulping it down and glancing at the copy of the *Washington Post* that sat on the corner of Sutter's secretary's desk. The Israelis were bombing Hamas bases in Gaza, which brought back memories of his own dealings with the Israelis and Palestinians over the years.

Hearing footsteps approach, he half turned, then felt a hand on his shoulder near where he'd been hit at OPM. It was Jim Anders, looking tanned and well rested. He said, "Good to see you again, Crocker. How was your Thanksgiving?"

Neal Stafford's funeral flashed in Crocker's mind—his wife and two tow-headed kids standing beside the coffin. He shook away the anger and grief, and answered, "Good. How was yours?"

"Excellent. My family met me in Hawaii for four days in paradise. You ever been to Maui?"

"Maui, yeah. Fabulous place," he said automatically. He'd spent two weeks there with a wild Australian chick between his first and second marriages, diving, windsurfing, and making love. Pretty much knew the island by heart. But that felt like another lifetime.

He was remembering a drive through the mist and fog up to Haleakala volcano as they took their seats in Sutter's office. The captain explained that he had just gotten off the phone with Jim Anders's boss at CIA, Chief of Operations Lou Donaldson.

Crocker winced at the mention of Donaldson's name. Although he'd been told many times by third parties how much Donaldson admired Crocker's team's work, the two men had never gotten along. Crocker thought of him as a headstrong, rude SOB.

Sutter cleared his throat and spoke with a smooth, deep Kentucky accent, which had the effect of putting people at ease. "Crocker, you get a chance to read the post-op report about the fighting at OPM in Nuristan?"

"No, I haven't, sir," he answered, bracing himself for what he thought was coming next and folding his hands in his lap. The office was large and outfitted with handsome nautical-style furniture.

"Apparently some of the RPGs and heavier artillery rounds fired were provided by a covert Iranian group called Unit 5000."

Crocker was intrigued. "Unit 5000. What's that?" he asked, running through a mental Rolodex of names and acronyms. "I thought the Iranians were working exclusively with the Shiite groups in western Afghanistan."

"Not when they have a chance to kill Americans."

"I've never heard of them before," Crocker said, leaning forward in the brown leather chair.

"We'll get back to them in a minute," Anders answered. "First, I want to talk to you about the car bombings in Bangkok and Athens last week. You hear about them?"

"I read something in the newspaper, that's all," Crocker answered, wondering why Anders had changed the subject.

"Take a look at this," Sutter said, handing Crocker a green folder. Inside were a series of photographs of the twisted, burned carcasses of eight cars and SUVs. His stomach started to turn. Beneath the photos was a list of the Americans killed and wounded. Glancing at it, he recognized one of the names—John Rinehart. He and Rinehart had met ten months ago in Kabul, while Rinehart was attending an economic conference there and Crocker was training the security detail assigned to protect President

Karzai. Rinehart had struck him as a gentle, intelligent, academic type.

"These bomb attacks resulted in more than a dozen deaths of U.S., Israeli, and Saudi diplomats, and those unfortunate individuals who were riding in the vehicles with them," Sutter said.

"Tragic," Crocker muttered, remembering the night run he and Rinehart had completed together around Bagram Airfield.

"And scores of locals who happened to be in the vicinity either killed or wounded," Anders added.

"Where did you say these bombings took place?" Crocker asked, looking from Sutter to Anders.

"Bangkok, Athens, Rome, Mumbai, and Cairo."

Bangkok is where Rinehart had told him he was stationed.

"Who was the perpetrator?" Crocker asked, thinking that most people didn't appreciate the risk diplomats took when they served overseas.

Anders said, "Unit 5000."

"Oh," Crocker groaned. "Again?"

"Unit 5000 is a special, ultrasecret branch of the Iranian Quds Force, and the brainchild of your old nemesis Farhed Alizadeh," Anders continued. "Code name the Falcon."

The mention of Alizadeh's name caused Crocker's whole body to heat up. Alizadeh was the evil fuck he'd first encountered trying to steal nuclear material from an Australian cargo ship off the coast of Somalia. Alizadeh later attempted another theft of nuclear material in Libya, which Crocker and his team thwarted, and hired a group of local militiamen to kidnap Crocker's wife. Now he was supplying heavy arms to the Taliban and killing American diplomats all over the world.

"The Falcon," Crocker repeated, picturing Alizadeh's sinister, dark, deep-set eyes, short stature, and acne-scarred face covered with a short black beard. "Where's that little bastard now?"

"I wish I knew," Anders answered, reaching into an aluminum briefcase.

"So do I. Tenfold."

"You ever see one of these?" Anders asked. He handed Crocker a black metal object that looked like a miniature hockey puck. The underside of it was covered with tiny silver-colored balls.

"No. What is it?" Crocker asked, running his finger over the little spheres.

"Those balls are magnetic," Anders said. "And that device is empty, which is a real good thing, because the operative ones are packed with a plastic form of CL-20, a small detonator, and a digital timer. Very powerful and extremely deadly."

CL-20 was the highest-energy solid explosive produced in the United States, 20 percent more powerful than HMX and extremely expensive to make. It had been called the most significant energetic discovery since the hydrogen bomb. Crocker knew it was used in high-rate detonating cord and high-performance gun propellants. But this was the first time he'd heard of it packed into a stand-alone explosive device.

Even more alarming to him was the news that it had fallen into the Falcon's hands.

"I didn't know that anyone besides us had access to CL-20 or other nitramine explosives," Crocker said.

"Apparently they do now," Sutter responded.

Anders said, "As far as we know, the only place that made it was the Thiokol Corporation in Ogden, Utah."

Crocker's head shook as he considered the implications. But investigating breaches of domestic security was not part of his job description. They fell under the purview of the FBI.

"Similar devices were used to kill Sunni leaders in Iraq. But those were packed with RDX and C-4," Anders added. "In each of the car bombings we're talking about now, someone on the back of a motorcycle attached one of these bad boys to a car's rear fender, near the vehicle's gas tank. The people inside didn't stand a chance."

A well of anger rose inside Crocker as he thought of the assassination of John Rinehart and the recent death of Neal Stafford and the other SEALs in Nuristan Province. He growled, "That evil, fucking bastard." Then, thinking of Rinehart, he asked, "Do you know why those particular people were targeted?"

"Most of them were diplomats. There seemed to be no reason they were selected, except to instill terror, fear, uncertainty," Anders answered.

Sutter added, "The Iranians are too clever to take us on directly. So they try to undermine us and rattle our cage with acts of terrorism or working through proxies. It's a coward's game, in my opinion."

Crocker growled, "I won't rest until I have Alizadeh's head on a stick."

"We feel the same," Anders added, meaning the CIA. "Which is why I'm here."

Anders reached into the metal briefcase and retrieved an envelope. Crocker was hoping it contained information regarding Alizadeh's current location. Inside were several stills of a modest-size hotel surrounded by tropical foliage, a name (Lieutenant Colonel Sarit Petsut), and an address in Bangkok.

"What's this?" he asked, feeling somewhat disappointed.

"The Special Operations Unit of the Royal Thai Police believe they have a lead on the terrorists who struck twice in Bangkok. We want Black Cell to go there and pursue whatever Thai officials can provide."

Black Cell was the name recently given to Crocker's six-man team—consisting of himself, Mancini, Ritchie, Akil, Davis, and Cal. They were a subgroup of the Naval Special Warfare Development Group, known as DEVGRU, specifically tasked with top-secret antiterrorist operations assigned by CIA and the White House.

"You want us to gather intel?" Crocker asked. He'd much rather go after Alizadeh directly.

"You don't understand," Anders answered. "We're taking the gloves off. So we expect intel, suspects, dead terrorists. We want to know what Unit 5000 is planning, and we want to punish the people who ordered the attacks, built the bombs, and carried out those attacks."

All of this was sweet music to Crocker's ears. He said, "Sir, you have my assurance that we'll go after these Unit 5000 characters as hard as possible."

"That's what we expect."

Sutter rubbed his chin with the back of his hand and added, "I suspect you'll find an intricate chain of connections that lead directly back to Iran."

Anders pointed at the contents of the envelope he had handed him and continued, "We've made reservations for the six of you at the Viengtai Hotel under assumed names. Those are your passports and travel documents. Your contact in Bangkok is an American businessman named Emile Anderson. Among other things, he runs a local tourist agency and is one of our assets. Anderson will help you get around and connect you with Lieutenant Colonel Petsut."

Crocker frowned.

"Is there a problem?" Anders asked.

"I was hoping you were sending us to get the Falcon," he answered.

"It's our hope, our suspicion in fact, that the trail you uncover will lead to him."

"I sincerely hope so. He and I have a score to settle."

"This isn't personal," Sutter added.

"In this case I respectfully disagree, sir." The more anti- and counterterrorism ops Crocker ran, the more he realized how personal it was—a clash of fundamental beliefs and will.

"We need you to launch within twenty-four hours," Anders said. "Can you do that?"

"Of course we can," Crocker answered.

"Then good luck."

There were always complications—usually minor, sometimes major—having to do with getting his men ready to leave on a few hours' notice. In this case, they were being asked to deploy a few days after a difficult mission in Afghanistan. Davis's wife was expecting their second child in four weeks. Mancini had recently buried his younger brother, who died of pancreatic cancer, and was dealing with paying off his medical bills. Cal's mother had died two months ago, and he was still settling her estate. Ritchie's girlfriend, Monica, a real estate developer, wanted to get married. Akil was helping his Egyptian father refurbish his Alexandria, Virginia, jewelry store.

Crocker returned to find Holly sitting on the edge of their bed changing into gym clothes and sneakers.

She said, "I'll pick up some salmon after my spin class. Do you mind grilling it with that lemon-mustard sauce you like?"

"Don't bother, sweetheart. I'm leaving tonight on a nine o'clock flight out of Dulles."

"Oh," she said sadly. "So soon?"

"Yeah." Crocker couldn't tell her what the mission was about or where he was going.

"Do you know how long you'll be gone?" Holly asked.

He couldn't tell her that, either. So he shook his head as he retrieved a black suitcase from the closet and zipped it open. It was prepacked with "business" clothes. He always kept his kit bags filled and ready for military deployments, and a suitcase for when he was traveling as a civilian. He checked to see if it contained garments appropriate for Bangkok. According to Yahoo! Weather, late November to early December was the beginning of the most temperate season, with lighter rainfall, average highs in the mid-eighties and the temperature dropping at night into the sixties.

When he turned to tell Holly that he hoped to be home before Christmas, her face was buried in her hands. He set the heavier-weight clothes he'd pulled from the suitcase on the bed and sat down beside her.

"What's wrong?" he asked her.

"Nothing, Tom," she answered, wiping her eyes with her sleeve. "I'm sorry."

"There's nothing to be sorry about," he said, gently. "What's bothering you—Neal's death, or Brian Shaw's, or the kidnapping?"

"All three," she sighed, squeezing his hand. In a low, even voice she told him that she was considering quitting her job at State Department Security and had recently discussed it with her boss. He'd suggested that she take a leave of absence and seek psychological counseling instead.

Crocker continued to switch out heavier clothes for lighter-weight wear—T-shirts, polo shirts, khaki pants—while staying mindful of the schedule he had to keep. "Maybe you should," he said.

"You mean, do the counseling?"

"Yeah."

"Do you think I'm being...selfish?"

"Absolutely not," Crocker said, stuffing his shaving kit in the suitcase and zipping up the outside pocket.

"I want to do the right thing, Tom," Holly said through tears. "I've been waiting for the right time to discuss this with you."

He didn't want to tell her she had waited too long as he rechecked his watch and realized that he had to be at the base airport in thirty-five minutes to catch a flight to Andrews Air Force Base, outside D.C. From there he and the other five members of Black Cell would be ferried to Dulles by helicopter.

Taking her hand in his, he said, "Maybe the best thing to do is take a couple of months off, do the counseling thing, and see how that works."

"What happens if a couple months isn't enough?"

"Try the counseling," he said. "Hopefully it works. If not, you can always ask for more time. Right?"

"I'm kind of scared to talk about it," Holly admitted. "You know, the incident. They tortured Brian and made me watch. It wasn't like what you see in a James Bond movie. You're there, and you see the cruelty and the pain on his face, and you want to disappear and die."

He put his arm around her, felt her trembling, and pulled her close. "Take all the time you need to heal yourself. Don't worry about what happens next."

"I'm afraid, Tom, and embarrassed."

He kissed her on the lips and she responded. But he had to pull free. "Whatever happens," he said, "I love you."

"You have to leave now?"

He stood, grabbed his bag, and nodded. "I'll call as soon as I can."

"Be careful, okay? And come back."

CHAPTER FIVE

*The man who removes a mountain begins by carrying
away small stones.*

— William Faulkner

JOHNNY CASH'S "Folsom Prison Blues" played on the stereo as
the pickup's tires crunched across the gravel driveway. It was
always difficult, pulling away from the ones you loved and not
knowing if you'd ever see them again.

The lyrics entered his head as though Cash was singing directly to him: "When I hear that whistle blowin', I hang my
head and cry."

Crocker wondered if he should have told Holly that he was
going after Farhed Alizadeh, the man who had planned her
kidnapping in Libya and ordered the killing of Brian Shaw.
Maybe it wouldn't have helped. Part of him wanted to stay
with her, but a stronger sense of obligation compelled him to
complete the mission and get Alizadeh.

How satisfying will that be, for Holly particularly? Crocker
asked himself as the pickup hurtled down a country road, past
modest houses where families were returning from work and

school and starting to prepare dinner. He hoped the death of his rival would give Holly some feeling of closure.

He was uncharacteristically unsure of himself when it came to dealing with emotional matters, and he scolded himself for not saying goodbye to his teenage daughter. He'd hardly had occasion to talk to her during the few days he'd been home. In the competition between family and SEAL team for his attention, it seemed as if the team always won.

Crocker stood at a magazine kiosk in Dulles International Airport, looking down at the face of disgraced general David Petraeus, when he remembered that his father's birthday was next week. He punched the button on his cell phone that speed-dialed his father's number.

"Dad?"

"Tom, what's wrong?" the eighty-two-year-old asked in a voice deepened and withered with time.

"Nothing. We missed you at Thanksgiving."

"Holly was kind enough to invite me, but I was too busy to drive up."

Tom's father lived in an apartment in Fairfax and had been kind of lost since Crocker's mother died three years ago. He spent most of his time volunteering at the local VFW, Post 8469, where he was commander.

"Too busy doing what?" Crocker asked.

"Serving turkey dinner to a bunch of beaten-down disabled vets."

He admired his dad and wished they had more time to spend together. "How are things?" he asked.

"I could complain, but no one would listen. Sure sucks, getting old. But I made a new friend. A young gal named Carla, who works as a waitress at the local diner. She's a single mom raising a son. Dale's his name. Nine years old and already teaching me how to play video games. Can you imagine, an old fart like me?"

Crocker heard his flight being called and saw Akil waving at him from near the gate.

"Dad, I've got to go."

"Where you calling from?"

"Dulles. I'm about to board a flight."

"I'd tell you to stay out of trouble, but I know you can't do that. Call me when you get back. Give my love to Hol and Jenny."

"Will do."

Approximately eight miles east of where Crocker's dad lived in Virginia, thirteen-year-old Alex Rinehart sat in front of a TV in his grandparents' basement, using a remote to flip through the channels. He was dressed in a black-and-white-striped shirt and jeans, and had a full face with a tangled mop of dark hair and sad, slightly Asian eyes. He looked like a normal, healthy, well-cared-for teenager. Hours earlier he had returned from his new school, the Bethesda–Chevy Chase Middle School.

Alex had been a student at the school for only two weeks and was already excelling in algebra, computer studies, and pre-calculus. But he was woefully behind in English, social science, and American history. A good deal of that had to do with his refusal to speak or write since the death of his parents in Bangkok.

A school-appointed developmental psychologist named Cathy Struthers sat in an armchair to his right observing him as he watched TV. She noticed that he quickly flipped past shows that dealt with personal relationships and, especially, family—*Friends, Seinfeld, 1600 Penn, Modern Family.* He paused at an old episode of *Law & Order*, but as soon as a distressed father appeared on the screen, Alex switched channels. He finally settled on a rebroadcast of *Jeopardy!*

His condition, which Dr. Struthers had diagnosed earlier, had a clinical name—reactive mutism—and was usually caused by trauma or abuse. RM was more prevalent among young people like Alex with an existing autism spectrum disorder. Treatment was problematic, especially for those in their teenage years.

Since Alex was already taking the serotonin reuptake inhibitor Paxil to help deal with his social anxiety, Struthers thought of recommending a medication designed to affect a broader range of neurotransmitters, such as Effexor or Serzone. But she suspected that they wouldn't work either. The more she observed Alex and realized how intelligent he was, the more strongly she believed that his mutism was a conscious choice—a silent angry protest against the cruel injustice of the world, for which there was no cure.

The six members of Black Cell flew United from Dulles seven hours and twenty minutes to Heathrow. They then boarded British Airways Flight 9, which covered another 5,928 miles in a little over eleven hours to Suvarnabhumi Airport.

Crocker passed the time playing chess with Mancini and

Akil, watching Mel Brooks's *High Anxiety* for about the fifteenth time, discussing the pluses and minuses of some new
handguns and sniper rifles with Cal, eating, drinking beer,
snoozing. He was dying to do a workout by the time he felt
the plane descend and saw the giant double hoops of the terminal rising from a vast expanse of vivid green marshland.

He loved the lushness of the tropics.

The high-tech, futuristic airport stood in striking contrast
to the wild marshland. It contained huge halls with soaring
metal arches lit with blue neon and white lights. As they
waited in line for immigration, a young woman on a video
screen on the wall explained that the terminal had been
opened in 2006 and boasted the world's tallest freestanding
control tower (434 feet), the world's fourth-largest single
building terminal (over six million square feet), and handled
approximately forty-eight million passengers a year.

"I feel like I've arrived on a friendlier planet," Akil said as
beautiful hostesses dressed in purple checked to make sure
they had filled out the appropriate forms and were standing
in the correct line.

After they passed through customs, the SEALs-turned-
businessmen arrived in the baggage claim area, where they
saw a medium-height white guy with a middleweight's muscular body and a thick mop of black hair standing next to a
nice-looking dark-skinned man holding a sign that read "Sonnex Petroleum."

Akil nodded toward the sign and whispered, "Look, boss."

"I see it."

Sonnex Petroleum was the name of the shell company the
six SEALs were allegedly working for. They were traveling

as oil company executives and engineers. Crocker's alias was Tom Mansfield, VP of exploration and research. What he really knew about oil exploration could fit on the head of a pin.

The taller of the two men introduced himself with a strong, confident handshake as Emile Anderson. Black Cell couldn't do what it did without the help and support of local agents.

"Welcome," he said to Crocker, full of nervous energy. "We're on kind of a tight schedule, so as soon as you get your bags, we'll take off into town to try to beat the traffic. Lieutenant Colonel Petsut of the Royal Thai Police is meeting you for dinner."

"The sooner we get started, the better," Crocker replied, looking down at his watch, which had adjusted automatically to the local time zone, 1652 hours.

He stood at Baggage Claim Station 3, surveying the international crowd—a polyglot of Asian, East Asian, European, young and old, dressed in business clothes and casual. The diversity reminded him of the movie *Blade Runner*, but here everything was clean, orderly, and efficient.

Including Anderson, who handed him a large manila envelope and said, "I've already prechecked you into your rooms. Your electronic room keys are in there, along with seven hundred bucks' worth of baht to get you started. My friend Daw here will be your driver."

"Hey, Daw. Nice to meet you, and much appreciated."

The short man with the round pockmarked face smiled back with a serene look in his eyes.

"Anything you need, you tell Daw or you call me on this," Anderson continued, handing Crocker a shiny new Samsung cell phone. "Both our numbers have been programmed into it, along with an emergency contact at the Station. Only use that in case of an emergency. Try to call one of us first. We'll be at your disposal twenty-four/seven. You need anything, and I mean anything, call."

"Thanks. What's the exchange rate?" Crocker asked.

"A hundred baht is worth about three dollars and twenty-six cents."

Large photos of a smiling King Bhumibol Adulyadej and Prime Minister Yingluck Shinawatra and her husband hung on the walls. The local people seemed amiable and gentle.

Within minutes the SEALs had packed their bags into the back of two Lexus SUVs and were racing down a modern, eight-lane expressway. Crocker sat in the passenger seat next to Anderson, who was driving 160 kilometers an hour, or approximately one hundred miles per hour.

"No speed limit?" Crocker asked.

"None that's enforced," Anderson replied with a grin that made his smashed-in nose stand out. "The freeways are F1 speed all the way."

As he drove, he explained that Lieutenant Colonel Petsut of the RTP was a proud man who generally frowned on letting foreigners operate on his turf but was making an exception in this case because of the severity of what had happened, the international implications, and the deaths of American diplomats.

"But he's only going to give you a small window to work in," Emile Anderson said. "So you've got to respect boundaries."

"In other words, you don't want me to argue with him."

"Like my daughter was taught in kindergarten: you get what you get, and you don't complain."

Crocker didn't say that once the SEALs launched the op there would be no stopping them. And he understood that the cooperation of local authorities was an enormous asset.

The hotel was a modern six-story joint a few blocks from the Chao Phraya River and close to the busy night scene centered around Khao San Road. Anderson explained that many of the city's attractions stood within walking distance—the National Museum, Grand Palace, Temple of the Emerald Buddha, and another spectacular gold-spired Buddhist temple called Wat Saket.

Mancini asked Anderson about Wat Phai Rong Wua, which he said was described as the "most bizarre tourist attraction on the planet" by a travel magazine he had read on the plane.

"If you're into graphic scenes of people being tortured by demons and monsters with blood and entrails hanging out, you'll love it," Anderson answered.

"Manny loves entrails of all kinds," Ritchie joked. "In fact, he was just telling me he wanted pig entrails for dinner."

"I know a great little place where they serve them raw, grilled, or sautéed," Anderson said, playing along as they passed through a cool caramel marble lobby decorated with tropical flowers.

Anderson left them there and said he'd be back to pick them up at seven.

"Cal, you still with us?" Ritchie asked as they rode the elevator up to the fourth floor.

"Yeah. Why?" Cal, their weapons expert and sniper, had

a Polynesian face that seemed creased in a perpetual smile. He was an enigma to most men on the team because he rarely said anything and kept to himself. Crocker knew him to be laser focused and extremely dependable during missions, which is all he cared about.

"You haven't said a freakin' word since we left D.C.," Ritchie said.

"That's because he's been sitting next to you, and he hates your guts," Akil said.

Cal: "Not true."

Electronic Asian music played over the elevator PA. "Sounds like a group of castrated gerbils," Akil commented.

"It actually fits into a genre called K-pop," Mancini said.

"What the fuck is that?" Ritchie asked.

"Electro pop-style music that originated in South Korea. Its best-known song is 'Gangnam Style,' by Psy. You're familiar with that, right?"

"Of course."

"Is there anything you don't know?" Akil asked. "What do you do, stay up nights and just study random shit?"

Mancini ignored him.

Ritchie slapped Cal on the shoulder as they exited the elevator and started down the beige carpeted hallway. "So. What's new?"

"Actually, I've been reading an interesting book."

"Tell me about it."

Cal reached into his backpack and pulled out a thick paperback entitled *The Creature from Jekyll Island*.

Ritchie looked at the cover and handed it back. "Who's the creature?"

"The creature is the Federal Reserve System. According to this, the whole thing is a scam cooked up and run by some big banks. The system isn't federal, and there aren't any reserves."

"Sounds like a real page-turner," Ritchie said with a smirk.

The room they entered was spacious and clean, with two king-sized beds, a TV mounted on the wall, and a bathroom that stank of lime-scented disinfectant and mold, Mancini quickly pointed out, being the fussiest member of the group. His wife, Teresa, described him as Martha Stewart in an alligator-wrestler's body.

"Two men to a room," Crocker announced. "Akil and I will take this one."

"How come you two always room together?" Ritchie asked. "Kind of makes me wonder."

"Because you can't fall asleep without the TV on, Manny snores like a wounded warthog, and Davis talks to his wife in his sleep," Crocker answered.

"It's true," Davis said.

"What about Cal?"

Crocker handed out the electronic key cards and said, "Unpack, wash up, jerk off, whatever....And reassemble here at 1855." That gave them roughly twenty minutes.

"You hear the part about washing up, Akil?" Ritchie cracked as he exited. "That's a not-so-subtle hint that you need to take a shower."

"Kiss my hairy Egyptian ass."

Crocker stacked his clothes carefully on the wooden shelves in the closet, showered, clipped his salt-and-pepper mustache, and changed into a fresh black polo and black cotton pants. Exiting the bathroom he found CNN News blaring from the TV and Akil on the floor by the window doing crunches.

He turned down the sound and said, "You'd better get ready."

On his way to the bathroom, Akil said, "I think I'm gonna like this city."

"We're not tourists," Crocker reminded him. He remembered leaving a bar early one morning the last time he'd been in Bangkok and coming to the aid of two drunken Aussies who were getting the shit pounded out of them by a gang of Thai toughs. The toughs claimed the Aussies hadn't paid their thousand-dollar bar bill. One of the Aussies shot back, "How could two skinny bums like us drink that much shitty Thai beer?"

He considered calling home, then realized it was something like 6 a.m. in Virginia. When the rest of the SEALs returned, Crocker quickly briefed them on the reason they were there and said, "I'm taking Mancini with me to meet the Thai colonel. I want the rest of you to grab some grub and return to the hotel. Hopefully, we'll get a location on the terrorists and execute a raid before the sun comes up. So no drinking or fucking around. I need all of you focused and ready. And don't expect to sleep tonight."

Ritchie turned to Mancini and asked, "Any place you'd recommend nearby for dinner?"

"For good Thai food try Tom Yum Kung on Khao San Road. If you want Italian, look for a place called Scoozi. They're both affordable."

Cal pointed to Ritchie's new watch and advised, "If we're going walking down Khao San Road, you might want to leave that in the hotel safe." It was a Jaeger-LeCoultre Master Compressor diving watch with a Super-LumiNova dial visible underwater, and it retailed for a little over ten thousand dollars—a marriage proposal gift from his girlfriend.

Cal, Ritchie, Davis, and Akil left first. When Crocker and Mancini descended to the lobby, they found Anderson dressed in a black silk shirt and cream blazer. With his hair slicked back, he looked like a character from *Miami Vice*.

They sat in the lounge and ordered Singha beer.

"What do you think of Admiral Olsen's statement about women performing combat roles in special ops?" Anderson asked out of the side of his mouth. Admiral Eric T. Olsen was the former head of U.S. Special Operations Command (USSOCOM), which oversees the various special operations commands of the army, air force, navy, and marine corps, including SEAL Team 6, Delta Force, and the air force's 24th Special Tactics Squadron. He had been replaced by the current commander, Admiral William McRaven, in August 2011.

"Asinine," Mancini answered.

"If they want to and can hack it, why not?" Crocker asked.

"Because it's wrong," Mancini answered.

Crocker, who was getting antsy, leaned toward Anderson and said, "We'd like to do this tonight, if possible. Can you get us everything we need?"

"Within reason, of course. Expect Colonel Petsut to set the parameters."

After paying the check, Anderson led the way to Khao San Road, a colorful stretch of shops, restaurants, sidewalk masseuses, sex parlors, bars, stalls hawking T-shirts, counterfeit watches, purses, bongs, and even Botox treatments, populated by tourists from all over the globe, including lots of young kids in tank tops and shorts, sporting cornrowed hair and bad tattoos. They pushed past shady local characters offering to sell them Armani suits for fifty dollars, "refurbished" iPhones and iPads, drugs, and every variety of sexual activity known to man. Several tuk-tuk drivers offered to take them on a tour of the city for twenty baht, the equivalent of sixty-five cents.

"It's gotta be a scam," Crocker said.

"No, mister," one of the drivers countered in Tinglish—a combination of Thai and bad English. "We get money from gov'ment for every tourist we take."

"Yeah, and I'm really a six-foot-six black basketball player named Michael Jordan. You ever hear of Michael Jordan?"

"You, Michael Jordan the basketball player? You crazy!"

A topless young woman waved to them from a window above a dress shop.

"Perky," Mancini commented.

"Friendly, too."

They turned into an alley that led to a wider street and the dark marble front of a somber, modern four-story structure. Anderson announced his name into the intercom and they were buzzed in. Two men in dark green uniforms checked them with metal detector wands, then pointed to a little elevator that took them to the top floor.

A pretty young woman in a tight white tunic and black skirt, her hair pulled back and decorated with a pink-and-yellow orchid, met them there.

Mancini whispered, "She smells nice," as they followed her

into a dark room that looked like an empty cocktail lounge. Norah Jones crooned "Come Away with Me" over the sound system. The young woman pointed her delicate arm at a tan banquette in the corner where three men in uniform sat. They bowed.

Recognizing Anderson, the man in the middle stood, smiled, and offered Crocker his hand. "Mr. Mansfield, welcome to my country."

"Thank you, Colonel. This is my associate Mr. Mark Jones."

"Sit down, please. What would you like to drink?"

Lieutenant Colonel Petsut of the Royal Thai Police was a little man with big ears and a scar that ran from the tip of his nose across his mouth to his chin. Short black hair greased back, mischievous dark eyes. He said something to one of his aides in Thai, and the man disappeared. Pointing to his other companion, he added, "I want you to meet my assistant, Captain Jakkri Phibulsongkram. You can call him Jack."

"Jack, it's a pleasure."

A lovely young waitress arrived with a tray of drinks, including a local tom yum, which featured lime vodka with Thai chili garnish. Crocker sipped it while Petsut talked about his time as a young man studying criminal justice at the University of California, Irvine, that apparently involved a love affair with a young Southern California girl named Linda and a proposal of marriage. He said that the two had not married but remained friends. As evidence he showed them a picture of Linda, her husband, and two daughters standing with him and his family in front of a huge reclining gold Buddha known as Wat Pho. As he stuffed the photo back in his wallet, he said,

"I suppose you won't have time to visit the temple and stroll around the grounds. It always puts my spirit at peace."

Crocker said, "We're here on business."

"Yes," Petsut answered, sounding sad. He spoke about the terrorist attacks and the panic they had caused, as appetizers were set on the table—*meang kum*, Baan Thai spring rolls, pumpkin *tod*, chicken satay, crispy tofu, and chicken served with sweet sauce and crushed peanuts. All done gracefully and without interrupting the flow of conversation.

When Petsut mentioned Thailand's Malay Muslim separatist movement, which had set off bombs that had killed and wounded more than three hundred people in the southern cities of Yala and Hat Yai, Anderson quickly pointed out that those attacks were not related to the recent car bombings in Bangkok. Those, he said, had likely been orchestrated by Iranian nationals.

"Yes, yes," Petsut answered, "but the violence perpetrated by the Malay Muslims should also be a concern to you Americans, because they have specifically targeted civilian foreigners. They're trying to upset the very active tourist industry in the south."

"I'm aware of that, Colonel," Anderson said. "But Mr. Mansfield and his men are here specifically to deal with the men who planned and orchestrated the attacks last month."

Dinner was served with green tea, rice wine, and white Australian wine. They ate seafood curry, *kaeng phet pet yang* (roast duck in curry), fried rice with crabmeat, noodles stir-fried with Thai basil, deep-fried fish with sweet and tangy tamarind sauce.

Crocker dined heartily while Captain Jack explained that

one of the men suspected of carrying out the attack against John Rinehart and his wife had been wounded in the face. This individual had sought medical attention at a clinic in Khlong Toei, a lower-class, crime-ridden area of the city. The injured man claimed to have been walking in the vicinity of the attack with his girlfriend. But the doctor who treated him became suspicious because he was a foreigner and had recent burn marks on his ankles that looked as if they'd been caused by a motorcycle exhaust pipe.

After several days the injured man recovered enough to take a train to Kanchanaburi. At the station there he was observed arguing with another foreigner, who then let him into his car and drove him to a small farm outside the town.

Members of the Special Operations Unit under the supervision of Captain Jack had placed the farm under surveillance. They had observed four men, all foreigners who looked Middle Eastern, coming and going, but they pretty much kept to themselves. The police also saw two motorcycles that resembled the bikes used in the bomb attacks parked in a barn. A CIA-installed listening device revealed that the men conversed in Farsi.

As Captain Jack spoke, Crocker grew progressively excited. The leads the Thais had developed sounded promising. He knew from a previous trip to Thailand that Kanchanaburi was only a two-hour drive northwest of Bangkok.

With the arrival of dessert, Petsut started to discuss parameters. Because the violence had been directed at American officials and the perpetrators appeared to have arrived from a third country, he said he was willing to allow Crocker and his team to deal with the situation. Ideally, the four foreigners would be detained and quickly flown out of Thailand, and nobody in his country would notice.

He asked that violence and gunfire, especially, be kept to the minimum, only what was required to subdue the suspects. He pointed out that local Royal Thai Police would be forced to respond to any gun battle or loud explosion.

"Can you ask them to respond slowly?" Anderson asked.

"Of course," Petsut replied. "We can do that." Then turning to Crocker, he ran a finger along the scar on his face and asked, "Mr. Mansfield, when are you planning to execute your raid?"

"As soon as possible," Crocker answered, looking around the room to find the source of the terrible stink that had suddenly reached his nostrils. It smelled like an overflowing toilet or broken sewage pipe. Petsut, Captain Jack, and Anderson ate the pastries, pastes, and fruits as though nothing were wrong.

Anderson noticed Crocker's unease and whispered, "It's the durian you're smelling."

"What's that?"

Anderson pointed to a plate of light-green melon sections in the middle of the table. "Taste it, it's delicious."

Crocker did his best to get past the smell and put a piece in his mouth. The durian tasted creamy and bittersweet. To his surprise, he actually liked it.

"Is there a problem?" Colonel Petsut asked with a very slight smile.

"Not at all," Crocker answered. "I was thinking about how much time my men and I will need. By end of the day tomorrow I think our mission will be completed."

"Excellent," Petsut said. "I wish you success."

After the meal concluded with coffee, tea, and brandy, the Americans were asked whether they wanted a relaxing massage from one of several pretty and strong-looking women who arrived at their table dressed in white pants and T-shirts.

The offer was enticing, but Crocker declined.

"Work before pleasure," Colonel Petsut commented.

"That's correct."

CHAPTER SIX

*We have forty million reasons for failure, but not a single
excuse.*

—Rudyard Kipling

FORTY MINUTES later Crocker, Anderson, and Mancini sat
in Crocker's room at the Viengtai Hotel, examining a map
of Thailand with three of the other four SEALs and Anderson's assistant Daw, a former sergeant in the antiterrorism
unit of the Royal Malaysia Police. Akil was the only one
missing.

"Where is he?" Crocker asked.

"Chatting up some Thai babe in the lobby," Ritchie responded. "Hopefully, it isn't a dude. I've heard some of the
best-looking girls here are really guys."

"Tell him to get his ass up here."

Daw was pointing out the location of the farm in Kanchanaburi when Akil entered quietly.

"Sorry, boss," Akil said.

"You're going to have to stop thinking about pussy until
this op is over."

"I was in the lobby. I didn't know you were back."

With a hand missing two fingers Daw traced Route 323 to the farm, which was a few miles east of Kanchanaburi, a rural town and popular tourist destination of roughly thirty thousand people located at the base of the western mountains.

Transportation wasn't a problem, thanks to the two Lexus SUVs Anderson had at his disposal. Mancini made a quick list of supplies, including automatic rifles and pistols with silencers, stun and tear-gas grenades, explosive material for breaching doors and windows, tie-ties, rope, axes, KA-BAR knives, and blowout patches.

Crocker and his men had raided dozens of buildings, houses, and apartments before, but the logistics and restrictions regarding this particular mission were unique. Turning to Anderson, he said, "We generally attack in quadrants. So if we hit the front first, we have men stationed at angles to cover any escape from windows or the back door."

Anderson said, "I don't see that as a problem."

"No, the problems are twofold. One, subduing the terrorists without a prolonged gunfight. And two, dealing with possible booby traps on doors and windows."

"Why's that a problem?" Ritchie asked. "As long as I can get my hands on some C-4, I'll blow right through them."

"Because Colonel Petsut wants us to do this as quietly as possible."

Akil posed the million-dollar question: "How do we accomplish that?"

"How about we have someone posing as a neighbor or local official knock on the door?" Davis asked. "That way we can catch them off guard."

"Good idea," Crocker said. "But who do we know who can pull that off?"

"You mean pass as a local?"

"Exactly."

He was waiting for Daw to volunteer. Cal spoke first.

"I can, boss."

Cal did look Asian, and could probably pass for Thai.

"You can?" Crocker asked.

"I speak some Thai," Cal added.

"Since when?"

"Since I lived with this Thai chick when I was stationed in Coronado with SEAL Team One."

This was news to Crocker and all the guys in Black Cell. Nobody had ever heard Cal refer to a girlfriend before— Thai or otherwise.

"You lived with a chick?" Ritchie asked. "No shit."

"Sarai Wattana."

"Pretty?"

"Beautiful."

Crocker was determined to shift everyone's attention back to the mission. Directing his question to Cal, who was leaning against the wall, he asked, "You sure you have no problem claiming to be a local official?"

"Not at all."

"And you speak enough Thai to pull it off?"

"I do. Yes."

Daw drew a detailed map of the farm based on surveillance photos. Then Crocker spelled out a modified version of the patrol leader's order, or PLO. First he covered points of engagement and firing positions. "Before Cal approaches the door, I want Akil and Davis positioned behind trees or bushes on the right side of the house. Akil, you'll try to establish line of sight through the right window."

"Got it."

"Ritchie and Mancini will be stationed out front. We'll try to get at least some of them to surrender. If that doesn't work, I'll give the order and we'll fire from the right-front quadrant, then shift to cut down or capture anyone fleeing the rear of the house."

Several of the men, who were seated on the desk and chairs, and leaning against the walls, nodded.

"Any targets we capture, we tie-tie or tape them, cover their mouths, and move on. Speed will be our friend." Turning to Anderson, Crocker said, "Cal is going to need a mike on him. I want to be able to communicate with each team front and back via radio."

"Handheld okay?" Anderson asked.

"Handheld is fine. We'll use the standard hand signals."

The men nodded.

"What about curious neighbors or other people arriving at the house while we're there?" Mancini asked.

"Neighbors we try to scare away. Point a weapon at them and use hand signals to tell them to keep their mouths shut. Same with dogs. Throw a rock at them, anything. Incessant, angry barking will have to be handled with a silenced round."

Several of the men were dog lovers, but they didn't protest.

Crocker looked at Davis and said, "The element of surprise is paramount. Anyone arriving at the house while we're at the farm will have to be subdued, or if they're armed or you suspect they're armed, taken out. Anything else?"

"Booby traps," Davis offered.

"Booby traps are a real danger. Clear all windows and doors before entering. Don't touch anything in the house or garage that you don't have to. Deal with the occupants first. We will be looking for at least four foreign nationals, Middle Eastern–looking men. After we've neutralized them, we'll do a quick sweep of the house and garage. Then we're out of there. Understood?"

"Yeah."

They decided that Cal would knock on the front door posing as a businessman from Bangkok who was lost and looking for a nearby property that was for sale. They dressed him in black pants and a long-sleeved blue oxford cloth shirt, and Anderson provided him with fake business cards and an actual real estate listing near the farm with an address and photo.

According to Plan A, Cal would lure the terrorists out to the front porch. On a signal from Crocker, the element in front would engage the enemy and try to arrest them. The element on the right side of the house would detain anyone escaping through the back. If for some reason Cal was asked or forced to enter the house, Plan B would go into effect on Crocker's order, which meant the men in front would rush through the forward door, while the ones on the side of the house covered the windows and back.

Gear and weapons secured, both plans talked through and rehearsed, the members of Black Cell set out from Bangkok at 0545 the next morning dressed in civilian clothes with their Dragon Skin body armor underneath.

Crocker noted that the sky was low loom, which meant a dark, moonless night.

He sat alone in the rear seat of the lead SUV going over everything in his head, checking to ensure that he hadn't forgotten some contingency. Daw drove, Cal sat beside him, and Ritchie and Mancini occupied the middle seats. Anderson followed in the second vehicle with Davis and Akil.

Within an hour the sun started to rise and Crocker saw that they were passing through a peaceful grove of evergreen trees. The violence of what they were about to do struck him.

"That river we're following on our left is the River Kwai," Mancini remarked as though he was a tour guide.

"The River Kwai from the movie?" Cal asked.

"Yes. Kanchanaburi was the setting of the David Lean movie starring Alec Guinness, *The Bridge on the River Kwai*. But the movie was shot in Sri Lanka."

"Whatever," Ritchie groaned, checking the chamber of his Benelli M4 Super 90 twelve-gauge shotgun with a laser illuminator mounted on the rail interface system on the barrel.

"Kanchanaburi was the location of the real POW labor camps," Mancini added.

"What camps?" Ritchie asked.

"You never saw the movie?"

"It was a long time ago. I forget."

Crocker'd seen it. It was one of his favorites, along with *The Godfather*, *Pulp Fiction*, and *Lawrence of Arabia*.

"The Japanese moved 61,700 allied prisoners—Brits, Americans, Aussies, Dutch—from POW camps in Singapore, Indonesia, and Malaysia to build a railroad from Thailand to Burma," Mancini explained. "The conditions they had to work under sucked, especially during the 1943 monsoon. And the Japs treated them like shit. Over sixteen thousand allied POWs died from sickness, malnutrition, and exhaustion."

"Did they ever finish the railroad?" Cal asked.

"Even though the prisoners had few pulleys, derricks, or other equipment, they managed to complete what became known as the Death Railway in about a year."

Daw pointed out that the town of Kanchanaburi became a popular tourist site after the movie came out in 1957. "Two museums were built," he explained. "But what the tourists who came here really wanted to see was the bridge. The problem was that the actual bridge didn't cross the River Khwae. It crossed a parallel river known as the Mae Klong. So what do you think Thai officials did to solve this problem?"

"You know the answer?" Ritchie asked Mancini.

"No, wiseguy."

"They switched the names of the two rivers," Daw said with a smile as he drove.

The road followed a limestone cliff covered with green foliage that ran along the river. Low tin-roofed buildings clung to the shore, indicating that they were entering the town. They passed temple caves, an elephant park, and even a tiger temple, where visitors could pet real Bengal tigers. But they hadn't come for the attractions.

The farm they were looking for sat on lower land on the opposite side of the river, so they crossed a narrow bridge. Rain started to fall as they turned off an asphalt road onto a mustard-colored dirt trail pitted with water-filled holes. The sun was trying to fight its way through dark clouds.

Crocker imagined that a rainbow would appear soon as his heartbeat sped up. He felt the tension building around him and heard the guys doing last-minute checks of their comms and weapons.

"You sure we're in the right place?" Ritchie asked as they bounced along.

"The entrance is over there, up ahead," Daw said, pointing to the right as he braked the vehicle to a stop.

Crocker said, "I'll hide on the floor. Manny, you, Daw, and Ritchie get out here."

Cal took the wheel and maneuvered the vehicle around a bend to a fence overrun with vines and weeds. He turned in the entrance, which had no sign, drove another two hundred feet through a patch of mango trees, and stopped about 150 feet from the house. The springs under the chassis creaked. A bird screeched.

Crocker waited about a minute, until he heard Akil's voice over the handheld radio telling him the men were in position. Then he slapped the back of the seat twice, which was the signal to go.

Cal left the engine running and the wipers slapping from side to side and got out. Crocker heard his footsteps on the wet dirt, then pulled himself up behind the seat and watched.

It was a low-slung, dilapidated structure painted pale yellow, with a porch in front and a rusted tin roof. A shed or garage with a red door peeked out from some bushes to the right. No cars, trucks, or motorcycles were visible through the light rain.

Through the earbud connected wirelessly to a tiny microphone in Cal's shirt pocket, Crocker heard a door creak open and Cal speaking in Thai. Then he heard a screen door snap shut.

"It looks like Cal has gone inside," Akil reported over the handheld radio. Anderson had joined Akil and Davis behind bushes on the right side of the house. Daw, Ritchie, and Mancini waited in front.

With Cal inside the house, Crocker waited and listened carefully. Things rarely went according to plan.

Through the earbud he heard a man talking aggressively in accented English, asking, "Who are you? Who sent you? What do you want?" At the end, he was almost shouting.

Cal started to answer in Thai, but the man cut him off. Then Crocker heard what sounded like a slap and scuffling, followed by two shots.

"Plan B!" Crocker shouted into the handheld. He burst out the side door of the SUV and ran as fast as he could to the front of the house. Arriving first, suppressed HK MP7A1 ready, he was about to push through the screen door when it opened and a very thin bearded man with a wild mop of hair stuck his head out. Crocker decked him with an elbow to the neck, then stepped over his prone body into the house.

He heard screams in what he thought was Farsi, and as his eyes adjusted to the darkness made out the shape of a man reaching for a pistol on the kitchen counter to his right. Crocker cut him down with four quick shots center of mass and one to the face. Mancini and Ritchie rushed in behind him.

The place was a shithole, with a sour, garlicky stench, discarded newspapers on the floor, clothes thrown over all available surfaces. He spotted a half-naked man scurrying out the back door; another was on his knees behind a sofa. A third stood near a mattress on the floor in front of Crocker, holding Cal in a headlock with his left arm. His right hand held a pistol to Cal's head.

"Surrender!" the man shouted in heavily accented English. "Drop the gun!"

Crocker shouted back with authority, "You're surrounded, asshole!"

The muscles on the terrorist's face tightened. Cal's nose bled down his chin onto the front of his shirt, but he appeared calm. The Middle Eastern man trembled as he pressed the gun harder against Cal's temple. Out of the corner of his right eye, Crocker saw the short barrel of the MK18 Mod 0 beyond the window. Then he heard a stream of 5.56x45mm bullets rip through the glass and saw them slam into the man's torso and head. The terrorist slumped and fell to the floor, leaving Cal frozen in place, covered with blood and brain matter.

"Cal, you okay?"

Crocker was aiming his gun at the man behind the sofa when a huge explosion went off behind the house, ripping through the back and sending debris and glass flying everywhere. He used his left arm and shoulder to shield his face. A piece of wood smacked into the Dragon Skin that covered his chest.

Crocker leaned against a cabinet to his right and caught his breath, then crossed to a big hole in the wall where the back window had been. "Wait here, Cal."

The sofa lay in shreds, and the man who had been hiding behind it was legless now and choking on his blood and dying. A long shard of metal had severed his throat. Through the smoke and falling debris Crocker saw something burning beyond the lemon trees behind the house.

"What blew?" he asked into the handheld.

"The garage," Akil reported. "The guy who ran out the back activated some kind of trigger before we could stop him."

"You see anyone else flee the house?"

"Negative."

"All our guys okay?"

"Anderson got some shit in his eye, a couple scratches. We're good."

"Search the back," Crocker shouted. "See what you can find. Then we'd better clear out."

Returning to the house, Crocker saw Ritchie and Mancini tie-tieing the man he had downed coming in the door. He was hyperventilating.

Crocker said, "Throw him in the truck, and help Cal. Tell Daw to stay with 'em. Then come back and help me look through this mess."

"Roger."

They gathered everything they could find—notebooks, laptops, thumb drives, maps, cell phones—threw them into plastic bags, and got the hell out of there, leaving behind four bodies and a burning garage. They had killed four suspected terrorists. A fifth lay on the floor in the backseat talking to himself in what sounded like Farsi.

Crocker said, "Slap some tape over his mouth. Shut him up."

The rain had stopped and the sun was trying to burn through the low clouds. Behind them black smoke rose into the gray-blue sky.

This was exactly what Colonel Petsut had told them to avoid—an explosion and fire. But shit happened.

As they tore through the front gate and turned left, Crocker heard sirens approaching. He turned to Daw and shouted, "Get us back on the highway to Bangkok. Fast!" If nothing else, they had taken out the terrorists who had killed John Rinehart, his wife, and the other U.S. officials.

CHAPTER SEVEN

Home is the place where, when you have to go there, they have to take you in.

—Robert Frost

BLACK CELL arrived home in Virginia Beach ten days before Christmas. It felt strange to Crocker, being back. Maybe it was the abrupt transition from death and destruction to lights and holiday music. Friends and family tried to sweep him up in the celebration and excitement, but something in him resisted.

He stood outside Banana Republic at the local mall looking at the faces of children lined up to see Santa Claus. The Santa the mall had hired this year had the same beak-shaped nose, oval face, and bushy eyebrows as ST-6 psychologist Dr. Neal Petrovian. Except Dr. Petrovian was a hundred pounds leaner and his eyebrows, beard, and hair were more salt-and-pepper than white. Holly and Jenny were inside shopping. He was thinking about Cal and how he was doing when his cell phone lit up.

His sister Karen on the other end of the line said, "Tom, did you hear? Dad's been arrested."

What Crocker had just heard sounded surreal, like maybe he wasn't hearing right. Or it was some kind of sick joke.

"Are you kidding me? Dad's been *arrested?*"

"That's what I just said."

"Our father? Are you sure?" he asked into the cell phone.

"Yes I am, Tom."

"Where is he now? What did he do?"

"He's being held in Alexandria County Jail on two counts of assault with a deadly weapon."

"Dad assaulted someone?" Those were words he had never expected to say.

"Yes, Tom. Our beloved father is in the slammer."

Message received, he knew immediately what he had to do, and said, "I'll drive there now."

It seemed incredible. His father was the kindest, most outgoing, empathetic man he knew. He liked people and loved entertaining them with stories. Except during his service in the navy, he'd never been in a fight, as far as Crocker knew. Only once or twice had his son even seen him lose his temper.

Threaten someone with a weapon? It seemed wildly out of character.

Holly seemed equally confounded when he told her. She looked at him with suspicion, as though he might be making up some crazy story so he could slip away from all the people and festivities.

Nothing could have been further from his mind. All he wanted was peace and quiet, and some time with his family, because his heart was still heavy from the ordeal in Nuristan Province. The four days and nights he'd been home had been good. Holly had started seeing a female psychotherapist and seemed better.

"Some people have to do what they've got to do," she had said to him last night as they sat in front of the fireplace. "You're like that, Tom. You almost can't help yourself. It's not a criticism. I admire your courage, and maybe I'm a little jealous of your sense of purpose." They held hands while watching the third season of *Deadwood*, then went to bed.

He'd awakened this morning feeling stronger mentally and physically than he had in months. Now this.

The desk sergeant was a Hispanic guy who burped into his hand as he checked the ledger, then escorted Crocker to a windowless room that needed repainting. Two black officers brought in his dad, looking small and embarrassed, and wearing handcuffs. Strands of limp white hair hung over his eyes.

It pissed Crocker off to see them treating his father like a criminal. "Dad, you okay?" he asked.

The old man avoided his son's eyes and shook his head. "I've been better. My back feels like I was hit by a car after last night."

"Jesus, Dad. They made you spend the night in jail?"

His father nodded, scratching his neck.

"Dad, what the hell happened?" Crocker asked.

The old man grimaced and ran his tongue over his teeth. "What'd your sister tell you?"

"Just that you were arrested and charged with assault."

His father nodded. "That much is true."

Crocker did a double take. "Dad, I can't imagine you assaulting anyone," he exclaimed. "What took place? I mean . . . how? why?"

"It's not your concern, son. I got in this mess, I'll get out of it myself."

"What are you talking about?" He sounded incredulous. "You're my father. I'm gonna help you and bail you out."

"That's not necessary."

"Yes it is!"

Their eyes met. Crocker saw the shame and anger in his father's as he slammed the little metal table with his fist. "It's an injustice! That's what it is, Tom. Carla—that poor girl served our country. And her German landlord had the gall to try to throw her out of her apartment. He's not even a citizen."

Crocker remembered his father mentioning her before but couldn't recall the details. "What about her?" he asked.

"Carla?" His dad curled his upper lip the way he always did when he was about to tell a story. "She's this young gal I told you about. Met her while volunteering at the Fairfax VA. She's a Gulf War vet suffering from PTSD and other medical problems. She works as a waitress at Applebee's, but she's been having trouble paying her bills. Last night I got a panicked call from her. Her landlord, this German guy, was in her apartment and threatening to evict her and her nine-year-old son. He was in the process of tossing her stuff out on the sidewalk. I drove over. Me and him, we got into a heated argument. He told me to get the hell out of there; I told him I wouldn't. He pushed me to the floor. I picked up a little wooden stool to defend myself and kind of by accident hit him in the face. He started bleeding and called the police."

*   *   *

What Crocker really wanted to do was find the landlord and kick the shit out of him. But he knew he couldn't do that.

So later that night he posted bail and drove his father back to his apartment, where they ordered takeout Chinese. The next morning he accompanied him to the courthouse, where the judge dismissed the charges because the landlord had forced his way into Carla's apartment without a legal eviction notice.

Crocker was sitting across from his dad at Applebee's, waiting to meet Carla and order lunch, when his cell phone rang. It was Captain Sutter's executive officer, telling him to return to the command as soon as possible.

So he climbed into his truck and drove as fast as he could down I-95, listening to Dave Brubeck, who had just passed away one day before his ninety-second birthday. As he arrived at the SEAL Six compound, Paul Desmond's alto sax solo in "Three to Get Ready" was still playing in his head. Sutter's XO looked annoyed as he walked with him down a hallway past framed photos of former COs. Sutter and Jim Anders stood waiting in the conference room with a man and woman in suits.

As soon as Crocker entered, Sutter said, "Sit down, Crocker. This is urgent."

"Sorry I was delayed, sir. I was dealing with a family matter."

"What we're about to discuss involves you and Black Cell. We need to know if you and your men are going to be able to deploy immediately."

"Yes, sir. The family matter's been handled," Crocker said, even though he had doubts. He also wasn't sure about Cal's mental state, since he hadn't spoken to him since the incident in Kanchanaburi.

Jim Anders cleared his throat, puffed out his chest, and started. "Nice work in Thailand, but the Thais are angry."

"I understand," Crocker countered. "The firefight, explosion, and fire couldn't be avoided. We attempted to surprise the terrorists, but things didn't go as planned."

"I said, nice work."

Crocker tended to be overly defensive about criticism from Langley. "Thanks."

Anders looked at Captain Sutter, who was seated at the head of the table and said, "We'll hold a hot wash later. There's also the matter of the Afghan major you detained at OP Memphis."

Crocker sat up. "Sir."

"In my opinion you're right about him, Crocker. But the disciplinary committee in Kabul wants a formal statement from you. When you have time, draft one. Include the reasons you became suspicious, what you saw, and the circumstances of his arrest."

"Yes, sir."

"Now, let's focus on the task in front of us."

Anders took this as his cue. "Yes," he said, pointing to his male companion, who dimmed the lights. A Smart Board illuminated on the front wall. On it appeared photos of the four terrorists who had died at Kanchanaburi.

The female CIA officer, wearing a blue blouse and a tight black jacket and skirt, stood up and spoke in a clipped voice.

"I expect you recognize these men, Warrant Officer Crocker."

"Yes I do," he answered.

A fifth photo appeared on the board—that of the man they had captured and turned over to the Royal Thai Police.

"This man claims to be Tino Farris. We've learned that his real name is Javad Mokri, and we believe he's the one who assembled the bombs in Thailand."

"The Thais are still holding him?" Crocker asked.

"Affirmative. And he refuses to talk."

Two of the three passports on the screen were partially burned. "All five of these individuals traveled to Thailand on Venezuelan passports," she continued. "We think they're part of the Quds Force Unit 5000 team operating out of Venezuela. And we have reason to believe they're planning more attacks against U.S. assets overseas and possibly even terrorist attacks inside the United States."

"Venezuela?" Crocker asked, alarmed that the Quds Force was operating in such close proximity to the States.

She said, "That's correct."

Anders said, "Thank you, Ms. Walker."

She sat beside Crocker and crossed her long legs.

"Ms. Walker is the assistant director of our Quds Force Working Group. Sy Blanc here is the director."

Crocker smiled as if to say "Nice to meet you."

The tall, gray-haired man named Blanc stood up. A picture of two men embracing appeared on the screen. He said, "Earlier this year Iranian president Mahmoud Ahmadinejad visited Venezuelan president Hugo Chávez in Caracas, and the two men lavished praise on each other and vowed to resist U.S. imperialism—specifically the tough sanctions we've imposed on Iran for continuing its nuclear program."

Chávez was a highly controversial demagogue who had taken power in 1998, nationalized foreign-owned businesses, and established alliances with the Castros in Cuba and President Evo Morales in Bolivia. He was now dying of cancer.

Said Blanc, "The Iranians have grown increasingly desperate. Not only are the economic sanctions hurting their economy, but we've also been running a number of covert operations aimed at their nuclear program. And they know it. They seem determined to hit us back, and Unit 5000 seems to be the means they've chosen to do that with. President Chávez, who has his own issues with us, has been helping them and allowing them to operate on his territory. With Chávez on his deathbed, the Iranians seem to be picking up the pace."

"What do you want from us?" Crocker asked.

Anders said, "You'll go into Venezuela in alias. Agency officials there will assist you. Basically we want to find out what Unit 5000 is doing there, what they've established in terms of resources, and what they're planning. To whatever degree is possible, we want you to thwart their operations."

"Happily," Crocker replied. "What about the Falcon?"

Ms. Walker clicked her red nails on the table and said, "We seem to have lost track of him temporarily."

Crocker was disappointed. He asked, "Isn't it fair to assume that he's behind Unit 5000's activities?"

"I would have to agree with that," she answered.

"Then why aren't we doing everything we can to go after him?"

"Because we think it's very likely that Farhed Alizadeh is back in Iran," Blanc asserted. "And since he's in Iran, he's out of reach. Besides, our immediate concern is what Unit 5000 is doing in Venezuela."

Crocker nodded. He understood, and he started thinking ahead. He had to contact his teammates, talk to Holly and Jenny, pack his gear.

It was 11 p.m. by the time he pulled into the driveway and found Holly sitting at the kitchen counter sipping a glass of rosé and looking forlorn.

"Something wrong?" he asked.

"You could have called," she said accusingly. "I expected you home at seven."

He said, "I just spent the last several hours with Captain Sutter."

"Really?" Holly said. "Work related?"

"Yeah. Important."

"Are you leaving again?" she asked anxiously.

"First thing tomorrow."

He noticed her hand trembling as she lifted the glass. She took a long sip and threw it toward the sink, where the glass shattered and wine splattered across the window and wall. "You might want to take a look at that!" she said, pointing to a letter on the counter.

"Holly, wait." He tried to stop her, but she avoided his grasp and left.

Over her shoulder she shouted, "I've had it! I'm exhausted. Don't ask me for any more help!"

He picked up the letter, unfolded it, and heard the bedroom door upstairs slam. Blood rising into his neck and face, he read the letter from Jenny's high school counselor. It said she was in danger of flunking two classes—biology and calculus—if she didn't perform better on her finals and turn in several missing assignments.

He sighed, refolded it, climbed the stairs, and knocked on Jenny's door.

"Honey?"

"Yeah?"

He pushed the door open. She sat up in bed, connected to her laptop via earbuds and wire.

"What are you listening to?" he asked.

She pulled the buds out, removed the retainer from her mouth, half smiled. "I'm studying."

"While listening to music?"

"Yeah." She was like a longer, younger version of his first wife, Kim—thin legs, big doelike eyes and reddish brown hair, dressed in gray sweatpants, a loose blue First Colonial High School T-shirt and socks. "It's that CD of yours that I downloaded," she said, offering him the earbuds.

He listened to the smooth modal changes of "So What" from the Miles Davis–Bill Evans masterpiece album *Kind of Blue*. It was one of Crocker's favorites, and to his mind the best Davis ever recorded.

"You really like it?" he asked.

"It's cool and…like…helps me relax."

He sat on a pink plastic stool across from her. "Sweetheart, let's talk about the letter that came from your counselor."

"Oh that…." As if the weight of the world had suddenly fallen on her seventeen-year-old shoulders.

He cut to the chase. "Is this about a boy, drugs, alcohol, or something else not related to school?"

"No, Dad," she answered. "Is that what Holly told you?"

"No."

"I'm not partying or fooling around," she said. "Maybe I go out on the weekends with my friends, but I come home every day after school and study."

"Then what's the problem?"

She sighed, "Dad, I'm trying. I'm just dealing with a lot of like…personal stuff."

He wanted to believe that, and knew it had to be tough having a mother who couldn't deal with her and sent her to live with a father who wasn't around most of the time. He tried to be involved, the way he was doing now, asking her what was going on at school, patiently waiting for her to explain. According to her, things weren't as bad as they seemed. Teachers in both classes had failed to enter some of her assignments into the computer grading system. And there were some tests and quizzes that she was planning to retake.

In the end, she accused Holly of overreacting.

Crocker begged her to be understanding. Holly, he explained, was going through a difficult time of her own.

Jenny nodded. "I know, Dad. I think she still feels guilty about her friend who died."

Both women were hypersensitive, especially with regard to each other.

He said, "I agree," then kissed her, told her he loved her, and that he had to leave the next morning.

"You think you'll be back for Christmas?" Jenny asked.

The holiday was four days away. "I don't know," he answered. "The odds aren't good."

"But you'll call?"

"Every opportunity I get."

"Thanks, Dad. I love you. Be safe."

He closed the door behind him, and padded down the hall to his bedroom, where Holly lay in bed with the reading lamp on beside her. He splashed water on his face, brushed his teeth, pulled off the sweater he'd worn all day, and sat down on the bed beside her.

"Holly," he whispered. "Sweetheart…"

She turned and he saw she'd been crying. He wanted to take her by the shoulders and tell her to snap out of it, but he knew that wouldn't work. So he wiped the tears from her eyes, told her he'd spoken to Jenny and she had assured him that her grades weren't as bad as they seemed. In fact, she thought she was getting A's in her three other classes.

"I can't help her, Tom," Holly said, squeezing his hand. "I'm too busy trying to deal with my own problems."

He kissed her on the lips. "I know, sweetheart. Don't be so hard on yourself."

CHAPTER EIGHT

*There is not a righteous man on earth who always does
what is right and never sins.*

—Ecclesiastes 7:20

THE SIX members of Black Cell sat in the Corona Beach
House in Terminal D of the Miami International Airport,
watching the Heat-Jazz game on TV, sipping beers and
snacking on nachos as they waited for their connecting flight.
The last time Crocker had been in Caracas he'd been part of
a security team guarding President George H. W. Bush back
in 1990 and not too long after he graduated from BUD/S.

That was before Hugo Chávez had assumed power and
become a thorn in the side of the United States. He even
blamed the States for causing the earthquake that devastated
Haiti in January 2010.

Crocker pulled Cal over to the salsa bar and asked, "You
okay?"

"Yeah. Why?"

"Just checking."

Working with the men on the team was easier than dealing

with people in civilian life. They bled, but they didn't complain. Their bones cracked, but they'd been trained not to break down psychologically.

He returned to the table as Ritchie was telling the others about a trip he'd made to New York City over the weekend with his fiancée, Monica, and how they'd enjoyed the Christmas show at Radio City Music Hall, ice skating at Rockefeller Center, shopping at Barney's and Bergdorf's. Monica had expensive tastes, and Ritchie, who had grown up in a trailer park on the outskirts of Dallas, seemed not to mind.

The two of them were planning an April wedding in D.C., and Crocker wondered after they were married how much longer a strong-willed, financially independent woman like Monica would want Ritchie to continue in SEAL teams. She'd want to have him around to travel with her, ski, play, have fun. Even though the pay was decent (around $100,000 a year, including his E-6 base pay, special skills pay, imminent danger pay, special assignment pay, and reenlistment installments), the hours sucked. It was the most exciting and challenging work Crocker could imagine. But the many days away from home wreaked havoc on relationships and families.

He was more aware of this than ever as he watched people pass by on their way to spend the Christmas holidays with loved ones. They had a right to be happy, especially this time of year. And a right to be protected, too, which is where he and his team fit in—to guard the sheep from the wolves.

Across the table he saw Mancini tearing into a huge mound of salad.

"You become a vegetarian?" Crocker asked.

"Teresa put me on a diet," the big man said, raising his thick eyebrows. "All the fresh veggies you can eat. A prescribed amount of protein. No rice, pasta, bread, cookies, or cake."

"Good luck." He had watched Mancini adopt and slip off numerous food regimens in the past. Not only was his wife an amazing cook, but the guy loved to eat.

"How many years you been on the teams?" Crocker asked him.

"Four years with Team Two. Eight fun-filled years now with Six—excuse me, DEVGRU. How about you?"

"Two years with Team One, three with Two, and twelve now with DEVGRU."

"We're the old-timers," Mancini said, glancing at Ritchie, Cal, Davis, and Akil sitting next to them, ribbing each other and cracking jokes. "Why'd you ask? You thinking of retiring?"

"Hell no," Crocker groaned. The idea repulsed him. Even though he was in his early forties, he had no plans for slowing down.

"Me neither," Mancini said, wiping salad dressing off his lips and beard. "And soon we're going to have some new toys to play with."

"What do you mean?"

"I spent a day last week with the people of DARPA." The Defense Advanced Research Projects Agency (DARPA), headquartered in Arlington, Virginia, was the most active and experimental military technology research facility on the planet.

"Yeah? What'd you see?" Part of DEVGRU's mission was to test the latest weapons and gear. For his part, Crocker tended to put more stock in the value of training and preparing first-class operators than in technology.

"They showed me some wicked cool new gadgets," Mancini said, grinning like a kid on Christmas morning. "I got to fire a BAE laser cannon, which shoots a laser blast as far as a mile and a half. They're developing a version of it to deploy on navy ships, to temporarily blind pirates and other terrorists. I fired a handheld version that shoots out this green beam of light like something out of *Star Wars*."

"No shit."

"But the most radical thing by far was the invisibility cloak they're developing."

"Invisibility? Really?" It sounded like something out of one of the Harry Potter movies he'd watched with his daughter.

Mancini said, "A couple years from now, you'll be able to wrap this cloak around you and walk into a building or enemy encampment completely unseen."

"Are you serious?" Crocker asked, checking the score on the TV beyond Manny's shoulder. The Heat were ahead by seven points with four minutes to play.

"It only works for a fraction of a second now, but the engineers at DARPA expect to improve it soon," Mancini explained.

Crocker feigned interest; his mind was elsewhere. "How's it work?"

"It's made of sheets of carbon wrapped up into tubes. Each page is barely the size of a single molecule, but it's hard as steel. The sheets are heated electronically, which causes light to bend away from the carbon nanotube sheet. It's basically the same as creating the pool-of-water effect you see when you're driving on a desert highway. They're also experimenting with metamaterials, natural materials that have a positive refractive index, to make tanks and ships invisible."

"Amazing," Crocker said, signaling the waitress.

"Isn't it?" Mancini leaned across the table and whispered in Crocker's ear. "And they gave me something for us to try out."

"What?"

"You'll see. They're tiny little drones, the size of my thumbnail. I've got two of them taped into the lining of my suitcase."

"Cool."

They landed early Christmas Eve morning at the Simón Bolívar International Airport. A tall Russian Venezuelan woman named Zoya from the Tara-Omega travel agency met them at the gate and helped them through Venezuelan immigration and customs. They were traveling as survival experts under the employ of a Canadian company called Balzac Expeditions and were purportedly in Venezuela to organize a trek into the Amazon jungle.

"I've booked you for a one-week stay at the InterContinental Tamanaco Caracas, which is right in the heart of one of the city's most prestigious shopping and business districts, Las Mercedes," Zoya said as her heels clicked down the terminal concourse. She seemed eager and efficient, and looked very young.

"If you need to extend your stay, you can continue at the same rate," she explained in perfect English.

"Great," Crocker said, half asleep. At 6 a.m. the terminal seemed vast and deserted. "And you got us a vehicle?"

"A one-year-old Honda Pilot. Will that meet your needs?"

"I don't see why not."

She led them to the silver SUV, which was parked in a three-story lot near the terminal. "One last thing," she said, handing over the keys. "The security situation in Caracas is deplorable. Currently we have an average of one murder per hour just in the capital. So keep your eyes open and don't travel alone, especially at night. Street gangs here like to rob and kidnap foreigners."

"Thanks for the warning," Crocker said.

She glanced at his biceps and added, "You guys look like you know how to defend yourselves, but be careful." Then she handed him her card. "Call me if you need anything. That's my cell phone."

"We will," Akil said with a smile. "Maybe you can show us around later tonight?"

"Tonight is Christmas Eve," she explained, holding her reddish-brown hair back and shielding her eyes from the early morning sun. "I'm spending it with my family."

"Then have a Merry Christmas."

"Merry Christmas to you, too."

Fog shrouded the emerald-green mountains on both sides of the Autopista Caracas–La Guaira. When it cleared, Crocker saw thousands of little shanties clinging to cliffs. The local government called them "informal settlements" but they were really enormous, sprawling slums. Modern office towers dotted the narrow valley ahead. The Garmin GPS map on the dashboard indicated that they were traveling roughly north to south, from the airport on the Caribbean coast to the capital city, which lay inland.

"Venezuela is a country of approximately twenty-nine million people," Mancini reported. "About a fourth of them live here in Caracas, which as you can see offers limited space because of its topography. So the city has an enormous housing problem on top of the huge disparity between rich and poor."

"Good to know," Ritchie said from the rear seat.

"Despite Chávez's socialist Bolivarian revolution, which was supposed to redistribute wealth to the poor, the country suffers from double-digit inflation, soaring crime, chronic shortages due to government meddling, and the expropriation of successful businesses and ranches," Mancini added.

Davis cut in. "Sounds like you're saying that despite Chávez's best intentions he's pretty much screwed things up."

"He's helped the poor, no question," Mancini answered. "But inefficient government management and expropriations have chased away local and foreign investment, and hinder the country from expanding past a single-resource economy."

"Oil, in other words," Davis added.

"Petroleum production. They pump something like 2.3 million barrels a day. Down from 3.5 million in '98 and continuing to plummet."

The female voice on the Garmin instructed Crocker to turn off the highway. They entered what looked like an upscale residential community, but bags of garbage were piled along the side of the road, many of the shops seemed empty, and pro- and anti-Chávez graffiti covered the walls.

Four blocks farther on they reached the elegant Las Mercedes district and turned down an alley to a nine-story modern sandstone structure shaped like a hexagon. Part of the aboveground parking structure was roped off.

A young man in shorts and flip-flops who stopped them

and offered to guard their car explained in Spanish that the roped-off area was occupied by squatters. He pointed out that he, his mother, brother, and three sisters lived in a twelve-by-twelve-foot wooden cubicle allocated to them by the Chávez government. His family and three dozen others shared a single bathroom with no hot water in the parking structure.

"How do you cook?" Crocker asked in broken Spanish.

"We have electricity, but no gas for cooking," the skinny man explained. "So the government delivers three meals a day and provides beds and furniture. They even bus my younger brother and sisters to a school three miles away."

Crocker handed the kid a five-dollar bill, parked the Pilot, and led the team down a flight of stairs to a modern lobby. Armed soldiers were stationed at either side of the front desk.

"What are they here for?" Crocker asked the male hotel clerk.

"They make sure we don't raise prices beyond those set by the government." The clerk went on to explain that the country had two exchange rates. The rate set for "priority" imports was 2.60 bolívars to the dollar and for nonessential items 4.30.

"I assume we're getting the nonessential rate," Crocker said.

"Yes you are, sir." But most of the benefit of the better rate quickly evaporated when the clerk explained that room prices had just been raised 15 percent.

A sign on the marble counter carried more warnings. In addition to the rampant street crime they had already heard about, the SEALs now learned that the country was experiencing a temporary energy shortage, which meant that guests could expect regular power outages.

"That's ridiculous," Ritchie commented as they rode up to the third floor.

"Especially in a country that's one of the top oil producers in the world."

The rooms were big and nicely appointed, with king-sized beds, LCD TVs, desks, safes, and balconies overlooking the garden and pool. But the trash cans hadn't been emptied, the sheets were stained, and Crocker and Akil's toilet didn't work. They used Mancini and Cal's while they waited for the plumber, who came four hours later, just as they were getting ready to leave for dinner.

Outside, the sidewalks were packed with strollers, partyers, and last-minute shoppers, especially tree-lined Avenida Principal de las Mercedes and inside the huge, multilevel Paseo shopping mall. The six fit men passed fashion boutiques, galleries, restaurants, discos, pubs, and beautiful young women displaying lots of tanned flesh even though it was Christmas Eve. Akil's head swiveled so rapidly to take in all the pulchritude that Crocker thought it might fall off.

Stores offered everything from Japanese anime dolls to Chinese noodles, haute French fashion, Turkish-made hookahs, NFL jerseys, English toffee, Colombian coffee, and Indian cotton.

The city boasted a modern subway system, yet the streets were clogged with traffic—mainly U.S.- and Japanese-made cars. From one of them Crocker heard a rap song blaring in Spanish, "People from the barrio ready to fight for a better life…"

Mancini stopped to sample the arepas—warm cornmeal patties filled with melted cheese—from a sidewalk vendor, and then they entered a traditional English pub. Crocker ordered fish-and-chips washed down with Newcastle Brown Ale. They bantered about the football season, basketball, trucks, motorcycles. Then the subject, as it always did, turned to women.

Akil turned to Ritchie: "You hear what Tommy Lee from Mötley Crüe said about marriage?"

Ritchie: "I know this is a setup. What?"

"Marriage is the only war where one sleeps with the enemy."

"And the enemy he got to sleep with was Pamela Anderson," Davis added.

Mancini: "That's before Kid Rock got hold of her and turned her into trailer trash."

"Monica isn't like that," Ritchie said. "She's classy, and we get along."

Akil: "Just wait."

"You know why marriage is like a violin?" Mancini asked. "After the music is over, the strings are still attached."

As the SEALs bantered back and forth, Cal used his fingernail to peel the label off a Dos Equis bottle.

"Cal, you dating anyone?" Ritchie asked.

"Not really. No."

"You keep in touch with that Thai girl?"

"Naw."

"You live by yourself?"

"I'm sharing a house in Lago Mar with two young waitresses who work at Hooters."

"Seriously?" Ritchie asked, raising his left eyebrow.

Cal nodded. "Yeah."

"What are they like?" Akil wanted to know.

"Beautiful but messy as all get-out. Leave their clothes and shit everywhere. Walk around in their panties."

"That's all?" Akil asked.

"Sometimes even less."

"And that's a problem?" Ritchie asked.

Cal smiled like the Cheshire cat. "Naw."

After dinner, he, Akil, and Ritchie ducked into a theater to catch the newest James Bond movie. Davis returned to the hotel to Skype his wife and year-old son. Crocker and Mancini entered a bar called Islands and found a young Hispanic man in a white polo with a Miami Dolphins logo on the front pocket sitting in a booth in the back.

"Ernesto Navarro. Most people call me Neto," he said, offering a hand with a large burn scar.

Crocker asked, "You the guy who's selling the beachfront property?"

"On Margarita Island. Yes."

Having dispensed with the bona fides, the SEALs sat. The room was dark and noisy, with most of the young patrons crowded around the bar.

Neto, who was with the Caracas CIA station, asked, "You guys okay to talk here, or do you want to go somewhere else?"

"This is fine," Crocker said, looking around and seeing that no one was seated close by. "Do we run any risk of being watched?"

"By SEBIN this time of year? About as much of a chance as the Wizards winning the NBA finals."

SEBIN (Servicio Bolivariano de Inteligencia Nacional) was the Venezuela secret police, previously known as DISIP. The Washington Wizards were the worst team in the NBA, with a record of two wins and fifteen losses.

"I assume you've been briefed on why we're here," Crocker said, cutting to the chase.

"Unit 5000," Neto answered, pointing to his head. "I've become an expert."

"Thanks for doing this on Christmas Eve."

"Duty, man. Whatever needs to be done. My kids are already in bed dreaming about Santa Claus."

"How many do you have?" Mancini asked.

"Two young boys. Total rascals."

Crocker: "I hope Santa's going to be generous."

"He will be."

The waitress, who wore a Hawaiian shirt tied above her waist, placed three bottles of cold beer on the table and smiled to reveal a metal ball in her tongue. She left behind a cloud of orchid-scented perfume.

"Here's to getting lucky," Neto said, raising his Corona.

Crocker leaned on his elbows and spoke directly into Neto's dark eyes. "What's the story with 5000?"

"It's an interesting one," Neto said, "with several new developments. Two things. One, we've been watching a house in Petare, which is one of the city's two major barrios. It's more like a shack on a hill. We've been tracking several known Unit 5000 operatives in and out of there for the past three weeks."

"Sounds like a good place to start," Crocker commented.

Neto said, "You'll never find it on your own. I'll have to show you."

"When?"

"How about Wednesday?" That was the day after Christmas.

"How about tomorrow night?" Crocker countered.

Neto frowned, then consulted his BlackBerry. "Christmas night? That might work."

"Good. We're gonna need gear."

"What, exactly?"

Crocker pointed to Mancini. "Talk to my colleague here."

Mancini grabbed a napkin and started writing. He said, "I'll give you a list right now."

Neto continued. "The barrios are dangerous, lawless places. Something like sixty percent of the city's population lives in them, and they're run by gangs."

"What kind of gangs?" Crocker asked.

"Primarily young punks who deal dope."

"You tell us how you want to handle getting in," Crocker said. "Maybe we're from a humanitarian organization handing out medicine. Maybe we give the gangs money to look the other way. Maybe we kick their asses. We don't care. We just want to get in and take a look at the house. Maybe grab a couple of the terrorists."

"You're talking about a raid, right?" Neto asked.

"Exactly." Crocker finished his beer and set the bottle down. "We're all about hitting 5000, capturing their asses, getting the guys we grab to talk, stopping them before they do more damage."

"I got it."

"What was the other thing?" Mancini asked Neto as he rubbed the stubble on his chin. "You said there were two."

"Yeah....We've picked up something from a source close to the minister of the interior. Seems like the Venezuela side of the Unit 5000 operation is being run by one of the president's top men—a colonel high up in SEBIN named Chavo Torres. A real shit-bag who we know is involved in drug dealing, prostitution, dogfighting, human trafficking, smuggling. Travels to Cuba frequently and hangs with the Castros. He happens to be the right-hand man of Nicolás Maduro, who is the current VP and will probably succeed Chávez when he croaks—which according to our sources could happen anytime."

"Torres sounds like a charmer," Crocker commented.

"A snake charmer, maybe."

"Can we assume that this Chavo character wouldn't be involved with Unit 5000 unless President Chávez and this Maduro guy approved?" Crocker asked.

"No question about it."

"And what is this Chavo guy doing for U-5000?"

"We're not sure," Neto answered, "but there's been a real marked step-up of activity now that Chávez is on his deathbed. I get the sense that they're building up to something big."

"A big attack, or a big expansion?" Crocker asked.

"Both."

He dreamt the wind was blowing and snow was piling up at the door and on the windowsill. The sky outside was black. Embers glowed in the fireplace. Seeing yellow eyes looking at him through the window, he reached under his bed for his pistol but found a stuffed toy animal instead.

In the morning, Crocker called Holly and Jenny to wish them a Merry Christmas. They were getting ready to go to her brother's house.

Holly said, "Your sister Karen called. She wants to talk to you about your dad."

"Tell her there's nothing I can do now. I'll call her when I get back."

He tried not to feel nostalgic but couldn't help it, with the colored lights and Christmas carols playing everywhere in the hotel. Biting into the grilled chicken sandwich he'd ordered from room service, he thought of his family gathered around the dining room table, his dad saying grace in his red Christmas sweater, the mom he loved so much serving the roast turkey, brussels sprouts, string beans, and potatoes. He remembered going outside in the cold to play touch football with his cousins from Ohio, then hunting for quail and rabbits with BB guns.

At sunset, rain started to fall. Minutes before seven, Neto arrived with an older Hispanic man named Sanchez, who had a flat, unexpressive face like a mask.

He said, "Sanchez knows the barrio far better than I do. We're probably going to need a four-wheel-drive vehicle in this weather, so I brought two Toyota FJ Cruisers."

While Mancini went down to inspect the gear and weapons, Neto and Crocker drew up a plan.

CHAPTER NINE

War may be an armed angel with a mission, but she has the personal habits of the slums.

—Rebecca Harding Davis

Black Cell set out an hour later, with Mancini in the passenger seat of the first Toyota dressed up as Santa Claus, complete with white wig and beard. The backs of both vehicles were packed with toys Neto had gotten from a storeowner friend.

"Feliz Navidad!" Mancini shouted out the window.

"Don't overdo it," Crocker groaned back.

They drove past modern apartment towers, through an upscale residential area, then off a major street to a smaller road that led up a steep hill into the barrio, which was dense and surprisingly colorful despite the falling rain and the slapdash quality of the shacks. They were put together with wooden packing crates, scraps of lumber, metal, and plastic, and featured corrugated tin roofs. Precariously clinging to steep slopes, the primitive structures were painted bright red, orange, and blue. Some were decorated with Christmas lights.

A few had beat-up cars and trucks parked in front or at the sides.

"Who lives here?" Davis asked.

"Poor people," Mancini shot back.

"Many of them are refugees from other countries— Ecuador, Colombia, Bolivia," Neto explained. "The barrios also get a lot of people from Central America. They come here because of the relative prosperity."

"Prosperity?" Davis asked skeptically.

"It's relative, man. Chávez might have been a nut job who broke into song during televised speeches, but he treated the poor well."

Crocker said, "He's not dead yet."

"Practically," Neto shot back.

"You said he treated the poor well," Mancini interjected. "How, in terms of specifics?"

"Land reform, improved public services like state-run gro-cery stores that sell discounted staple foods, soup kitchens, open clinics, free education."

Crocker had an intrinsic distrust of politicians. "Socialism," "freedom," "democracy," and "justice" were words they twisted to justify different agendas.

Sanchez spun the SUV ahead of them up a steep turn. The road was now a river of muddy water and sewage.

Mancini was in a jolly mood, befitting his new role. "Did I tell you what happened to my next-door neighbor Sam?"

"What?" Crocker asked.

"He forgot his wedding anniversary, and his wife was really pissed. She told him, 'Tomorrow morning, I expect to find a gift in the driveway that goes from zero to two hundred in less than ten seconds!' The next morning Sam got up early and left for work. When his wife woke up she looked out the window and found a gift-wrapped box in the middle of the driveway. So she ran out in her robe, ripped open the box, and found a brand-new bathroom scale inside. Sam has been missing ever since."

Crocker and Davis were still laughing when they arrived at a makeshift plaza where five narrower dirt trails converged. It was lined with a few little bodegas, two bar/restaurants, a bicycle repair stand, and a *peluquería*.

Neto said, "This is El Centro. We'll distribute the toys here."

Sanchez got out of the lead vehicle, and he and Neto walked into one of the bodegas. A few minutes later a half dozen boys and girls in shorts and dresses ran out into the rain. Seeing Santa Claus, they pounded aggressively on the Toyota's doors and hood. Mancini got out "Ho-ho-hoing" and started handing out toys, one per kid.

The number of children grew exponentially—like the raindrops. They seemed to come from all directions, shouting with excitement. The SEALs couldn't hand out the toys fast enough. When they ran out of gifts, they gave the kids dollar bills until they had no more.

It all happened in a fifteen-minute frenzy of hands, pleas, and squeals of delight. Then, shouting "Feliz Navidad!" the men piled back into the trucks and raced up one of the trails into the dark.

"What about the gangs?" Crocker asked, checking the SIG Sauer P226R 9mm pistol Neto had given him and concealing it in the inside-the-waist holster under his black shirt.

"Seems like they're taking the night off."

As they climbed, the shacks seemed to be packed closer together and the trail became so narrow they could barely squeeze through. Sanchez, who was driving the lead vehicle, braked at a steep turn that veered to the left and cut the lights.

Neto stopped behind him. With the wipers flapping frantically, he said, "It's just ahead, at the top of this hill. We should get out here."

"Okay."

Mancini slipped out of the beard and Santa suit, and they armed themselves with handguns, a few MP7 submachine guns, and night-vision goggles.

"Do you think they've been warned that we're coming?" Crocker asked.

"It's possible," Neto answered.

"Let's move fast."

Davis and Cal stayed behind to guard the vehicles. Sanchez led the way, with Crocker and Mancini behind him. Neto took Ritchie and Akil down another trail to cover the rear of the shack, which hung precariously on a ledge to the right of the trail at the top of the hill. The shack was little more than a patched-together wood-and-tin-siding structure with a big blue plastic tarp covering most of the right side. The whole thing was perhaps thirty feet wide in front, accessed by a door on the right side next to a narrow debris-filled dirt alley that separated it from the shack beside it. The left side of the building bordered the edge of a cliff, and though it was difficult to see, there appeared to be a whole slew of shacks behind it.

A pale yellow light shone through the soiled and cracked

window. Crocker and Mancini took up preassigned firing positions as Sanchez rapped on the door.

A woman appeared, wide and dark-skinned, midtwenties, her dark hair pulled back, wearing what looked like panties and a blue sports bra. A very young boy and girl stood behind her. She held the screen door open and was waving her hands and explaining something in Spanish when Crocker heard the sound of scraping wood in the narrow alley, then footsteps. Turning to Mancini, he whispered, "You and Sanchez inspect the house. I'm going into the alley."

He took off, pushing past Sanchez, and tried to find the object moving in the narrow space. Everything he saw was either black or shades of green through the night-vision goggles.

Hearing something being dragged across the roof, he looked up and saw a dark object the size and shape of a length of sewer pipe falling toward his head. There was no room to jump back and no time to lunge forward, so he tried to push it away with his hands.

The cement pipe grazed his left forearm, tearing away skin. Gritting his teeth against the pain, Crocker jumped back against the opposite wall so the pipe wouldn't hit his feet. He wanted to scream, but focused on scooting around the big pipe and following the sound of feet scurrying across the tin roof, then jumping and landing farther down the alley.

He quickly reached the back of the house and, seeing a moving shadow to his left, turned and squeezed into a little passageway, past a latrine overrun with rats. As he stepped around them, he heard three quick gunshots from the house, followed by a woman's screams.

Crocker had no radio. For a second he considered entering

the shack from the rear, but decided to continue pursuing the person running away. He wondered what had happened to Neto and the others, then saw the back of his assailant's head sliding down a ledge and disappearing from sight.

He ran fast, and when he tried to stop on the muddy ground, his feet slid out from under him and he fell off the cliff. He saw the tops of skyscrapers and clouds in the distance, and had enough presence of mind to twist his body and get his arms under him to break his fall. Still, he hit the wet grassy turf with a thud that jarred his neck and caused him to tumble sideways into the back of his assailant's legs.

He realized it was a male when he saw a densely bearded face. Then he felt the man's hot breath and fingernails digging into his neck. Crocker couldn't reach his pistol, which had dislodged from his holster during the fall and landed somewhere in the high grass. Nor could he think clearly, because the abrupt landing had winded him.

His instincts took over, and his body carried out the un-armed defensive tactics drilled into his head fifteen years ago by an overweight, badass instructor named Al Morrel, who had been Elvis Presley's personal bodyguard.

"At any point or any situation, there will be some vulnerable point of your enemy's body open to attack," Morrel had said. "Attack this point with all your strength—while screaming, if the situation allows. Screaming serves two purposes. One, it frightens and confuses your enemy. And two, screaming allows you to take a deep breath, which will put more oxygen in your bloodstream."

It was hard to scream with the savage's dirty hands around his neck, but still Crocker drew air through his nasal passages and tried. At the same time he drove the heel of his right hand into his enemy's nose with a tremendous upward motion, shoving the nasal bone into the man's brain. Crocker's attacker groaned his final breath and loosened his grip, which allowed Crocker to bellow.

His roar echoed as the man's body twitched. Crocker took a deep breath, shoved him off, then tried to move his own body to assess the damage he'd sustained.

Luckily, he hadn't suffered an injury to his spinal column or broken any bones—just scratches, abrasions, a severely bruised left forearm, and a sore ass and lower back. Searching the dead man's body, in the inside pocket of his gray plastic rain poncho he found a plastic pouch containing a Venezuelan passport and other documents. According to the passport, the man's name was Octavo Alvarez.

Something about his thick black eyebrows and the shade of his skin caused Crocker to doubt he was an Alvarez, or even Venezuelan. The little gold pendant the man wore around his neck confirmed Crocker's suspicions when Crocker ripped it off and examined it closely with the night-vision goggles he found nearby in the grass. It was stamped with the image of a hand raising an AK-47 with a globe in the background—the logo of the Iranian Revolutionary Guards.

Known as Sepah or IRGC, members of this militant Shiite Muslim group took their orders from the Iranian mullahs, whose authority they believed superseded those of the elected government. Contained under the umbrella of the IRGC was the Quds Force, a special forces element tasked with unconventional warfare (i.e., terrorism). Unit 5000 was the aggressive new Quds Force element run by Colonel Farhed Alizadeh—the Falcon.

"Makes sense…" Crocker said, looking down at the grimace on the dead man's face, which was being pelted with rain. He stuck the plastic sleeve with the man's passport and other documents in the front waistband of his pants and felt in the wet grass for his weapon.

Locating it, he wiped the action dry with his shirttail, and clicked off the safety so it was ready to use. Hearing people above, he crawled up the embankment and hid by the lip.

He recognized Akil's voice whispering, "Let's look down here."

"Akil?" he whispered back.

"Boss?"

Akil slid down with Ritchie behind him, both clutching MP5s.

"Who the fuck is he?" Akil asked, pointing at the dead man.

"Some guy who called himself Alvarez but is really IRGC."

"You get his Iranian name?"

"Don't worry about that now," Crocker whispered, grimacing.

"You hurt?"

"A couple bumps and bruises, but I'm fine."

They reached the top, where Neto informed them that the Venezuelan police would probably be arriving soon.

"Let's go then," Crocker said. "Get in the trucks."

At 0705 the next morning, the six members of Black Cell were back at the hotel packing their bags when Crocker got a call from Neto.

"What's up?" he asked, swallowing two Advils with a glass of water to help ease the pain in his lower back.

"The chief wants to see you."

"The station chief? When?"

"Now."

"We're in the process of moving to another hotel," Crocker said, assuming this summons had something to do with the previous night's raid. He'd handed the documents he had taken from the terrorist over to Neto. Maybe the Agency had gleaned some important info from them.

"There's been a change of plans," Neto said.

Plans always changed. Crocker was okay with that. "No problem, Neto. Just tell me what you want me to do."

Neto explained, "We have an office not far from where you are. Go to Las Mercedes Avenue and turn right. You'll see a tall Banco Popular building halfway down the street. Go up to the ninth floor and look for Global Partners Investments."

"What time?" Crocker asked.

"ASAP. We're here now."

"You want me to come alone?" Crocker asked.

"Let me check," Neto said, then put the phone on hold.

Crocker and his men had returned shortly after 0400, napped, and had ordered breakfast from room service. Now the two hours they had spent after they had left the slum of Petare replayed in his head, a movie of Caracas side streets, back alleys, byways and highways. Neto and Sanchez had made sure to shake off any SEBIN or Venezuelan police tails before dropping them off at their hotel.

Neto's deep voice came back on the line. "Bring your deputy."

"Mancini and I will be there in ten."

Crocker didn't have time to change his clothes or shave. He limped down Avenida Principal de las Mercedes in his dirty black pants and T-shirt, with Mancini by his side talking about the recent announcement that President Chávez had slipped into a coma.

"Any chance he'll recover?" Crocker asked, scanning the street for plainclothes police and seeing men in brown uniforms throwing plastic bags of garbage into a large green truck.

"Unlikely," Mancini answered. "Apparently he's got stage-four colon cancer. He had a baseball-sized tumor removed several years ago, along with chemotherapy. During the recent election campaign he claimed he was cancer free, which turned out to be a lie."

Another kind of cancer—lung cancer—had afflicted Crocker's mother. But before it had taken her, she had died in a freak accident. Crocker's sister hypothesized that maybe the accident was a blessing, which angered Crocker at the time. But now, as he pushed through the revolving doors of the modern Banco Popular building, he thought maybe his sister had been right.

He and Mancini rode up in the elevator with a group of men in business suits, then walked down the carpeted hall to the door at the end of the corridor. Crocker hit the buzzer on the call box and waited.

"Quién es?"

"It's Tom Mansfield and his associate from Balzac Expeditions."

A Hispanic woman in a tight black skirt and heels led them

to a waiting room with a view of the city bathed in yellow sunlight. A tired-looking Ernesto Navarro shuffled in holding a stack of papers.

"This way, gentlemen," he said.

They entered a generic conference room. The shades were pulled over the windows. Two men sat at the table, which was crowded with papers and coffee cups.

The thinner of the two looked up and said, "Gentlemen, my name is Chase Rappaport. I'm the chief of station here." He pointed to a swarthier, thicker-built man seated across from him. "This is my deputy, Hal Melkasian."

Melkasian looked over his shoulder at the SEALs. "Welcome."

"Which one of you two is Warrant Officer Crocker?" Rappaport asked. He had a sharp, mean face and piercing blue eyes.

"That's me."

"Take a seat. Neto here will pour you some coffee. Melky and I, along with a number of analysts back at Langley, have been reviewing the packet of documents you recovered last night."

"Yeah?" Crocker said, sipping the bitter coffee and running a hand through his thinning, close-cropped hair. "What'd you find?"

Rappaport pushed his chair back, placed his shoes on the edge of the table, then glanced at some papers in his lap. "You hear about the president's condition?"

"Critical, right? My teammate and I were just talking about that," Crocker said with a nod.

"It might seem unrelated, but I can assure you that it underlies everything we're dealing with here," Rappaport said ominously.

Crocker shifted his weight in the leather-covered swivel chair and fought off the feeling of fatigue. "I'm not sure what that means."

Rappaport turned his Doberman pinscher–shaped face toward him. "It means that this program will be accelerated," he intoned, pointing to the documents on his lap. "When Chávez dies, Maduro will take over. They'll hold a special election, but the vote will be rigged. Maduro isn't Chávez. He has none of his charisma. He's a leftist labor organizer who never finished high school, loves Led Zeppelin, and worships a dead guru named Sai Baba. So nobody knows how long before the opposition rises and kicks his ass out."

"What program are you referring to?" Crocker asked.

"The Iranian-Venezuelan program. Unit 5000. What did you think? Now that we know—"

Melkasian cut him off. "Chase, I don't believe these gentlemen had a chance to peruse the documents in question."

Rappaport looked at Crocker, confused. "You recovered them, didn't you?"

"I did, yes," Crocker answered. "But I immediately handed them over to Mr. Navarro. I expected that we would be leaving our hotel first thing this morning because of the violence that took place in Petare."

In addition to the man Crocker had killed with his bare hands, another presumed terrorist had been gunned down inside the house—something the Venezuelans wouldn't be too pleased about, especially if they found out that the men had been offed by U.S. operatives.

"Oh," Rappaport said, cleaning his gold-framed glasses with the tail of his shirt, then placing them back on his nose. "Then Melky, you have some filling in to do."

"Yes," his deputy said, arching his spine and rubbing the back of his neck. He pointed to a pile of documents on the table. "From what I've been able to learn so far, it looks like Unit 5000 is in the process of organizing a substantial base here in Venezuela with the help of people in the Chávez-Maduro government."

"Colonel Torres," Mancini muttered.

"Yes, Colonel Chavo Torres. He's helping the Iranians build a terrorist base in Venezuela capable of delivering attacks on the U.S. and other targets. The men you killed last night were Iranian Unit 5000 functionaries who had been given new identities and Venezuelan citizenship."

As he tried to follow Melkasian's train of thought, Crocker's head hurt—a result of the trauma his body had suffered and the pain medication he had taken for his back. Mancini, seated beside him, poured another cup of black coffee and downed it. The skin around his eyes was swollen and gray.

"How big a base are we talking about?" Crocker asked, trying to appear alert.

"Let him finish," Rappaport snapped.

Crocker wanted to reach across the table and punch him in the face. He used a paper clip to dig the dried blood from under his fingernails.

"The men you killed were probably lower-level people in charge of distributing money and documents," Melkasian continued, picking a stack of Xeroxes off the table. "Couriers, basically. Inside the packet you recovered was a coded log and copies of visa applications and travel documents. From them we've been able to ascertain that the group contains at least a dozen individuals of Iranian origin who have been given Venezuelan citizenship and new identities, which allows them to travel throughout the region without raising suspicion."

Crocker immediately thought of the Falcon, because this sounded like one of the devious plans he had cooked up in the past. The proximity of this new program to the United States alarmed him.

Then Melkasian said, "Obviously, they're planning something, but we don't know what."

Crocker leaned forward and said aggressively, "We can't sit back and wait."

"We're cross-checking recent immigration records and flight manifests, hoping to ID some of these cats," Melkasian continued.

"Alizadeh is dangerous. You have to move fast."

Rappaport shot back, "When we find out something, we'll tell you what you need to know."

Crocker felt his anger rise. He wanted to tell Rappaport that he didn't appreciate his snippy attitude, but he was disciplined enough to know this would serve no purpose.

He asked, "What do you want from us?"

"You're to stay in-country and await further orders," Rappaport responded. "This thing is red hot. Insidious. We plan to give you a chance to do what you do, which is to kick some ass."

"Excellent," Crocker said. "I assume you've cleared this with my CO."

"You can be sure about that. Captain Sutter, Jim Anders, Lou Donaldson—they're all on board."

"Good."

"Melky and Neto will be your point men. Be ready to deploy."

CHAPTER TEN

Character is power.

—Booker T. Washington

FIRST, **HE** and his men checked out of the InterContinental Tamanaco Caracas and moved their gear to a safe house in the nearby La Florida section of the city. Then they slept.

Crocker dreamt he was swimming against a strong current with a huge white shark close behind. When the beast opened its mouth, he saw teeth made of serrated steel. The shark closed in on his legs and snapped its jaws, causing Crocker to wake with a start and grab his cramping right foot. Sore from head to toe and running a slight fever, he downed two more Advil with a glass of H2O and then met his men in the kitchen, where they were feasting on takeout from a local Taco Bell.

Through the large patio door he watched two big green parrots sail through a bolt of sunshine and land in the backyard. He thought he might be dreaming but realized he wasn't when Neto walked in, leaned on his shoulder, and whispered, "I need to talk to you alone."

Crocker took a last bite of the cold beef taco and wiped his mouth. As he walked over cool tiles in his bare feet, he noticed he still had on the same black polo and pants he'd worn on the raid last night.

They sat on a back patio with a view of big flowering hibiscus bushes. The last couple of weeks were becoming a blur.

"Did I tell you about the Iranian official who arrived two days ago?" Neto asked, his dark eyes searching Crocker's face.

Crocker thought back to the conversation they'd had in the bar on Christmas Eve and the waitress with the metal ball in her tongue. "No, I don't think so."

"Rappaport didn't mention it?"

"He might have, but I don't remember. No."

"Well, this Iranian big shot has been meeting with Colonel Torres and other Venezuelan officials. In fact, we think he's staying at the colonel's house."

"Do you know the Iranian's identity?" Crocker asked, standing and lowering his head in an attempt to get blood into his brain.

"All we have is what we assume is a fake name from the flight manifest. Cy Norath."

"You get a photo of him?" Crocker asked, stretching his arms over his head.

"No, he arrived on a private jet."

"He's here in Caracas now?" Crocker asked, bending from the waist.

"Yeah, staying at Torres's residence, which borders the Caracas Country Club," Neto answered. "We've got a surveillance team stationed outside."

"He could be important. Show me the house."

"Now?" Neto asked.

"Give me a minute to shower and change."

Crocker left Akil and Davis behind to coordinate with the station chief and inform him about new developments. He took the four Spanish speakers on his team—Cal, Ritchie, Mancini, and himself. Cal and Mancini were fluent; his and Ritchie's version was rudimentary but good enough.

With Neto at the wheel of the Pilot and the GPS guiding them, they drove east along the *autopista* and entered a very upscale neighborhood of gated mansions, stately cedar trees, and manicured gardens. Colonel Torres's estate stood on a small road off Avenida los Cedros. The red-tiled roof of the two-story house was visible from the street, but they couldn't see the front gate because the access road was blocked by two jeeps and half a dozen uniformed soldiers.

The level of security was fitting, given that Colonel Chavo Torres was Chávez's man in charge of SEBIN's external operations, and the whole country was on alert. As he drove past the estate, Neto explained that Torres and Chávez had graduated from the Venezuelan military academy and served in that army's counterinsurgency unit together.

"Back in the late seventies the enemy was local Marxist insurgents. But when Chávez read the works of Marx, Lenin, and Mao Zedong, he took a sharp turn to the left and founded a revolutionary movement," Neto explained. "Colonel Torres followed in lockstep behind him. Unlike those of the president, it's hard to determine the colonel's true politics. What we do know is that he's an opportunist who loves power and wealth, likes to inflict pain on people, and like Chávez and Maduro hates the United States."

"Let's go get him," Ritchie said.

"We're not here to start a war in Venezuela," Crocker reminded him. "Our mission is to track and disrupt the activities of Unit 5000."

"I know."

A tall sandy-haired woman and a bald man from the station sat in a Toyota Camry parked at the end of the block, approximately four hundred yards from the house. While the man waited in the Camry, the woman got into the Pilot with them. Neto turned right at the corner and parked at the intersection of Avenida Lecuna, next to a man with a bicycle who was sharpening knives and scissors.

"The visitor has been inside since last night," the female officer reported. "Colonel Torres left about an hour ago, but the visitor didn't accompany him."

"You sure about that?" Crocker asked.

She nodded. "Not only have we maintained twenty-four/seven visuals on the front entrance, but we also had someone attach a tracking device to his briefcase at the airport."

"There's no other exit?" Crocker asked.

"No, there isn't."

"What's the best possible way to clandestinely access the house?"

She had soft green eyes and an easy smile. "If I were trying to get in, I'd approach from the back, the side that borders the golf course."

"Thanks," Crocker said.

Neto added, "Stay on the radio. Let us know if you see the visitor exit."

"Sanchez is relieving us in an hour," she reported. "He'll be on a motorcycle and get a flat, which he'll take his time to re-pair. We have another team following after him."

Crocker liked her immediately. "Good," he said. "Pass on the message about informing us if the visitor leaves the prop-erty."

"Yes, sir. I will."

"Let's go," Crocker ordered.

"Where?" Neto asked.

"Inside the club."

"How?"

"We'll figure something out."

It turned out to be not all that difficult. Neto flashed his diplomatic credentials to the guard at the country club gate and said they were meeting the American ambassador for lunch. An outright fabrication—luckily, the guard didn't bother to check.

They entered through luxurious grounds past strolling pea-cocks, flowering plants, and women in golf carts, and parked near the stately sand-hued clubhouse.

"Classy setup," Ritchie commented as he got out.

Mancini, who was carrying a black briefcase, said, "It's the opposite side of the social spectrum from what we saw last night."

"How many of the residents of Petare would you guessti-mate have memberships here?" Crocker asked facetiously as they walked past the pool, which overlooked the city.

"Zero," Neto responded with a grin.

He led them to the edge of the golf course, along a stone path to the fifteenth tee. The fairway was a beautifully cared-for brilliant green carpet bordered by bushy twenty- to thirty-foot trees. A mustached man in a blue blazer stopped them and asked where they were going.

Neto told him that Crocker, Mancini, Cal, and Ritchie were golf course engineers from California who were inspecting the layout of the greens.

"*Es esplendido,*" Crocker said in gringo-accented Spanish.

"*Gracias,*" the man responded, then sent them on their way.

They waited for a foursome of men to tee off and drive away in their carts before they entered a grove of trees to the right of the fairway. Approximately a hundred feet down where it dog-legged left, Neto pointed out a large two-story house past the trees on the right. It was separated from the golf course by an eight-foot stone fence topped with metal spikes.

Mancini snapped some digital photos. Ritchie determined the best place to climb the wall. Crocker took mental note of the deep second-story balcony facing the fairway, the lone soldier with a submachine gun lazily patrolling the yard, the antennas on the roof, and asked, "How sure are you that the visitor is lodging here and not in a hotel?"

"About eighty percent," Neto answered.

"Let's grab some surveillance equipment and return after dark."

There was no problem entering the club this time, because Neto got an embassy officer who was a member to invite them to dinner. The four SEALs, Neto, and the officer—a man named Skip Haffner—sat outside on a patio near the pool feasting on carne asada and shrimp.

Not a bad life, Crocker thought, watching the sun set beyond the mountains.

"Skip here used to be a professional golfer," Neto said out of nowhere.

"I was on the team at Duke," Skip offered with a smile. "Right after I graduated, I joined the amateur tour, then turned pro."

"You must have been good," Crocker said.

"Good wasn't good enough, but I had fun."

Ritchie asked, "You ever party with Tiger Woods?"

"Closest I got to him was in 2002, when he entered the clubhouse at Congressional as I was being escorted out."

"What's the highest you ever placed in a tournament?" Cal asked.

"I won some amateur and college tournaments, but the highest I got in a PGA event was twenty-fourth."

They waited until the city lights glittered in the distance and stars shone above. Crocker checked his watch, which read 9 p.m.

He said, "Thanks, Skip. It's been fun."

"If any of you guys want to play tomorrow, I've got a tee time at eight fifteen."

"Thanks, but we're busy."

"Another time, then."

While Skip settled the bill, Neto moved the Pilot to an empty lot near the golf course, and the SEALs stripped off their shirts to the tees underneath. Dressed all in black, they geared up and deployed, seeking cover in the trees along the fifteenth fairway and behind the high wall separating the course from Colonel Torres's house.

Neto used a handheld radio to check with CIA surveillance out front, which reported that the colonel had returned and the visitor was still inside.

Light glowed from both floors, but the brightest space was the room behind the second-story balcony. The door was open, and strains of music drifted out.

Cal snapped together the twenty-inch parabolic dish of a KB-DETEAR listening device, aimed it at the open balcony door, and listened through headphones. Even though the room was approximately 150 feet away and well within the device's 300-yard range, he wasn't able to hear past the water splashing in the balcony fountain and the easy-listening jazz playing inside.

Meanwhile, Mancini launched the two experimental nano quadrotor drones that DARPA had given him to test. They ran on tiny lithium batteries, were the size of human fingernails, and looked like little metal insects. Manny succeeded in maneuvering them through the balcony door via a handheld wireless joystick but was unable to get the video they beamed back to appear on the eight-channel portable DVR monitor he had set up on the ground.

"What's the problem?" Crocker whispered over his shoulder.

"The software's not working," Mancini answered, adjusting the knobs on the DVR. "It's always the software."

Mancini had also brought an RQ-11 Raven, a bird-shaped unmanned aerial vehicle used by the U.S. military, but because its wingspan exceeded four feet he didn't think the Raven could hover in front of the window without being seen.

Crocker was willing to try anyway.

Monitoring the dials on the gadget in his briefcase, Manny replied, "Probably won't work anyway. The house is protected by a spectrum analyzer and signal process block."

"What's that mean in plain English?" Crocker asked.

"Any type of digital or analog-based surveillance we launch will be interfered with and risks being detected."

They were too close for Crocker to even think of giving up. Noticing a low-hanging tree branch that was reachable from the top of the wall, he decided to access the house the old-fashioned way—by climbing into the yard.

Neto, however, had reservations. "I don't know about this, Crocker," he said. "There's too high a risk you'll be discovered."

"Don't worry. We do this shit all the time."

"What happens if you're discovered?"

"Blame it on me."

Although Crocker was the team's lead climber, he was moving awkwardly because of his injured back, so Ritchie volunteered. They armed him with a silenced subcompact SIG Sauer P239, smeared black nonglare cammo on his face, handed him a small digital camera, and wished him luck.

As he was ready to launch, Neto whispered, "Establish a quick ID and pull out."

"Yes, sir," Ritchie said.

Crocker watched Ritchie scale the wall and from the top of it jump and grab the branch. He shimmied along it and dropped into the yard.

The wall prevented them from observing Ritchie roll on the lawn, hide behind a bush, and spot the lone guard standing with his back to him sixty feet away. He appeared again in their line of vision using a trellis and a drainpipe to climb to the balcony. He vaulted over the balcony railing, entered the house, and disappeared from view.

Crocker counted the minutes on his watch. Three… five…ten…his anxiety growing. He was starting to think that this might have been a bad idea when he saw a black shape scurry over the balcony rail and reach with his foot for the trellis. Ritchie paused to flash them a thumbs-up, then slipped and fell.

Crocker heard a sickening thud when Ritchie hit the ground, then footsteps running across the yard. He was already halfway up the wall, ignoring Neto's anxious whispering at his back. Within three seconds he had jumped up and grabbed the cedar branch, pulling himself toward the yard.

Hearing a gunshot and then a man shouting in Spanish, he looked down and saw a Venezuelan soldier standing over Ritchie, pointing an AK-47 at his head.

Completely vulnerable as he hung from the branch, Crocker took a deep breath, shifted his weight to his left arm, and used his right to find the HK45CT pistol with full-sized Ti-RANT suppressor. From fifty feet away he aimed and squeezed three rounds into the soldier's back and watched him buckle at the knees and fall.

Letting go of the branch, he hit the ground and rolled. Ignoring the lightning bolt of pain from the base of his spine, he got up and crossed to Ritchie.

Ritchie's eyes were open, and his right hand held his jaw. When Crocker carefully pulled Ritchie's hand away, he saw his jawbone and a row of lower molars. The round had hit him near the chin and exited near his ear.

Crocker used his index and middle fingers to fish the shattered teeth and bone out of Ritchie's windpipe. The injury didn't appear life threatening, since the bullet hadn't hit a major artery. Nevertheless, Crocker quickly completed the last three steps of the medical ABCD checklist.

Ritchie's breathing was regular, his pulse was strong, and there appeared to be no damage to his spinal cord or neck. However, his tongue was probably fucked up, because he was trying to speak but having trouble.

Crocker held a finger to his mouth to tell him not to try, then pulled off his T-shirt and tied it around Ritchie's head. The wound, though ugly, was not likely to produce a great loss of blood because the injured vessels weren't large. Nor was there much risk of secondary hemorrhage, though it was important to keep his head elevated.

The next challenge was to get the two of them out of there alive.

As Crocker lifted Ritchie up and hoisted him over his left shoulder, a flash of pain ran down his spine into his legs. That was the least of his problems. He retreated to the shadows at the back of the house and quickly appraised his situation. Mancini had climbed onto the wall and was reaching for the tree. Crocker waved him back.

There was no fucking way he'd be able to lift Ritchie high enough, even if he put him on his shoulders, because the cedar branch was at least sixteen feet from the ground. His options were limited. Other guards had been alerted. He heard hurried footsteps approaching from his left and turned right with the HK45CT clutched in his right hand and an extra magazine in his left. With Ritchie's warm blood dripping down his chest, he crossed to the other side of the balcony and stopped. More footsteps were coming from the right.

Five feet ahead stood a white door leading to the bottom floor. He tried it. Locked. He kicked it in and entered, all his senses alert. Loud rock music reverberated through the narrow hallway—Lynyrd-fucking-Skynyrd singing "Free Bird." It happened to be one of the songs he worked out to in his dad's garage.

He passed from a dark passageway to a brightly lit kitchen. A stout young woman in a white uniform stood at a giant sink washing dishes. She stopped midbreath when she saw the two men. Her eyes locked onto Crocker's. What a sight he was—bare-chested, with an injured, bleeding man slung across one shoulder, a pistol in the other. He grinned and raised the .45 to his lips as a signal to be quiet. She nodded.

He pushed through a swinging door that led to a formal dining room. The lights were out and the room was filled with shadows. He crossed quickly to another room, past a portrait of President Chávez as a young man, to a sitting room that opened through an arch to the front hall.

An ornate wooden stairway rose to his right. He was so pumped up on adrenaline that he considered climbing it, finding the colonel and his visitor, and finishing them off right then. But he had Ritchie on his shoulder moaning quietly, as if humming a song.

People were moving above. Angry voices drifted down. Crocker clutched the extra magazine of .45 rounds in his teeth, grabbed the front doorknob, turned it with his left hand, took a deep breath, and pulled it open.

It was as though his whole life and all of his training had been leading to this moment. In warp-speed time, he took in everything. To his left stood an armed soldier with his back to him. Beyond the soldier was a partially open metal gate with blue jeeps parked on either side of it.

The soldier turned in slow motion and opened his mouth. Before any words came out, Crocker fired three bullets into his side and chest. The soldier's eyes darkened, and he fell backward into a pot of white geraniums.

Crocker hurried down three steps, making sure to keep his balance, and turned sideways to squeeze through the half-opened gate. That's when he spotted another soldier crouched in front of one of the jeeps, speaking urgently into a radio. Crocker raised the HK45CT, ran to the front of the jeep, and fired until the gun was empty. Ejected the warm, empty mag and inserted the second. Another soldier standing across the street aimed his AK-47 and squeezed off a round that whizzed over Crocker's head and slammed into the wall and gate.

He knelt alongside the jeep. Ritchie was trying to whisper something in his ear. Tactical advice, no doubt, which amused Crocker in a graveyard humor kind of way.

"I got this one, Ritchie. Conserve your energy."

On the other side of the jeep, in the driver's-side mirror, he saw the soldier run a few feet down the street, stop, and shout something over his shoulder. Desperate words in Spanish that ended when Crocker stood and fired a silenced burst from the pistol that took him down.

The alley was narrow, flanked by high walls covered with vines and ivy, and topped with brass owls. One direction led to the street; the other to more houses and a dead end. But he couldn't tell which one went where, so he had to decide which to take.

Eeny-meeny-miny....

Getting out on foot was going to be a problem. Looking inside the jeep, he saw no keys in the ignition. Still, he sat Ritchie in the front seat and buckled him in. Crocker had hot-wired so many cars as a wild punk growing up in New England that starting it was relatively easy. After locating the access cover under the steering wheel, he smashed the plastic lid with the butt of his pistol and pulled it off. Then he reached behind the ignition switch harness, located two red wires, used his teeth to strip about an inch of insulation from both, and twisted them together.

He heard a vehicle approaching, but didn't look up. Finding the brown ignition wire, he pulled it out of its harness and touched it to the two red wires.

The jeep started with a growl. Now, which way to go? Ritchie raised his arm and pointed right.

"You'd better be correct," Crocker whispered, gunning the engine, the pistol now clutched in his right hand.

Almost immediately he was blinded by headlights that swung into the alley. He turned the wheel sharply right, causing the side of the jeep to graze the wall and sending up a shower of sparks that cascaded onto Ritchie's head. The other vehicle passed, then screeched to a stop. He heard boots hitting the street, mags slamming into rifles, men shouting in Spanish.

"Alto! Alto!"

He turned sharply right onto Avenida los Cedros and floored the accelerator. The jeep swerved and skidded past another military truck. The driver stared at Crocker with big saucer eyes, then ducked as Crocker opened fire, shattering the side window.

Bullets sailed over Crocker's head as he shifted into fourth and sped past the entrance to the country club through a red traffic light, then burned serious rubber onto another street, then another and another, and stopped, breathless.

Ritchie moaned something that sounded like a question. Fishing a phone from his pocket, Crocker punched Neto's number.

"It's Crocker," he said, out of breath.

"Where the fuck *are* you?" Neto asked urgently. "What happened? Where's Ritchie?"

"He's with me. He's injured. We need to get him to an emergency room ASAP!"

"What's your current location?" Neto asked.

"I'm in a stolen military jeep. I'm about a mile or so west of the country club."

"Use the GPS on your phone and give me the name of the street."

Crocker checked as sirens screamed in the distance and echoed off the walls around him. "We're on Calle Garcia, near Avenida Cuello."

"All right, turn onto Cuello," Neto said. "Take the first left. There's a restaurant on the corner. Pull into the parking lot. Find a dark corner in the back. I'll meet you there in five."

CHAPTER ELEVEN

Despite all these lucky breaks, why do I still feel that I got screwed somehow?

—Woody Allen

THE **LIGHT** from the fluorescent bulbs burned Crocker's weary, bloodshot eyes. He leaned on the edge of a gurney at a comfortable angle for his aching back while a nurse with thick glasses used cotton swabs dipped in alcohol to clean the blood off his chest. His mind shifted to the golf course, to the meeting with Rappaport, to the fevered drive in the jeep, in no rational order, picking up speed. A voice in the background screamed, *Why did you do it?*

He didn't have an answer. The green curtain parted and Mancini stuck in his head, looking like a cartoon criminal with his neck and face covered with a dense stubble of dark whiskers. He said, "Boss, they're about to wheel Ritchie into surgery. He wants to see you."

"Where?"

The nurse tried to stop Crocker from pulling on a light blue robe and following Manny out of the room, but she failed.

They trotted down a yellow hall to a little room where Ritchie sat in a wheelchair with a white bandage covering half his face.

"Ritchie?" Crocker whispered. "How's it hanging?"

He opened his left eye, tried to smile, mouthed the words "It's still hanging," then pointed to a yellow legal pad and pen on the table to Crocker's right.

"You'll be fine," Crocker said as he gave it to him and noticed Ritchie's dried blood all over his hand. Hiding it behind his back, he said, "There's no major structural or neurologic damage. They'll patch you up, fix that ugly mug of yours, and you'll end up looking better than before."

Ritchie's concentration was focused on the pad and what he was slowly writing. He held it up for Crocker to read. The letters were thin, long, and slanted to the right. They read: "I saw Alizadeh, the Falcon. He was in the house."

Crocker felt a sudden burst of energy. "Alizadeh? You sure it was him?"

Ritchie nodded and attempted to mouth the word "Yes." He wrote, "I'd know his ugly face anywhere."

Crocker wanted to hug him, but only said, "That's great, Ritchie. Very important. Good job."

A doctor and orderly in white jackets arrived to wheel Ritchie away. He quickly scribbled one last message, which he handed to Crocker. It read: "Tell Monica we have to postpone the wedding, if she still wants me like this."

"I'll tell her, Ritchie. Don't worry about anything. You'll be fine."

Crocker wanted time to sit back, process, heal, and think, but events were moving too quickly. Seconds after Ritchie was wheeled into surgery, he telephoned Neto to tell him the news about Alizadeh. Neto spoke to Melkasian at the station, and a meeting was set for midnight.

Crocker grabbed a few winks in the car. He woke up remembering that he had never had a chance to do his Christmas shopping—an iPad for Jenny, a crystal-and-amethyst necklace he'd picked out for Holly at a Virginia Beach jewelry store. He hated being late with presents but couldn't help it this time.

As soon as they arrived at the office in the Banco Popular building, Neto ordered pizza with everything and sodas from an all-night fast food joint. They were chowing down when Rappaport and Melkasian walked in clutching briefcases and dressed in rumpled business clothes. It looked as though they'd been working all night.

Rappaport said, "You sure kicked up a shit storm, Crocker."

"Couldn't avoid it."

"Who authorized you to go into the colonel's house?"

Neto spoke up. "I did, sir."

Crocker cut in, "That's bullshit. I did. I take full responsibility. I felt that it was important to try to identify the Iranian, and I ordered my man to scale the wall. Unfortunately, he had an accident and was discovered and shot. I deeply regret that now. But I'm also pleased that we've established that it's Alizadeh himself who is setting up the Unit 5000 operation here."

"It often works that way, doesn't it, Crocker?" Rappaport asked. "The good mixed with the bad."

"Yes it does, sir," Crocker replied, struck by the sincere tone in his voice.

Rappaport reached across, laid a hand on Crocker's shoulder, and said, "I'm sorry about your teammate. I pray he recovers quickly."

"I appreciate that, sir." Maybe Rappaport wasn't a total asshole.

"As far as pissing off the Venezuelans, I say: fuck them," Rappaport growled. "They had it coming. And as far as the Falcon goes, I'm ready to go to war."

Crocker liked Rappaport's new attitude and nodded in agreement. "Me, too, sir. Let's kick his ass."

Briefcases clicked open, pizza boxes were cleared from the table, and a secure phone line was opened to Langley, where an analyst named Sue from the Crime and Narcotics Center (CNC) reported that the names of three of the individuals mentioned in the Xeroxed documents captured in Petare had been matched to a computer printout of recent arrivals to Mexico from Venezuela.

"What's that mean?" Rappaport asked.

"I don't know."

"Do you have any idea where they are now?" Melkasian asked, using a device to project a map of Mexico on the screen at the front of the room.

"Mexican PFM has tracked them to the town of San Miguel de Allende, which is about a hundred and seventy miles north of Mexico City," Sue said over the speakerphone. PFM was the Mexican version of the FBI.

At the mention of San Miguel de Allende, Crocker smiled inwardly. Before they married he and Holly had spent a romantic week in that village in an inn overlooking the lake.

"What are they doing there?" Rappaport asked.

"We've been treating them as potential drug traffickers," Sue answered. "They claim to be Venezuelan financial advisors looking for business investments. Their behavior is suspicious because they stick together, spend a lot of time in their hotel room, eat at cheap restaurants, don't drink alcohol, and are constantly looking over their shoulders to see if they're being watched."

"Potential drug traffickers?" Melkasian asked skeptically.

"Yes, our intelligent operational probabilities computer program gave that a probability of forty percent, which is high. But it's possible they could be up to something else."

"You mean some other sort of illegal activity?" Rappaport asked. "And you say Mexican PFM is keeping an eye on them?"

"That's correct, sir."

"Can they be trusted?"

"Not really, no. That's why we've dispatched a two-person DEA team from Mexico City. They should be there within the hour."

"Good," Rappaport said, checking his watch. "We think these men might be Iranian members of the IRGC, so inform us immediately regarding their movements or anything else you learn."

"I will, sir."

"You have anything else?" he asked.

Sue said, "The names of two other individuals on the list you sent us—Jorge Alvarez Nazra and Raul Abaid Lopez— correspond to two men who recently passed the PPL and CPL exams in Venezuela."

The speed of the new information was dizzying.

"What are the PPL and CPL?" Melkasian asked.

"Those are the exams required by the ICAO, the International Civic Aviation Organization, to qualify for private and commercial pilot licenses," Sue replied.

The moment he heard "commercial pilot licenses," Crocker traveled back to 9/11, an event that had profoundly changed his life. Prior to that time, the pace of ST-6 operations had been so slow he'd been thinking about leaving the navy and starting a private security firm. Following 9/11, ST-6 ops increased exponentially. He had been deploying overseas an average of 280 days a year.

Rappaport asked, "What do we know about the real identities of these men?"

"Practically nothing," Sue answered. "Since we found them on the papers you recovered, we assume they are Iranians who have been granted Venezuelan citizenship and given new identities."

Melkasian's cell phone rang. As he listened to the person on the other end, his forehead furrowed. He put his hand over the phone and, turning to Rappaport, said, "It's Sanchez. He says the Learjet the Iranian flew in on is getting ready to leave from Simón Bolívar Airport."

"Excuse us for a minute, Sue," Rappaport grunted into the speakerphone. Then, to Melkasian, "Is Alizadeh aboard?"

"Unclear."

"Where's the plane headed?"

"According to the flight manifest, the destination is Ciudad del Este, Paraguay."

"Why the fuck is he going there?" Rappaport asked, thinking out loud.

Crocker chewed on the same question. What business

might Alizadeh or the other Iranians possibly have in that lawless, corrupt city?

Rappaport bid goodbye to Sue for the time being, and the four men spent the next forty minutes discussing possibilities. Then they called Reston, Virginia, and woke up the head of CIA's Quds Force Working Group, Sy Blanc. Though Sy was suffering from a fever and flu-related symptoms, his mind remained sharp. He pointed out that Ciudad del Este had approximately twenty-five thousand Shiite Muslim residents who had emigrated from Lebanon during the 1948 Arab-Israeli War and the 1985 Lebanese Civil War. It was known that the Iranian-backed Hezbollah militia had built an active smuggling network operating out of the remote tri-border region and that it funneled large sums of money to fund operations in the Middle East, also financing training camps, propaganda campaigns, and bomb attacks in South America.

"What kind of smuggling?" Rappaport asked.

"Cigarettes, marijuana, and cocaine. It's smuggled across the border to Brazil, then shipped to Europe," Blanc reported. "Profits are huge, anywhere from an estimated two to four billion a year."

It was the perfect place, Crocker thought, for Alizadeh to find money to support Unit 5000's activities. If he was looking for an illegal means for funding his new organization, what better place to look than the lawless tri-state border region of Paraguay, Brazil, and Argentina?

Blanc agreed, concluding that "Ciudad del Este is essentially a free zone for significant criminal activity, including people who are organized to commit acts of terrorism."

"Great," Rappaport said with a groan. "What should we do?"

Blanc pointed out that since Hezbollah terrorists operating out of Ciudad del Este had bombed several Jewish synagogues, killing more than a hundred people in nearby Argentina in the 1990s, Mossad had maintained a presence there. The CIA also had assets in Ciudad del Este.

Blanc said, "I'll make sure they're alerted to look for the aircraft and monitor Alizadeh's activities."

"But we're not sure he's on the plane," Melkasian reminded him.

"No, we're not."

Crocker argued that he should travel there immediately to help support local CIA assets. Sy Blanc agreed.

Emergency visas were issued for Crocker and Akil (who spoke fluent Farsi) and tickets booked on a 6:37 p.m. flight to São Paulo. Crocker hurried back to the safe house, packed, instructed Mancini to coordinate with Melkasian and Neto regarding what they needed to do until he returned, then called a taxi to drive them to the airport.

Traveling as Tom Mansfield and Jerid Salam, they flew to Bogotá via Avianca Airlines, and after a six-hour layover, which they spent mostly surfing the Internet and drinking beer, the flight continued another six hours to Guarulhos International Airport in São Paulo. They arrived just before seven the following morning, then transferred to a small TAM Airlines jet to Ciudad del Este.

By the time they reached Aeropuerto Internacional Guaraní, they were half asleep. A young Paraguayan customs official stopped them and asked where they had gotten their visas.

"Caracas, Venezuela," Crocker answered.

"What were you doing there?" the official asked in accented English.

"We were there on business, organizing an expedition."

The official explained that their visas hadn't been entered into the Paraguayan system, which meant that they couldn't enter the country without each man paying a hundred-dollar expediting fee. What system he was talking about wasn't clear. Akil pointed out that the computer screen he appeared to be looking at was blank.

They were traveling in alias, so Crocker didn't want to attract attention, but he didn't feel like being ripped off, either. A Brazilian man who stood behind them in line sweating profusely whispered, "I recommend that you pay it. Otherwise he will keep you here all day."

Crocker handed the official twenty dollars, which he said should cover both men. The official shook his head no, he wouldn't accept it.

Akil reached into his wallet and produced three more twenties, whereupon the official stamped their passports and waved them through.

"Nice place," Akil whispered.

"Yeah. Be alert."

The baggage claim was packed with travelers from Europe and Asia who were going to visit the famous Iguazu Falls. Akil's suitcase, which he had had to check in São Paulo because of its size, was a no-show, so he filled out a form at the information desk.

"Good luck with that," Crocker commented.

"Yeah, right."

The woman working the desk had a message for Mr. Mansfield, which read, "This is DZ from the agency. Because of circumstances, I'm not able to meet you at the airport. Hire a taxi to take you to Hotel Casablanca. I'll see you there. Don't let the driver charge you more than $30."

The only two taxi drivers stationed outside the terminal both demanded a fifty-dollar fare. Crocker and Akil chose the newer and cleaner-looking of the two cars—a fairly comfortable Toyota Corolla sedan. The overweight driver drove it as if it was stolen, tearing down the freeway at eighty miles an hour.

The air outside the window was hot and sticky, the ground dotted with mud-colored puddles. Storm clouds formed impressive towers of gray, white, and black, while the landscape was festooned with exuberant tropical foliage. Man's footprint could best be described as tacky—broken-down cars and buses, mud-encrusted shacks, large lurid signs advertising sex shows, casinos, electronics stores, and "five-star" Italian, Japanese, and Chinese restaurants.

Out of the corner of his eye, Crocker saw a motorcycle tear out of a side street toward their car and screamed, "Watch out!"

The driver, who was speaking nonstop Spanish into a cell phone and didn't see the motorcycle until the last second, swerved to avoid a head-on collision. From the backseat, Crocker watched the young rider's face smash into the passenger-side window. Then the bike and rider flew into the air.

The driver slammed on the brakes, got out, examined the scratches on the side panel of his car, and started cursing.

Crocker ran over to the motorcycle rider, who wasn't wearing a helmet and was lying facedown in the dirt. He assumed he was dead, but as Crocker knelt to examine him, the long-haired kid got up, rubbed his dislocated kneecap, which appeared to be his only injury, then limped over to the bike, picked it up, and wheeled it to a footpath. Crocker tried to stop him, but the kid was intent on confronting the driver. The two men stood nose to nose, shouting at each other.

A crowd of onlookers gathered and stared. Crocker wandered back to the taxi, where Akil asked, "What do we do now?"

"Let's find alternate transportation," Crocker answered as flies started to form a moving halo around his head.

When he asked the driver to pop open the trunk so he could retrieve his suitcase, he threw his arms up in disgust, walked back to the car, and started the engine. Neither man had insurance, he explained.

"What a shock," Akil whispered.

Once again they were flying down the highway at eighty. Approaching the city, traffic slowed to a crawl. The streets narrowed and became clogged with people carrying boxes containing TVs, stereos, and DVD players, and huge sacks of what looked to be newly purchased goods on their backs. The driver said that smugglers made a very good living by purchasing goods made in China and Japan on the Paraguayan side of the border, then crossing the Ciudad del Este Friendship Bridge into Brazil and selling them for a two hundred percent profit.

How they were able to do that, he didn't say. Instead, he pulled over to the curb and started asking for directions to the hotel. Nobody seemed to recognize the name of the establishment or know how to get there. Vendors approached the taxi windows and offered to sell the two Americans see-through panties, porno videos, Viagra, and tool sets.

"Unbelievable," Crocker said.

"Maybe we should tell the driver to turn this thing around and beat it out of here," Akil suggested.

"That's not gonna happen," Crocker said, examining the map he had picked up at the airport. On it he found a small ad for the Hotel Casablanca, which was part of something called the Parana Country Club.

They continued ten more minutes to a gate, where a guard wrote down their names and passport numbers, and gave them directions to the hotel, which was past another golf course.

"We should have brought our clubs," Crocker joked.

Neither of the big men played golf.

They walked through the open front door and found no one at the desk. A man with short dreadlocks and a Real Madrid soccer jersey sauntered over sipping a can of coconut water, offered his hand, and said, "My name's David. Call me DZ."

"Tom Mansfield and Jerid Salam."

"Cool, man. Follow me."

The room was clean and large, with a magnificent view of the Guaraní River. Crocker and Akil were more or less the same size, six feet two and 210 pounds, so Crocker lent him some underwear, a pair of black chinos, and a black T-shirt, which Akil said looked a hell of a lot better on him.

A half hour later the three men were in town, sitting at an

outdoor café across from something called the Jebai Shopping Center. It could have been lifted out of Beirut, Cairo, or any other Middle Eastern city. Stands sold hummus, *shawarma*, and roasted lamb; Lebanese flags hung everywhere. Pasted over walls and windows were slogans from the Koran: "The curse of God on the infidels!" "Take not Christians or Jews as friends." "Fight for the cause of God!"

They drank coffee, then Crocker and Akil followed DZ into a store with high aluminum shelves packed with bottles of J&B, Johnnie Walker, Marlboros, portable CD players, and cell phones. Watching them through a cracked glass partition was a guard cradling a pump-action Mitchell Escalade 12-gauge shotgun.

Two Middle Eastern–looking men sat behind a high counter. One read a newspaper and puffed on a hookah. The other measured bags of pistachios on a scale.

"I'm looking for Hamid," DZ said in Spanish.

The man operating the scale pushed a buzzer that unlocked a door to a stairway and held up three fingers. At the third-floor landing they entered a door covered with Arabic script. An old man with a jeweler's loupe on his eyeglasses looked up.

DZ pointed to Crocker and said, "My friend here wants to buy a bracelet for his wife. I was hoping that Hamid could help us."

The jeweler pushed a button, spoke into an intercom on the wall beside his desk, and nodded at four dirty black leather chairs, indicating that they should take a seat. Two minutes later a short, skinny young man bounced out of the back room in a ball of energy. He looked liked a grown-up kid, with yellow streaks in black hair worn in a pompadour, tight black jeans, and a tight blue shirt with skull and crossbones printed on it.

"Hamid, this is my friend Tom Mansfield," DZ said. "He's looking for a bracelet for his wife. I told him you could hook him up at a reasonable price."

Hamid pointed to the room behind him. "Step inside, Mr. Mansfield. I think I can help you."

It was small, with a high ceiling and a large frosted window along one wall. At the back sat an old wooden desk. On either side of it were tall cabinets with rows of little drawers.

"What did you have in mind?" Hamid asked, meeting Crocker's eyes.

"I'm not sure."

"They're the ones who are looking for a Learjet that landed yesterday from Caracas," DZ explained.

"Which side of the border?" Hamid asked, rubbing his sharp chin.

Crocker: "We don't know."

"Walk around and meet me at the Pietro Santo for lunch at one o'clock," Hamid said. "DZ knows where it is."

"Thanks."

Once they were outside, DZ whispered in Crocker's ear, "Hamid works for Israeli intelligence." Crocker had worked with Mossad in the past, and had found it overrated.

The restaurant was appropriately dark and foreboding. Glass-covered red-checked tablecloths, an old map of the boot of Italy on one wall, faded frescoes of the Leaning Tower of Pisa, Michelangelo's *David*, and Mount Vesuvius and the Bay of Naples decorating the others. They sat eating breadsticks and kalamata olives, and talking sports. Crocker thought finding the Iranians in a place like this would be like looking for a needle in a haystack.

But when Hamid arrived twenty minutes late, he said he had a lead. Two men who had arrived last night from Venezuela had met up with two other men. The four of them were staying in a guesthouse behind a Shiite mosque and religious center called Ali Hassam. The Learjet they had arrived in had left early in the morning and returned to Venezuela. He didn't know whether it was carrying cargo or passengers.

"Do you know if any of the men is named Farhad Alizadeh?" Crocker asked.

"I didn't get names, but I believe the men are Iranian," Hamid answered.

"Let's go visit the mosque."

CHAPTER TWELVE

One loyal friend is worth ten thousand relatives.
—Euripides

THAT NIGHT the two SEALs sat alone in the rear of the hotel lobby watching a rebroadcast of the Barcelona-Athletico Madrid soccer game on a big-screen TV. Crocker didn't follow international soccer, but Akil was a fan. He explained that Barcelona was one of the greatest teams in the history of the sport, led by two of the most talented forwards who had ever played the game, Lionel Messi (an Argentine) and Andrés Iniesta (a Spaniard).

Barcelona had just pulled ahead 2 to 1 when Hamid, wearing a gray hoodie and jeans, waved at them from the front desk. They met him out front as a steady rain started to fall, lowering the temperature and producing a relaxing calm.

"Reminds me of summer showers in northern Virginia," Akil remarked as they climbed into Hamid's dark green Ford Explorer.

"DZ is gonna meet us there," said Hamid as he navigated the SUV through dark, narrow streets.

The rain evoked Crocker's childhood memories—sitting on the back porch at night listening to the owls, exploring the woods behind his parents' house, catching fireflies with his brother.

The mosque sat in a high-walled compound in a residential part of town. There were two entrances, front and back.

Hamid volunteered to watch the back, while Crocker and Akil joined DZ, who had arrived in a Volkswagen Jetta that was now parked across the street and down the block from the front gate.

Once Hamid was in position, Akil walked to the blue gate and, standing in a pool of light from the lone streetlamp, rang the bell. A short stooped man with a short white beard and a long dark robe appeared looking like he'd just walked out of the Arabian desert. Akil addressed him in Farsi. The old man nodded, looked left and right along the street, then stepped aside and let him in.

Akil returned twenty minutes later to report that the guest-house stood at the back left corner of the compound. He had walked by the one-story structure and seen through a window three men smoking cigarettes and drinking tea at a table.

"You recognize any of them?" Crocker asked.

"I only saw the sides of their heads."

"What did you tell the old man at the gate?" Crocker asked.

"I told him I wanted to pray."

As they sat in the car waiting for the men to leave or others to arrive, the conversation drifted to James Bond movies.

"Who's your favorite Bond girl?" Akil asked.

"Ursula Andress in *Dr. No,*" Crocker said. "I was a kid when I first saw her coming out of the water wearing that white bikini. Suddenly a whole world of fantasies opened up to me."

"I bet."

"What about the orange bikini Halle Berry wore?" DZ asked.

"Outstanding as well."

Crocker watched an old dog with sagging tits cross the street and disappear in the shadows next to the walled mosque. The rain had subsided to a gentle spray when he heard Hamid's voice over the push-pull radio in DZ's lap. He said, "Four men have just exited the back gate and are getting into a black Ford Ranger."

Akil leaned over the back of the front seat and said, "That might be them."

"What do you think?" Crocker asked Hamid over the radio.

"They have suitcases with them. Looks like they're leaving."

"Let's follow," Crocker said.

They did, in both vehicles—Hamid and Akil in the Explorer, DZ and Crocker in the Jetta—over the rusting iron International Friendship Bridge to the Brazilian border, where they were stopped by four Brazilian Federal Police officers wearing jeans and bulletproof vests who asked to examine their passports, then waved them in. DZ pointed out that they were in Foz do Iguaçu now, which seemed to be a slightly more upscale version of what they'd seen on the Paraguayan side.

They followed a hundred feet behind the Ford Ranger down a two-lane highway through a field of sugarcane. The half moon hung off kilter to their right, peeking through cumulus clouds.

The rain stopped and the wind picked up, whipping the high cane on both sides of the road. Crocker saw the brake lights on the Ranger light up, then the vehicle take a right past what looked like a little farmhouse.

"Where are they going?" he asked.

DZ shook his head. "I don't know this area."

The road narrowed and circled behind long, dilapidated, industrial-looking buildings to an unmanned gate. They lost the Ranger in a grove of mature avocado trees. Hamid's voice over the radio barked, "Cut your lights!"

Crocker, in the passenger seat, spotted the Ranger two hundred feet ahead. "They're turning left," he said urgently.

DZ drove past the intersection, parked the Jetta off the road under a big tree, and got out.

"Why are we stopping here?" Crocker asked.

Hamid hurried over and spoke through the open driver's window, the wind playing with his hair. "There's an airstrip back there that's used by Brazilian charters," he said. "It's not sufficiently lit, and closes after dark."

Crocker said, "Let's hide the vehicles and take a look."

"Yes."

They armed themselves with pistols, then Hamid led the way through a sea of high sawgrass. Frogs croaked and crickets chirped around them. Two hundred yards along, he raised his right hand, pushed the foliage in front of him aside, and pointed. "There they are, over there."

Crocker saw a runway with portable klieg lights powered by a generator and an old aluminum 737 with "Aero Tetra" stenciled in black on its tail. Two large covered trucks were parked beside it. Men in short sleeves were tossing suitcase-sized bales of something wrapped in clear plastic from the back of the trucks into the jet's forward and aft cargo doors. An empty jeep sat fifty feet behind the jet.

"Aero Tetra? Never heard of it," Akil said.

"They couldn't get away with calling it Aero Terror," DZ commented.

"Who couldn't get away with calling it that?" Akil asked.

"The Iranians, man, the Iranians." There was no time to explain.

Crocker counted eight guards in shorts, armed with AK-47s, standing near the airplane and trucks.

"You think it's cocaine?" DZ whispered to Crocker.

"If it is, they're hauling hundreds of millions of dollars' worth."

"Where do you think they're planning to take it?" Akil asked.

"Europe, probably."

Akil: "What do we do now?"

"We stop it," Crocker answered.

"The aircraft? How?"

An excellent question. Armed only with pistols, they were grossly outgunned and outnumbered, had no body armor or backup, and there was a strong probability that Brazilian authorities had been paid off.

Crocker stuck out his chin and looked to his right along the runway to the terminal, which was completely dark. Then he pushed a button that illuminated the dial on his watch. It read 2308 hours.

The men loading the plane were moving quickly. The cockpit lights were on, which meant that the pilot, copilot, and navigator were inside and probably doing a preflight instrument check before they started the engines. That gave Crocker and the three men with him ten to twenty minutes to stop the plane from taking off.

The time it would take to alert the CIA stations in Asunción, Brasília, or Buenos Aires didn't seem worth it. Besides, all three cities were far away.

Turning to Akil, Crocker whispered, "Grab one of the radios and come with me. You guys wait here and stay alert," he said to DZ and Hamid.

"What are you gonna do?" DZ asked.

"Don't know yet, but I'll keep you informed."

He led the way through the sawgrass with his head tucked down and arms in front of him so the serrated blades wouldn't cut his face to shreds. *We've got to stop it. Somehow we've got to stop it*, he repeated over and over in his head.

After two hundred feet the field opened onto a large cement parking lot. A one-story terminal topped with a seventy-foot-tall control tower stood to his left. No lights. No sign of people inside. Akil breathed heavily behind him.

"What do you see, boss?" Akil whispered, sweat running down his forehead.

"Nothing. Follow me."

Crocker readied his 9mm Glock, dashed to the six-foot chain-link fence separating the parking lot from the runway, climbed it, and landed on the other side. He knelt on the concrete and scanned the area. On the tarmac on the runway side of the tower rested two trucks with "Petrobas" painted on them. One was a fuel truck; the other was a flatbed. Judging by the height of the tank above its suspension system, the fuel truck was empty.

"See if that one has keys inside," Crocker whispered, pushing Akil to the flatbed.

Neither of them did.

Akil joined Crocker near the cab of the tanker. "Boss, what are you thinking?" he asked.

"I checked, and the tank is empty."

"So?"

"I'm considering hot-wiring this baby and driving right at 'em. See how close we can get."

"Then what?"

"I don't know."

"If we drive at 'em, they're going to shoot us to shreds," Akil warned. "I counted eight armed guards, another half-dozen loaders. They could be armed, too."

"What's your gut say? You think Alizadeh's on the plane?" Crocker asked.

"My gut's not working."

He wanted this guy so bad he could feel it in his bones. No fucking way he was going to let him slip away again, even though he wasn't sure he was on the plane. It was a chance. A shot. That's all you got. Bold action was always clouded with danger and uncertainty. He said, "Radio DZ and tell him and Hamid to get ready. We're gonna need them to support us when the guards open fire."

Akil nodded. "Whatever you say, boss."

Crocker climbed into the cab and reached under the steering column to locate the starter wires. Access to the ignition switch involved removing the panel and cover around the ignition tumbler, which was directly below the lock. He located the wires and stripped the ends, then looked up as Akil hopped in the passenger-side door.

"What?" Akil asked, reading the uncharacteristic uncertainty on Crocker's face.

Crocker whispered, "We'd better wait."

"Wait for what? A miracle? An act of God?"

"That would be nice."

A fatalistic grin spread across Akil's wide face. "We launch now, it's a suicide mission, which I'm okay with if that's what you choose. But we gotta hope some vestal virgins are waiting for us."

"Shut up. I'm thinking...."

"Think hard."

Crocker twisted the ends of the two red wires together. "When I give the signal, you touch these to the end of this one," he said, pointing to the brown ignition wire.

"You want me to drive?" Akil asked.

"Yeah, you're driving. I'm gonna hide on top of the tank."

"I wish we had a Blackhawk about now, armed with Hellfire missiles," Akil whispered.

"And I wish I was Superman."

They sat in the stillness and watched from approximately two hundred yards away as the men continued loading. When the pilot fired up the 737-300's twin CFM56 turbofan engines, Crocker was jolted to a higher level of readiness.

The loading stopped. Someone inside the fuselage pulled

the cargo doors shut. The jet engine revved higher, screaming into the night, burning into Crocker's head, demanding that he do something fast.

The tension in the cab grew. "Now?' Akil asked.

"Not yet," Crocker whispered back.

He wanted to act, but the eight armed guards were still ranged in a perimeter around the trucks. Someone leaned out the cockpit window and was shouting something to one of the men on the ground. He threw him a packet. The man who caught it flashed a thumbs-up to the cockpit and ran to one of the trucks. Four guards jumped in, leaving another four standing around the jet. The trucks backed up and started to leave.

"Let's go!" Crocker said.

Akil gritted his teeth and nodded. He shifted into the driver's seat as Crocker opened the door and got out.

"When I slap the top of the cab, that's the signal to launch."

"Got it."

"I want you to drive straight toward the jet. If the guards stop you, talk to them in Farsi. They probably won't under-stand, but they might get confused and think you're with the men flying the plane."

"Okay."

"See if you can get all four of the guards to come over to you. Keep your pistol ready on the seat. I'm going to try to take out as many as I can."

"Then what?"

"Then you take out the rest and we stop the plane." At the very least it was an illegal flight carrying Iranians holding Venezuelan passports and trying to leave under cover of night.

"Sounds like fun."

"Start the engine, now!" Crocker said.

He scurried up the ladder and lay belly down on the front of the cylindrical tank. The trucks that had carried the drugs were gone. All that remained was the jeep, the 737, which was in the process of swinging its nose toward the runway, and four AK-47–wielding guards who were backing away from the jet.

Crocker reached out and slapped the cab of the tanker. Akil put it in gear. The truck lurched forward, and Crocker held on.

He was trying to fix the location of the guards, but the powerful wing lights on the 737 blinded him. He thought he heard shots above the noise of the grinding truck engine and the whine of the jet.

Hamid and DZ?

As the truck picked up speed, a hot wind hit his face, causing his eyes to water. The gunfire was coming from his left, somewhere in the high grass, maybe near the road where they had parked. What was transpiring there, he didn't know.

He had to focus on what was in front of him—the jet, the jeep, and the armed men. The tanker truck was now sixty feet from them. He heard Akil shouting out the window in Farsi and waving. One of the guards fired into the air. Akil slammed on the brakes and the tanker screeched to a stop. Crocker had to hold on with all his strength to prevent being thrown forward over the hood.

Two armed guards ran toward them, pointing their AK-47s at Akil, who emerged from the cab with his hands held over his head. One of them ordered him to lie prone on the ground. Akil shouted back at him in Farsi. He didn't want to lie down, and when Crocker saw the pistol stuck in the back waistband of his pants, he understood why.

One of the guards aimed his AK at Akil's head, while the second guard stepped forward and used the butt of his gun to pound Akil in the chest. Crocker aimed the Glock at the first guard and pumped four rounds into his torso. The man spun and fell, surprising his companion, who was standing over Akil, now lying on his back.

The second guard turned for a split second to look back at his colleague, and as he did, Akil cocked his leg back and kicked him in the groin. The guard doubled over. Crocker leaned over the edge of the tank to get a clear shot, but as he aimed the Glock, a third guard fired from somewhere near the plane. A bullet sailed past Crocker's ear. Others slammed into the metal around him.

He ducked, flipped his body over to the right, grabbed the rail that ran along the other side of the tank, and let himself down. Akil and the second guard were wrestling on the opposite side of the truck. Ignoring his colleague's safety, the third guard sprayed the truck, causing bullets to ricochet off the tank and hood.

Crocker crouched by the front right wheel and fired at Guard #3, but the intense light in his face made it hard to see. The jet was bearing down on them. Turning and looking up, he saw the pilot's and copilot's eyes, their determined faces. Guard #4 now opened fire at him from near the parked jeep. Bullets skidded off the concrete around him, throwing up long sparks.

But he couldn't hear the shots, because the roar of the engines drowned out all other sound. The jet picked up speed. Its wing was practically overhead.

With bullets whizzing past him and slamming into the side of the truck, Crocker opened the passenger door and climbed in. The engine was still running. He glanced out the side window and saw Guard #1 reaching for his AK. Crocker leaned out and shot him three times in the head.

As he put the truck in reverse, bullets shattered the windshield. He ducked. The plane's wings were behind him now. Crocker saw Akil pulling himself up off the tarmac and knew he was in danger of being sucked up into the jet's engine. So he opened the door, leaned down, grabbed Akil around the torso with his left arm, lifted him into the cab, and pushed him over his lap into the passenger seat.

"Nice fucking plan," Akil groaned, wiping blood from his face with the back of his hand.

"Sloppy execution," Crocker countered, shifting the vehicle into first and pushing down on the accelerator. He realized that bullets were no longer hitting the truck.

Maybe DZ or Hamid took the other guards out from behind.

"Now what?" Akil grimaced.

"Buckle your seat belt and hold on!"

He had the truck in fourth gear. The left front fender was about twenty feet wide of and thirty feet behind the oscillating red light on the tip of the jet's wing. Crocker gunned the engine and pulled even. Just then someone in the cockpit leaned out with an AK-47 and started shooting. Crocker ducked behind the dashboard as bullets slammed into the vehicle's hood and grille.

They were passing the terminal, and the jet was moving fast. Crocker thought, *Now's the time!*

With bullets ricocheting off the hood and tearing into the dash, he turned the steering wheel sharply left just as the plane started to lift off. The top of the tanker grazed the side of the jet engine, then slammed into the landing gear with a tremendous explosion of sparks.

"Fuck, yeah!" Akil shouted.

Crocker felt an incredible jolt and tried to hold on to the steering wheel, but lost control. The tanker was knocked off its wheels and rolled once, twice, then flipped again and landed in the grass with a thud that jarred him so powerfully he passed out. He gained consciousness briefly at the sound of an enormous explosion that lifted the truck off the ground.

"Akil?" he called weakly.

CHAPTER THIRTEEN

People are made of flesh and blood, and a miracle fiber called courage.

—Mignon McLaughlin

HE WOKE up in a hospital. Blinked. Felt his legs and arms, which were still intact. It took him a couple of seconds to focus on the yellow walls and the man sitting in the corner in a green chair, talking into a cell phone in what he recognized as Portuguese. The first things about him that registered were the short dreadlocks and the tattoo on his neck. Then Crocker remembered his name.

"DZ," he said, trying to sit up. "What the fuck happened? Where am I?"

The left side of his head hurt. He lifted his left arm and touched the bandage that ran from the top of his head to his ear.

DZ put the phone away and said, "You're one crazy lucky motherfucker."

"Why?"

"*Why?*" DZ threw back his head and laughed. "I can't believe you asked that."

"Where are we?"

"Dude, we're in a hospital in Puerto Iguazú, on the Argentine side of the falls. You suffered a pretty bad concussion, a crack in your skull that's been closed up with staples, some lacerations to your wrist, and a couple of bruised ribs. Otherwise you're okay, which is totally unbelievable."

"Okay?" Crocker asked, trying to recall what had transpired to split his head open and land him in the hospital.

"I saw the whole thing happen, man, and I still can't believe it," DZ continued. "Are you Irish?"

"Irish? No, some French, German, Scottish, and Norwegian mixed together. Why?"

"You know the saying, the luck of the Irish. Never mind."

Crocker looked for his watch, which wasn't on his wrist. The place where it used to be was covered with another white bandage. "What time is it?"

"A couple ticks shy of noon."

Noon. The last thing he remembered was the jet taking off at the airport last night. He'd been driving a truck. Akil sat beside him. "Akil. How's he?" Crocker asked, realizing that his mouth was bone dry, and reaching for the bottle of water on the table beside him.

"Akil was taken to the airport in Ciudad del Este about an hour ago," DZ answered, standing and adjusting the hems of his pant legs. Crocker noticed for the first time that the young man was wearing a cast on his left foot. "His right arm and wrist are both broken, and his right foot is messed up." DZ pointed to the night table to Crocker's right. "Oh, and he left you his watch."

Crocker leaned over and saw the black Luminox Color-mark 3050 Series watch on the table's gray enamel surface. The Luminox wasn't as tricked out as his Suunto, but it was rugged, water resistant, and featured continuous-glow dive bezel, hands, and hour markers. "What happened to mine?"

"It got totaled, man. Big surprise."

He liked that watch, which had been a present from Holly. "Totaled how?"

"Smashed to shit when the truck tumbled over like a toy, a little metal toy flicked by Godzilla. I never in a million years expected anyone to walk away from that alive."

"Where's Akil going?" he asked, stretching his arms over his head.

"We're taking him back to the States to get his arm properly set."

"Oh." Crocker was starting to feel tired and wanted to rest, but there was one more question he needed answered first. "What happened to the guys on the plane?"

"You don't remember?"

"Nope."

"The plane crashed and burned," DZ answered. "Everyone aboard died."

"Alizadeh, too?" Crocker asked excitedly. "Was he on it?"

"Who's he?"

"Farhed Alizadeh, a.k.a. the Falcon."

"The Brazilians haven't released any names so far. All they said was that everyone aboard burned to death. They also confirmed that the aircraft was packed with cocaine. They're saying about two hundred million dollars' worth. But they don't know shit about you, or us, or why the plane crashed, which is one of the reasons you're not in their custody."

Crocker's eyelids started to feel heavy. "Where am I, again?"

"Argentina."

"That's right. Argentina."

He closed his eyes and fell asleep.

He was sitting alone in a boat on a lake eating a bowl of chocolate ice cream. The surface of the lake shone like a piece of glass. He saw his reflection, then, looking up, realized the lake was vast, maybe endless. He couldn't make out a shore past the bluish mist in the far distance. He thought, *Maybe I'm dead. But even if I am, I trust in God.*

Crocker woke in a sweat, sitting on the edge of the bed in his underwear. Hands were holding him up and pulling on a pair of pants and a shirt. The hands belonged to DZ, Hamid, and a woman he'd never met.

"What's going on?" he asked, trying to focus.

"The Brazilian authorities are looking for you, so we're going to move you," DZ answered.

"We're taking you to a house we have in the city," Hamid added.

Crocker's head felt swollen and heavy. His entire body felt numb from the medication he'd been given. "Who's she?" he asked, nodding at the dark-haired woman tying his sneakers.

"Her name is Mercedes," DZ answered.

The walls looked a richer shade of yellow than before. The fluorescent light that glanced off them bothered his eyes. "Mercedes, like the car?"

"Correct."

"Hi, Mercedes."

"Ciao."

*   *   *

He remembered bouncing on the backseat of the SUV. The woman, illuminated by the headlights, opening a rusted green gate. She wore dark green pants and a cream-colored sweater.

Now he was seated outside by a swimming pool, and a doctor with a shaved head and a deep crease between his friendly blue eyes was taking his blood pressure. He pressed a stethoscope to Crocker's chest and back, then started asking questions. "Where were you born? What are your parents' names? Where did you go to school?"

He had no problem answering, but was starting to feel impatient.

He saw DZ standing off to one side, seemingly intent on the leaves floating in the pool. Mercedes, who was short, with round hips, stood behind him smoking a cigarette. Her hair was cut parallel to the line of her jaw, and he thought she looked vaguely French. Crocker waved DZ over.

"What's going on?" he asked.

DZ said, "The doctor's checking to see if you're healthy enough to fly."

"Where am I going?"

"We don't know yet."

"What have you learned about the three men on the plane?" Crocker asked.

"The Brazilians recovered four bodies. They haven't released any information about them, but we've heard they're communicating with both the Venezuelan and Iranian embassies."

"That's a good sign," Crocker said. The fact that the Iranians had been notified meant that some of their people were involved. He remembered the two sets of dark eyes glaring at him from the cockpit window. Something about them—the thickness of the brows, the way they were set, the pride and outrage in them—told him they were Iranian eyes, not Venezuelan.

An hour later he was in the same terminal he and Akil had entered the city in two days ago. This time he felt slightly dizzy as he stood with DZ and the dark-haired woman. "Mercedes will travel with you to Bogotá," DZ explained. "She's going to act like your girlfriend and never leave your side."

She had a pretty face. Pouty lips, thick wavy hair, sparkling dark eyes, smooth skin. When she spoke, her accent was Brazilian. "You need anything, you tell me," she said with confidence.

"Okay. But why Bogotá?"

"So the embassy doctor there can examine you again," DZ answered. "See if you're fit to return to Venezuela. You've also got two cracked molars that need to be fixed."

Crocker said, "I want to return to Venezuela. My men are still there, right?"

"Yes."

"I'll take care of the teeth later."

"The doctor will decide that."

The whine of the jet's engine bothered him, and when it gained speed down the runway, he had to resist a panicked urge to get up from his seat. In a flash it all came back to him, the man shooting at him from the cockpit, him at the wheel of the tanker truck, the blinking red light on the end of the 737's wing. Then the powerful jolt as the truck hit the jet.

He found Brubeck on his iPod and let the 5/4 swing of "Take Five" work its magic. The melody and rhythm calmed him, and he started to feel like himself. Music was transcendent. He wanted to learn more about it and understand how it worked. Not the hard rock and metal he'd listened to as a kid, but jazz, especially cool fifties jazz and bebop—Stan Getz, Dizzy Gillespie, Zoot Sims, Charlie Byrd, Art Tatum, Ben Webster, Lester Young.

Crocker never graduated from college, having gone straight from high school into the navy. Not that he had any regrets, except that he hadn't rubbed shoulders with people who were knowledgeable about a wide range of subjects, particularly the arts and music.

Drinks were served. He ordered a Diet Coke, then turned to Mercedes, tapped her on the shoulder, and asked what she was listening to.

"Music," she said grinning.

"No kidding." At least she had a sense of humor.

"If you really want to know, his name is Caetano Veloso." She had a tough, self-possessed demeanor that he found appealing.

"Caetano...who?"

Her eyes glistened with mischief. "You've never heard of Caetano Veloso?" she asked, tossing back her hair and pursing her full lips.

"No. You ever hear of Malcolm and Angus Young?"

"Caetano is a huge international star."

"So are Malcolm and Angus Young. They're the ass-kicking leaders of AC/DC."

"Tell me about it, Thomas."

He laughed inside. The last person who'd called him Thomas was his high school girlfriend Natalie, who was married now and living in Northern California. She had dark eyes, too, and an insatiable sexual appetite that got them both in trouble when they were caught making love on her parents' sofa. Natalie had not been allowed to see him after that, which pissed him off to the point that he got drunk and banged on her front door one night, only to be chased away by her shotgun-wielding father. Mercedes was like a shorter, curvier, Brazilian version of her.

He didn't mind that she shared a room with him, or that she walked around in a tank top and shorts, or that when they went out to dinner that night she peppered him with questions about his background, his failed first marriage, and what it was like to kill someone. Nor did it bother him when later that night she crawled into the other king-sized bed, and he was tempted to cross the space between them and take her in his arms. It made part of him feel alive. And also helped him remember how much he loved his wife and missed her.

"Love the One You're With" by Stephen Stills played in his head. He sat up, watched shadows wash across the walls, and recalled that he had now suffered seven—or was it eight?—concussions. Every severe impact to his head caused more brain cells to die. And every life taken left another scar on his soul.

In the morning he visited the embassy doctor, who like Crocker happened to be a former navy corpsman who had served in Japan. They discussed the strange obsessions of Japanese people—manga comic books, electronic games, Chinese dumplings, S&M—and their respective visits to the ancient city of Kyoto. The doctor cleared Crocker to travel to Venezuela, but warned him to take things easy.

Fat chance of that, Crocker thought, before answering, "Sure, Doc. Thanks."

That afternoon he and Mercedes swam laps in the hotel pool, then took a taxi to the airport. He was unable to shake the image of her round ass hugged by the tight red bathing suit. It screamed at him during the flight to Venezuela while she told him she had been born in Salvador de Bahia to an Italian economist father and Brazilian mother. They had split when she was ten. Her father was now living in Paris.

"Do you see him often?" Crocker asked. He was starting to understand how her background had made her worldly and self-reliant.

"About once a year. He's remarried. Because of him I'm always seeking men's approval, sometimes in self-destructive ways."

He found her honesty and confidence kind of sexy.

Later, when she fell asleep with her head on his shoulder, he debated whether she was inviting him to take things further, and whether he was a fool for letting an opportunity like this slip away or mature and intelligent for not giving in to temptation, risking his career, and destroying his marriage.

It bothered him that the answer wasn't as clear as he thought it should be. Maybe it was the medication he was still taking. Or maybe he was just being a red-blooded man genetically programmed to find attractive, fertile women and drag them back to his cave.

When he hugged her goodbye at the airport, she held on and whispered, "I hope I get to see you again, Thomas."

"Me, too," he answered, even though she was seventeen years younger than he and had trouble written all over her.

Pulling her suitcase, she disappeared into the crowd, taking with her the answers to many questions that popped into his head: How did she get into this line of work? How long had she been working for the Agency? Did she have a boyfriend? Where was she based?

He saw Sanchez waving above the bobbing heads, and raised his hand to acknowledge him. The sexual charge subsided.

Caracas seemed calm and orderly compared to Ciudad del Este. The city was starting to feel familiar—Miami with mountains instead of a coastline. Sanchez, at the wheel of the Ford Taurus, said, "Mr. Rappaport wants to see you later."

"I figured," he responded, remembering Mercedes getting out of the pool.

"Chávez is on life support. The rumor is that his family wants the doctors to pull the plug. Meanwhile, his VP, Maduro, is running the government, and everything seems to be the same as before—except the whole city is on edge."

"The Iranians, too?" Crocker asked as the glittering skyline came into view.

"Are they on edge? Yes. Especially after what you guys did to them in Brazil."

Crocker smiled to himself and thought, *Score one for us.* He knew he'd feel even better if they found Alizadeh's body in the wreckage in Foz do Iguaçu.

"You want me to stop somewhere so you can pick up something to eat first?" Sanchez asked, turning off the *autopista*.

"I'll be okay."

Davis was the only member of the team still living at the La Florida safe house. He explained that Cal and Mancini had left with Neto that morning for the southwestern state of Barinas.

"Why?" Crocker asked.

"Because Unit 5000 is building a base there," Davis answered, running a hand through his blond surfer hair, which didn't match the darker color of his beard.

"What about Ritchie? What's the word on him?"

"He's back home healing and feeling sorry for himself," Davis reported. "He says he's sick of watching TV and eating applesauce and yogurt."

Crocker detected torment in his young teammate's eyes. "What about you? You okay?"

"I'm fine," Davis answered. "I just got off a Skype call with Sandy." Sandy was his blond, former USC cheerleader wife. "She's freaking out because Tyler is running a 104-degree fever and she can't get hold of the pediatrician."

Tyler was their one-year-old. "I told her to use a wet washcloth to cool him down, give him some baby aspirin, and let him sleep. He'll probably be better in the morning, right?"

Crocker said, "Tell her to check in on him every so often, and that kids bounce back fast. If he's still running a high fever in the morning she might want to take him to the hospital."

"That'll reassure her. Thanks."

Crocker unpacked, nuked some canned soup he found in

the kitchen, then had Sanchez drive him over to the Banco Popular building, which looked deserted. It was the week between Christmas and New Year's, and a lot of people seemed to have left the city.

He rode up to the ninth-floor office and found Melkasian in a blue tracksuit and sneakers talking to someone on the phone. Crocker picked up a recent issue of *Time*, which had a smiling Egyptian president Mohamed Morsi on the cover. He didn't trust him. To his mind anyone whose political beliefs were determined by religious dogma, especially if it was Muslim, had to be carefully watched.

Melkasian put his phone away and threw Crocker a bottle of water. "How's your head?" he asked.

"Still seems to work, as far as I can tell. How's yours?"

"Heavy with concerns, problems. I heard about that wild stunt you pulled in Foz."

"I'm still trying to remember the details," Crocker said. "Anything new about the identities of the men on the plane?"

Melkasian shook his head. "Doubt if there ever will be," he answered. "They were burned to a crisp. But we do know that the Iranians requested the remains."

"But they haven't been ID'd?"

"No."

Rappaport arrived, popped open his metal briefcase, and they got down to business. Crocker was shown satellite photos of a plot in Barinas where Unit 5000 was reportedly building a base and landing strip. There wasn't much to see, except for a couple of tin-roofed structures and a swath of reddish dirt carved into what looked to be a flat grassy plain.

"Where's Bolinas?" Crocker asked.

Rappaport snorted. "Bolinas is a town on the Northern California coast. Barinas is a state southwest of here."

"What's this?" Crocker asked, pointing to what looked like a country club, with a large house and pool area, on one of the surveillance photos.

"That's the Hugo Chávez family estate, La Chavera," Melkasian said. "He was born nearby in the house of his paternal grandmother, and grew up there until he came to Caracas at seventeen to attend the Venezuelan military academy."

"Interesting that the Iranians decided to build their base there."

"Also interesting is the fact that the Iranians are building a landing strip in Barinas, which is near the Colombian border and close to hundreds of cocaine labs."

"How convenient," Crocker observed.

"Exactly."

CHAPTER FOURTEEN

Lost causes are the only ones worth fighting for.
— Clarence Darrow

CROCKER, DAVIS, and Sanchez set out early the following morning in one of the white Toyota FJ Cruisers they had used the night they raided the shack in Petare. The four-lane "super" highway was paved and relatively new. Sanchez explained that the Chávez-Maduro government had removed all the tollbooths so that anyone regardless of their social or economic status could afford to take the country's best roads. This explained the heavy traffic. Crocker also saw disrepair in several places and wrecked, abandoned cars along the side of the road.

The sun was starting to set when they arrived at the state capital of Barinas, which featured open fields, groves of trees, and gated estates. Sanchez said that since they were close to the Colombian border, the area was frequented by FARC (Fuerzas Armadas Revolucionarias de Colombia) soldiers, and therefore considered dangerous at night.

"I've dealt with them before," Crocker said, recalling past missions against FARC bases in eastern Colombia.

"The guerrillas cross the border to steal stuff and kidnap people. So all the ranchers in the area are armed and on alert. They lock up their cattle and equipment after dark."

The FARC, which called itself a peasant army whose goal was to overthrow the Colombian government and establish an agrarian Marxist-Leninist state, financed its operations by kidnapping wealthy Colombians and foreigners for ransom, growing coca, and processing, trafficking, and transshipping cocaine. One of its leaders, Guillermo Torres, had been captured near Barinas in June of the previous year.

"Interesting place for Unit 5000 to establish a base," Crocker said, thinking out loud. "They're in Venezuela, so they're protected, Barinas is in the middle of nowhere, and there's an endless supply of cheap cocaine that they can sell overseas to fund their operations."

He was starting to understand how the Falcon thought.

"I was thinking the same thing, boss," Davis said. "Instead of having to ship the drugs out of places like Ciudad del Este, they'll soon be able to fly it to Europe right out of here."

"Good point."

They stopped at a farmhouse with a big garden and were greeted by large barking dogs. The proprietor, Señor Tomás, looked like a wizened, white-haired Indiana Jones, complete with safari jacket and straw fedora. Crocker learned that he was a Cuban American cattle rancher and CIA asset. He also had two extra bedrooms, one of which was being used by Mancini, Cal, and Neto. Crocker, Davis, and Sanchez took the other one, which seemed to belong to a huge black dog named Chico, who slept in a large wicker basket under the window.

After washing up and unpacking, Crocker and Davis met the other members of Black Cell and Neto on the rear veranda, where they drank rum punch and beer, and listened to Señor Tomás talk about how the government was ruining the country by driving rich Venezuelans and foreign capital out, and thereby shutting down new business investment.

"You think Maduro will change anything?" Mancini asked.

"Probably not," Tomás answered. "He's a fucking communist demagogue, too. Spends a lot of time with the Castro brothers in Cuba looking for ways to screw the U.S. As a matter of fact, he might be worse."

After dinner of roast lamb and baby potatoes, their host showed them photos of his family's house in Havana, where he had been born in 1940. His father, he explained, had been arrested and shot by Che Guevara shortly after the Cuban Revolution. He himself had returned to Cuba as a teenager as part of the CIA-trained Brigade 2506 during the Bay of Pigs Invasion on April 17, 1961. He was one of an estimated 1,202 Cuban anti-Castro rebels who were captured a few days later, after the Kennedy administration failed to assist the invading force with much-needed air support. He spent a year and a half rotting in a Cuban prison before he was released and returned to Miami.

He hated the Kennedys for their betrayal but said he despised Fidel Castro even more, which is why he had worked with the CIA to help defeat communists throughout Latin America ever since.

With his blond American wife humming along, Tomás played a guitar and sang plaintive songs in Spanish. One of them, "Guantanamera," a love song to a woman from a country town in Cuba, caused tears to spill from his eyes. He wiped them away, ran into the yard, and starting lighting something with a torch.

"What's he doing now?" Crocker whispered to Mancini.

"He's setting off fireworks. It's about two minutes shy of the New Year." With all the excitement, injuries, and activity, Crocker had lost track of time.

They watched rockets explode in the sky, drank champagne, and sang "Auld Lang Syne."

After midnight, Crocker, Mancini, and Neto piled into the Toyota for a drive past the Unit 5000 base, which was a couple of miles west. All they could see from the narrow road was a high aluminum fence topped with barbed wire. Guarding the gate were Venezuelan soldiers armed with automatic rifles who were passing a bottle of whiskey.

Back at the house, Neto and Crocker examined the latest satellite photos. Neto pointed out that while all that had been built so far were two barracks and an admin building, construction on the airstrip, small control tower, and storage hangars was moving fast.

"How soon before the airstrip is operational?" Crocker asked.

"They're already landing smaller planes on this dirt strip over here," Neto answered, pointing to another photo. "But the longer asphalt one probably won't be ready for another three or four months."

Bush and field crickets chirped through the screened window and a string of firecrackers went off in the distance as Crocker sat down at a laptop in Señor Tomás's office and typed out a report on the Brazilian raid for Captain Sutter back at command. He still owed him one about his arrest of the major in Afghanistan, too. He thought, *Maybe I'll get to that tomorrow.*

The white stucco walls and tops of the old credenza, desk, and bookcase were covered with framed pictures of Tomás's life and adventures—smiling in the back of a boat with a large sailfish in one hand and his arm around a beautiful woman; standing with a group of shorter Cuban-looking men; shooting skeet; waterskiing. One of the black dogs snored on the round faded rug near Crocker's feet.

He was starting to stand when he heard something move outside and he stopped to listen. The dog lifted its big head for a moment, then subsided. Another dog barked in the distance. It stopped, and all he heard were crickets again and the leaves rattling in the breeze.

Crocker looked at the watch he'd received from Akil: 0324. He was still wide awake.

He liked the house, the semitropical setting, the languid feeling in the air, the sense of being surrounded by memories. Projecting at least fifteen years into the future, he wondered what it would be like to retire to an outpost like this with Holly. If she didn't want to come with him, he might try living there on his own. Maybe find a younger Venezuelan family to help him run the ranch. Maybe learn to play the saxophone, which he'd always wanted to do.

He saved his document, shut down the computer, and was walking down the hall to the bedroom when he heard a vehicle enter through the gate and stop. Footsteps hurried over the gravel. The dogs barked.

Someone was pounding on the front door. He heard Tomás shout in Spanish and ran to see what was going on. A single gunshot reverberated down the hall, followed by the horrible yelp of a dog in pain.

More men shouted from the bedroom area. Crocker ran back to the office, grabbed the old .38 revolver he'd seen in the top drawer of the desk, and checked to see that it was loaded. With his back pressed along the wall, he made his way to the front room.

From the hallway, he saw Tomás wrestling with two men wearing black ski masks. Tomás punched one of them in the face; the other grabbed him around the neck and threw him to the ground. While the two masked men kicked him in the chest and groin, another man with a big belly watched. He laughed, then leaned over to smack Tomás in the face with the big black pistol he was holding.

Crocker stepped forward and heard the wooden floor creak behind him. He stopped and pivoted into the barrels of two AK-47s pointed at his head. "Drop your gun," a masked man growled in Spanish-accented English.

Crocker bent down to lay the pistol on the floor, then threw himself at the men's knees. He was reaching around in the dark trying to locate one of the men when something smashed into the small of his back and a bolt of pain shot into his legs and up his spine to his head. His arms and legs went numb. Hands grabbed him by the neck and roughly pulled him to his feet.

He kicked and tried to pull away when something hit him

in the stomach, forcing the air out of his diaphragm and striking the vagus nerve in his stomach, which made him want to throw up.

Gasping for breath and unable to summon the energy to fight back, Crocker was hog-tied at the wrists and ankles, his mouth was taped shut, and he was dragged outside past a dead dog and thrown into the back of a covered truck. He saw Cal beside him bleeding from a wound on his forehead. When he heard Mancini moaning, he tried to turn and look over his left shoulder, but a soldier kicked him back.

The truck they were in started moving and picking up speed. As Crocker sweated through his clothes, he counted the seconds in his head. Simultaneously he was trying to remember the route—down a straight road, right, up an incline, another right, past what smelled like a barn. They stopped when he reached 243-Mississippi.

Two soldiers dragged him across a dirt field and down fifteen concrete steps. A metal door creaked open. He was pushed into a little room that stunk of human waste and rot. It was completely dark and barely long enough to accommodate his long body.

Three soldiers wearing black masks entered. One used a large pair of scissors to cut his clothes off while another removed his watch, shoes, and the tape from his mouth. A third placed a large tin can filled with water on the floor, and all three left.

Crocker heard a muffled scream from another cell and thought it sounded like Cal. He wanted desperately to help him. His windowless room was completely devoid of light. With his wrists still tied behind his back, he measured the space with his leg and the side of his face. He found rough cement, a metal door with a one-inch gap at the bottom, human waste, and some bones in one corner. *Nice way to start the new year,* he said to himself as he saw a rat squeeze under the door and scurry around his cell. When it ran across his shoulder to his chest he shook it off, then used his knees to crush it against the wall.

Sitting naked with his back against the wall, he measured his breath. Square breathing, they called it in yoga—counting to four as he inhaled, holding his breath in his lungs for another four, exhaling in four, then counting to four before he inhaled again.

He tried to stay positive and chased out of his head all thoughts of long-term captivity, torture, and death.

They'll come and get me. Something will happen. An opportunity will present itself, and I'll strike.

Hours passed before three men in olive uniforms with black hoods over their heads entered. They dragged Crocker down a dark, narrow hallway to a larger room with bright lights. The men sat him in a metal chair facing a long metal table.

The light burned his eyes as he waited for perhaps an hour, with soldiers standing guard behind him. Then a door to his right opened and three more men filed in, also wearing black hoods but dressed in civilian clothes. The one with the big belly carried a gray folder, which he slapped onto the table as the other two took their seats on either side of him. The guards moved forward to stand parallel with Crocker. He noticed automatic handguns in the holsters on their waists.

The man with the big belly opened the folder, grabbed a

pen from his pocket, clicked it, and looking up at Crocker asked in English, "Name?"

"Thomas Mansfield."

"Name?"

Crocker had volunteered for SERE (meaning Survival, Evasion, Resistance, and Escape) training soon after he'd been assigned to SEAL Team One. At the age of twenty-four, he'd spent weeks in a mock POW camp in Warner Springs, California, where he was interrogated, deprived of food and sleep, and waterboarded. He had also served as a SERE instructor at the same camp a few years back. So he knew what to expect during an enemy interrogation, and had committed to memory the six articles of the military code of conduct.

Article Three stated: If I am captured, I will continue to resist by all means available. I will make every effort to escape and aid others to escape. I will accept neither parole nor special favors from the enemy.

"Name?" the man at the table barked again.

"Thomas Mansfield."

"If you tell us the truth, we can make this easy," the man said. "Name?"

"Thomas Mansfield."

"Nationality?"

"Canadian."

"Occupation?"

"Businessman."

"What's the name of your company?"

"Balzac Expeditions."

A shorter man at the left end of the table with a silver Swiss military watch on his left wrist cleared his throat and spoke with a Middle Eastern accent: "I know this criminal. His name is Tom Crocker, and he's an assault team leader with SEAL Team Six, also known as DEVGRU."

Crocker focused on the voice and the silver watch. The man said he knew him. *Could it be Farhed Alizadeh, the Falcon?*

The man with the belly asked, "Is this true?"

"No," Crocker answered, trying to recall the names, faces, and voices of Iranian VEVAK and Quds Force agents he had run into during the course of his career.

"Mr. Crocker is a very dangerous man. A cold-blooded killer," the man at the end of the table continued. "Why are you in Barinas, Mr. Crocker?"

"My name isn't Crocker."

"What are you doing in Barinas?"

"Me and some of my business associates stopped here on our way to scout an expedition into the jungle."

The short man pointed to the dirty, tattered bandage on the left side of Crocker's head and asked, "What happened to your head?"

"I fell down some stairs."

"You're a liar."

The man's accent, short stature, air of self-importance, and the cold menace in his voice all led Crocker to conclude that he was Alizadeh, who he'd seen face-to-face in Tripoli the previous year.

"Are you lying?" the fat man asked.

"No."

Knowing that Alizadeh was there heightened the stakes and Crocker's desire to escape. It also heightened his disappointment. The Falcon wasn't dead.

"If you answer one question correctly, I will have you moved to a room with a bed and maybe even give you clean clothes and a shower," the fat man offered.

Crocker nodded.

The men at the table conferred in whispers, then the fat man in the middle sat back and spoke again. "I'm going to ask you one more time. Name?"

"Thomas Mansfield."

Article Four: If I become a prisoner of war, I will keep faith with my fellow prisoners. I will give no information or take part in any action which might be harmful to my comrades.

"Nationality?"

"Canadian."

"Occupation?"

"Businessman."

"Liar," Alizadeh said.

"I'm a Canadian businessman."

"What's more important to you, Mr. Crocker, defending a lie or being able to ever make love to your wife again?"

The men at the table rose together and exited through the door to Crocker's right. As the door closed behind them, the guards on either side of him went to work. First they strapped him spread-eagle on a set of bedsprings on the floor. Then they took turns pissing on him. Then they beat the bottom of his feet with sticks. Then they burned the skin on his chest with cigarettes. Finally, they hooked up the metal bedsprings to a portable generator, threw water on his body, and turned on the current, which made his muscles clench to the point that he felt his body was squeezing in on itself.

His gums bled, his head and ass hurt, and he felt sick and exhausted.

Smoke rising from Crocker's body, the guards moved him back to the metal chair. The three interrogators reentered and asked him the same questions. Crocker repeated the same answers. He hated all three men, especially Alizadeh, on the left. The interrogators filed out and the guards hooked up the electricity again, this time applying it directly to his scrotum, nipples, and anus.

Another round of questions from the interrogators, then a session of waterboarding, which Crocker didn't mind as much, since he'd trained himself to hold his breath for nearly three minutes. When they strapped him on a slanted board and pushed his head under water and held it there, he came up pretending to be suffering although he wasn't.

Two more sessions of questioning and electricity, then Crocker was dragged back to his cell starving, exhausted, and barely conscious. He drank the greasy water, threw up, and defecated in the corner.

He knew in his heart that he would never give up information. They'd have to kill him. Maybe they would.

CHAPTER FIFTEEN

*Today is victory over yourself of yesterday. Tomorrow is
your victory over lesser men.*

— Miyamoto Musashi

HE FELL asleep and woke up with an idea. Feeling around
in the dark and locating the bones in the corner of the cell,
he selected two strong, thin, short ones. Holding them in his
teeth because his wrists were still handcuffed behind him, he
dragged them along the rough concrete wall for hours, until
his neck, teeth, and mouth were so sore and tired that he had
to rest. Ten minutes later he resumed, scraping for hours until the bones had been honed down to sharp, lethal points that
were short enough to hide in his palms.

He covered the tips of the bones with his shit, hid them in
his hands, curled into a ball on the bare cement floor, and fell
asleep. He dreamt that Ritchie was telling him about a vin-
tage Indian Chief Roadmaster motorcycle he had just bought.
He explained that it was an exact copy of one that had been
owned by his father—cream colored and beautifully detailed,

with an inline four-cylinder IOE engine and four-speed over-drive transmission.

"My dad had an Indian, too," Crocker responded. "Once he lost control of it on some ice and slid under an oncoming truck. The big front prevented him from being crushed."

As he said these words, he experienced them. He was under the truck, smelling the gasoline and feeling the hot engine.

Ritchie grabbed him by the wrists and started to drag him out, which at first Crocker welcomed. But when the back of his feet started to burn from the scraping, he shouted at Ritchie to stop. That's when he opened his eyes and realized he'd been hallucinating and he was in the interrogation room again.

A guard slapped him so hard he saw stars. Opening his eyes, he registered the three men sitting behind the table. Blood dripped from his nose onto his bare chest.

Alizadeh said, "You keep this up and you'll be useless to anyone soon, Mr. Crocker."

"My name's not Crocker. It's Mr. Mansfield."

Alizadeh pointed at the guard, who slapped him again. Crocker lost consciousness, but remembered to keep the bones clenched in his fists.

When he came to, his interrogators were gone and the two guards were unlocking the handcuffs around his wrists.

"Water," he muttered. "I need water."

"No water," the taller of the two guards growled, putting him in a headlock and dragging him over to the bedsprings for another session of shocks. Crocker moved his fingers to make sure the sharpened bones were still in his hands. *It's now or never*, said an authoritative voice in his head.

The voice was right, because when the guard let Crocker go his legs were so weak that he crumpled to the wet floor, hitting the side of his head. They laughed, then bent over on either side of him to pull him onto the bedsprings and chain him down.

His head still reeling, Crocker turned to the guard on his right, who was holding him by the back of the head, and focused on the guard's neck. Locating the carotid artery, he cocked his arm at the elbow and drove the bone into the artery with all the strength he had left. The guard screamed, went into immediate toxic shock, and collapsed.

The second guard reached for his gun and hurried over to his colleague. Crocker moved quickly, grabbing him by the front of his uniform and pulling him to the ground. Then he shifted the second bone into his right hand. The guard saw the crude weapon coming and shielded himself with his arm, deflecting Crocker's thrust just enough that the bone drove into his windpipe instead. He fell backward and shouted something in Spanish.

Hearing someone moving toward him, Crocker spun. On the floor he spotted the chain the guards were about to use, picked it up, and swung it wildly. It struck a third guard who had run into the room, momentarily stunning him. As Crocker scrambled to his feet, he saw the man who was doubled over reaching for the pistol in his holster, then realizing he wasn't moving fast enough to stop the chain that hit him in the face with a loud crack. His right eye exploded and he screamed desperate pleas in Spanish that ended when Crocker wrapped the chain around his neck and tightened it until he stopped breathing.

His heart beating wildly, Crocker grabbed his pistol, a knife, another pistol, and a set of keys from the belt of the first man he had killed. Then he stripped off the guard's olive uniform, and pulled it on. Still barefoot and with no time to button the uniform, he opened the door behind him, slipped out, limped down the hallway as fast as his bruised feet would take him, breathing hard, not knowing where he was going.

He came to the end and a bare cinder-block wall. A single light bulb hung from the ceiling, illuminating another hallway. Crocker was disoriented, but thought the cell he wanted was located to the right. From the opposite direction came muffled voices shouting behind him. His head pounding, he checked to make sure the pistol in his hand was loaded, then shook the first metal door.

"It's Crocker. Who's in there?"

"Boss?" the weary voice responded.

"Yeah, it's me. Hold on."

Crocker's hands were covered with blood and his head was messed up, but he kept it together long enough to try seven of the dozen keys until he found the one that fit. The cell was dark and emitted a horrible stench. He found Mancini huddled in the near corner and helped him up. His face was badly bruised and he had trouble standing.

Mancini mumbled something, then repeated it. "Sanchez is dead."

"Lean on me. How do you know?"

"They shot him in front of me, then cut his dick off…"

Crocker shook him and whispered urgently, "Manny, listen. Listen. I need your help."

"Yeah, boss. What?"

"I need you to stand on your own. Can you do that?"

"I'll try. They killed Sanchez."

"I know. You told me. Now, take this pistol, and lean on the wall if you have to. I need you to guard the entrance to the hallway while I get the other guys out."

Mancini nodded, grabbed the pistol, stumbled naked to where the main hallway branched off, and waved. Crocker saw burn marks covering his torso. He waved back, then unlocked the next cell, where he found Davis lying on the ground unconscious. He dragged him over to the bucket and splashed dirty water on his face.

Davis struggled wildly to pull free. "Stop!" he growled. "Let go!"

Crocker slapped him. "Davis, it's me!"

Everything happened fast. One moment he was holding Davis, the next the two of them had located Neto and Cal in another cell. Cal, who was slipping in and out of consciousness, had to be carried. They heard a pistol discharge behind them. Mancini fired back, then shouted, "They're coming, boss! They're here!"

Davis: "Oh, fuck!"

Neto peered down the murky passageway in front of them and pointed, saying, "I saw a stairway down this way."

Davis, numbly: "A stairway?"

Crocker waved vigorously to Mancini and shouted, "Cover us, then run! Can you run?"

"I'll try!"

Crocker slung Cal over his shoulder and they moved as fast as their broken, exhausted bodies could take them, down the hallway, to a door with safety glass that Crocker had to punch out with the butt of the pistol so he could reach through and undo the lock from the other side.

"Watch the glass! Feet! Watch your feet!"

None of them had shoes, and all were naked except Crocker. They stumbled up the concrete stairs, pushed open a metal hatch, and tasted fresh air.

Pain emanated from every part of Crocker's body. He leaned against a metal lamppost for a few seconds. Neto, panting beside him, pointed at the sky and muttered, "Look."

"Yeah, stars."

"Where's Mancini?"

Crocker considered going back for him, but seeing someone standing near a truck at ten o'clock, placed his hand over Cal's mouth. He motioned to the other men to hide behind some plastic garbage bins to the right. The soldier was sixty feet away and had his back toward them. He turned and shone a light in their direction. Curious, he took several steps forward.

From behind one of the bins, Crocker watched him raise his rifle. He was aiming it at Mancini, whose big head had just emerged from the stairway. Before the soldier had a chance to pull the trigger, Crocker rose and shot him three times in the chest.

Turning to Davis, he said, "Grab his gun and his uniform, then meet us in the truck."

"Okay."

It was a two-ton military cargo truck with a winch in front. He and Mancini helped Cal into the bed and covered him with a tarp. "Stay with him," Crocker instructed.

Then he hurried to the cab and found a single key in the ignition, but when he turned it and pushed down on the gas, the engine whined and died. He tried it a second time with the same result.

Crocker heard men behind them shouting in Spanish, pushed away rising panic, and noticed that the truck was parked on a slight incline. He told Neto and Davis to go to the back and push.

The shadows of men were emerging from the stairway. "They're coming," Mancini warned through the open back window.

"Stay down!" Crocker growled back.

As the truck picked up a little speed on the narrow dirt road, Crocker shifted into second and pressed down on the accelerator. The truck lurched, and the engine coughed and started. Crocker shouted, "Get in!" as guns fired behind them and a bullet shattered the side mirror, spraying shards of glass across the front of his stolen uniform.

In the moonlight he saw they had a chance if they could make it to the bottom of the hill, where the road turned sharply right and was shielded by a stand of tall trees. More bullets slammed into the back of the truck. In spite of the mayhem, Crocker welcomed the sweet, pungent smell of eucalyptus, the fresh night air, and the moments of freedom.

"How's Cal?" Crocker shouted over his shoulder.

"He's still out, but his heart rate seems normal."

Neto opened the glove compartment and found a pack of Marlboros and a BlackBerry.

"Don't use it," Crocker warned.

"But we need to call for—"

He reached over with his right hand and slapped it away. "Don't!"

He spotted headlights in the rearview mirror.

"Boss!" Davis shouted from the seat beside him.

"I see them."

The engine coughed, missed, and started again. The grove they had entered was dense and dark. He floored the accelerator but the truck didn't gain speed. Forty appeared to be as fast as it could go.

Crocker cut the headlights and turned onto a dirt path that continued for a hundred feet into the forest, descending sharply and becoming narrower and overgrown. He pushed the truck through and down a steep embankment that stopped at a dark body of water.

"Why are we stopping here?" Neto asked.

"Because this thing won't float."

He had to jam the door into encroaching high bushes to get out. The canopy was so thick they couldn't be spotted from above. Moonlight shone off the surface of the water. Frogs croaked.

Rampant foliage cloaked the lake, making it a good place to hide. He thought, *A lake this size is probably fed by a stream or river, which means that there's some form of town or hamlet nearby.*

He looked at Davis's gaunt, bruised face and said, "Help everyone get out. You'll wait here while Neto and I get help."

He pocketed the BlackBerry, then released the truck's parking brake and with Neto's help pushed it into the lake. Turning to the four men, he saw they looked weak and dehydrated. He tried the water, which tasted clean.

"Drink," he whispered. "We all need water."

The water seemed to revive them. They circled right into even denser foliage and stopped. Cal, who Crocker had been carrying, continued to slip into and out of consciousness. His heartbeat seemed normal, but his pulse felt weak. No apparent fractures to his skull; no major wounds to his body.

Must be some sort of blunt force injury or concussion, Crocker concluded, holding Cal up, giving him water, and washing the shit off his face.

Cal opened his gray eyes, blinked, and asked, "Boss, where are we?"

"You're gonna wait here with Manny and the others. I'm going to get help."

"I want to come with you."

Crocker smiled to himself. "No, you stay here."

He led the way through the shallow edge of the lake to the other side, then up an embankment to a spot that was heavily wooded and defendable.

Cal looked around and asked, "Where's Sanchez? We forgot Sanchez. He was with us."

"Sanchez is dead," Neto said, clenching his jaw and looking down at his feet.

They left two of the pistols with Mancini and Davis. Crocker and Neto took the other pistol and the knife, slid down the embankment, and found the feeder stream, which they followed for half an hour to a small village.

Crocker said, "You take the knife and see if you can find a phone."

Neto: "Where should I tell them to meet us?"

Crocker: "Tell them we'll be waiting by the path that leads into the forest. If you're coming from the prison, it's about thirty yards after the first big bend in the road. Tell them to flash their headlights three times and I'll come out."

"Got it."

Two and a half hours later, just as the sun was starting to light up the sky and men with dogs and flashlights were searching the other side of the road, Crocker saw three black SUVs stop about two hundred feet away. After the lead vehicle flashed its lights three times, he stepped out onto the road and waved. They pulled closer, and six heavily armed men dressed in black emerged to start loading them in. No questions asked; no words exchanged. They sped twenty minutes to an airstrip, where the four SEALs and Neto boarded a Gulfstream IV.

A half hour later, Crocker, Mancini, and Neto deplaned in Caracas. Davis and Cal stayed on the jet, which continued to Panama City, where the two men were taken by ambulance to Hospital Punta Pacifica.

CHAPTER SIXTEEN

Rectitude is one's power to decide upon a course of conduct in accordance with reason, without wavering; to die when to die is right, to strike when to strike is right.

—Nitobe Inazo

CROCKER, MANCINI, and Neto were examined, X-rayed, and patched up by a doctor and nurse at a clinic, then driven to the safe house in La Florida, where they crashed. Crocker heard Mancini shouting in his sleep, "They're coming! Quick! Find a place to hide!"

That afternoon after he woke and was limping from the living room to the kitchen, he heard rap music, then saw a big young African American man sitting on the sofa, typing on a laptop.

Recognizing him, Crocker said, "Tré, what the fuck are you doing here?"

Tré's real name was Dante Tremaine. Why the former marine and University of Nevada, Las Vegas basketball player was called Tré had never been explained to him. Maybe it was because he'd been an excellent three-point shooter in college, or maybe it was because Tré was an abbreviation of his last name, which was pronounced *Tree*-maine, not *Tray*-maine. Crocker knew him as an expert munitions and weapons man, a tireless worker, and a fun guy to be around despite his complicated personal life, which involved three children with two women.

"Captain Sutter sent me 'cause of what went down with Ritchie," Tré responded with a toothy smile.

"How's Rich?"

"He's making slow progress, but it's gonna take a while."

"How long you been here in Caracas?"

"Two days, one night."

"Well, it might be a short deployment," Crocker observed.

"Whatever happens is cool with me," Tré responded. "Oh, and the Captain wants you to call him when you're awake."

"I'm awake now."

"If you say so." Tré smiled.

Crocker had suspected he might be hearing from his CO after what had happened in Foz and Barinas. Pointing to the half-eaten protein bar on the wooden coffee table, he asked, "Where'd you find the Promax bar?"

"There's a whole box in the kitchen," Tré responded. "Help yourself."

He gobbled one down with a quart of milk he found in the refrigerator.

Tré pointed to the multiple burn marks and bandages crisscrossing Crocker's torso and said, "Fuck, man. Looks like someone used you as a dartboard."

"I ran into some lit cigarettes."

"Hope you punished them sons-a-bitches."

Crocker grinned. "Some of them, yeah."

Tré chuckled. "That's what I dig about you, chief. The glass might be a drip or so from empty, but you always see the silver lining. Like the movie, right?"

Crocker hadn't seen a movie in months. He lifted the receiver of the STU secure telephone, picked up the key that lay beside it, inserted it into the hole at the top of the phone, and turned it. Then he pointed at the stereo and said, "Turn it down."

Tré said, "Those are my brothers Kanye and Jay-Z."

As Crocker punched in the numbers, he muttered, "It's all the same nasty rap shit to my ears."

"Then you need some educating to appreciate where it's coming from—lyrically, I mean."

"Turn it down or plug in."

Captain Sutter picked up in his office at SEAL Six command and spoke in his distinctive Kentucky drawl, "Sutter here. Who's this?"

"It's Warrant Officer Crocker, sir, calling from Caracas."

"Chief Tom Crocker, speak of the devil. Several of us here were just talking about you. We expected you and Mancini to continue to Panama City with the rest of your team."

"There was no need, sir," Crocker said. "The two of us are ready and able to continue with the mission."

"Jesus Christ, Crocker, don't you ever stop?" Sutter asked.

"Stop, sir? What for?"

"Stop, as in take a break, heal, attend to your mental health, smell the friggin' roses."

"Sir?"

"I know you, Crocker, and I know you push yourself beyond the breaking point. I've heard your motto: Blood from every orifice. I admire your dedication and courage, but everyone has their limits."

Crocker said, "I know that, sir, but maybe my limits aren't as narrow as you or I think they are. The point is, I only suffered minor cuts and bruises. I'm rested and ready to go."

Sutter snorted. "Bullshit."

"Sir?"

"Maybe I heard wrong, but I was told on good authority that you suffered a major concussion, then spent a day and a half being tortured. Now you're ready to go? Go where? An insane asylum?"

"Proceed with the mission, sir. Continue our pursuit of the Falcon and Unit 5000."

Sutter chuckled and drawled, "We have a saying in Kentucky that goes: Don't give cherries to pigs or advice to fools."

"Are you calling me a fool, sir?"

"Draw your own conclusions," Sutter answered. "I'm not sure who's being more irrational here, you for wanting to continue after you've gotten the shit kicked out of you, or me for letting you."

"Did I hear you correctly, sir?" Crocker asked. "Are you giving us approval to proceed?"

"I probably should have my head examined, but yes I am, Crocker. Check in with the station when you're ready. Call me if you need anything."

"I will, sir."

"Dante Tremaine should be there by now."

"He is."

"Then Godspeed."

As Crocker hung up, he noticed a number written on a pad by the phone. "What's this?" he asked Tré.

"That Melkasian cat left it. Wants you to call him in the morning."

"Tomorrow morning?"

"Yeah, mañana."

Why waste time? Crocker thought. He was motivated, energized, and ready to jump back into the fray.

Melkasian picked up at home, where he was helping his wife assemble her new Fuji bicycle. "Hey, Crocker, you know anything about installing the axle on a Fuji mountain bike?" he asked.

"Yeah, it's pretty simple. After you insert the skewer through the front axle, make sure you put the spring in narrow side first, and don't tighten it too much or you'll damage the bearings."

"I think I need help."

"You got it. I'm ready to meet with you and Rappaport when you are," Crocker answered. "Bring the bike."

"Now?" Melkasian asked. "You sure you don't want to rest up and do this in the morning?"

"I'm fine."

"All right," Melkasian answered. "Give me forty minutes. You need me to send someone to pick you up?"

"Not necessary."

Crocker showered, dressed, downed another Promax bar, two apples, some old roast chicken he found in the fridge, and half a gallon of water. Refreshed and energized, he decided to walk the mile or so to the bank building on Avenida Principal de las Mercedes. The coincidence of names amused him as he recalled the tight ass in the red bathing suit.

The more he got to know this upscale part of the city, the more it reminded him of Miami, a city he'd spent a lot of time in over the years and liked.

Rappaport and Melkasian sat waiting in the conference room, coffee cups and plastic-wrapped sandwiches in front of them on the table.

"We got you a roast beef and half a tuna," Rappaport said.

Crocker bit into both, popped the tab on a Diet Coke, took a seat. "You bring the bike?" he asked Melkasian.

"What bike?" Rappaport wanted to know.

"The mountain bike I bought for my wife. Crocker wanted to see it. It's downstairs in the back of my car."

"I thought we were here to discuss operations," Rappaport growled.

"We are."

"How's Ernesto? I mean, Neto," Crocker asked, changing the subject.

"He's taking some time off," Rappaport shot back. "He's still shaken up."

"Give him my best. And I regret what happened to Sanchez. I wanted at least to recover his body, but that wasn't an option," Crocker said.

"Good man," Rappaport observed. "Not your fault. We'll get his body, one way or another."

"He left a family?" Crocker asked.

"A wife and three-year-old son."

"Damn." Crocker hung his head. Losing friends and colleagues was the worst part of the job. "If there's any way I can help them…"

Rappaport: "Let's talk about that later."

"And Señor Tomás?" Crocker asked, remembering their host in Barinas, a place he hoped never to have to visit again. "What happened to him?"

Rappaport grinned. "That's a man who knows how to take care of himself."

Melkasian: "He manages to make friends on every side of any conflict."

Crocker was about to ask how he did that when Rappaport cut him off. "Tomás was arrested and held in a local jail. Claimed that he knew nothing about you guys, but was simply renting out rooms. Venezuelan authorities released him this morning. He thinks they bought his story. I'm not so sure."

"Interesting character," Crocker said, pivoting in the chair and grabbing another Diet Coke off the table, popping it open, and downing it. His thirst seemed unending.

Rappaport leaned back in the chair and, holding his hands behind his head, said, "You sure you want to continue, or have you had enough?"

"I don't plan to stop until we get the Falcon," Crocker said, remembering the short man sitting at the table in the interrogation room and involuntarily clenching his teeth. "I spoke to my CO. My two associates and I are cleared to go."

"Then pay close attention, because things just got a lot more complicated," Rappaport said, reaching into a manila envelope and tossing a BlackBerry on the table. "Where'd you recover this bad boy?"

Crocker stared at the phone for a second before his memory kicked in. "Isn't that the one we found in the truck we stole outside the interrogation center?"

"Correct," Melkasian answered.

"We found some interesting e-mails on it," Rappaport offered.

Crocker finished chewing and wiped his mouth with the back of his hand. "You gonna tell me, or do I have to guess?"

Rappaport said, "Save your aggression for the field, Crocker." Then, turning to Melkasian, he growled, "Get Sue from the Crime and Narcotics Center and Sy Blanc on the secure phone."

"Done and dusted."

While Melkasian dialed the number in Langley, his boss continued, "Remember the three suspected Unit 5000 operatives who were staying in Mexico under assumed names?"

Crocker's memory was a bit cloudy. A lot had happened since the last time he and Rappaport and Melkasian had met.

"The guys in San Miguel de Allende," Rappaport offered, trying to help him.

"Yes, sir. I remember."

"Well, they seem to be referred to in some of the e-mails on here," he said pointing to the BlackBerry. "One of the most recent messages reads, and I translate: 'Time to move the furniture from SMA to TX.' "

"SMA as in San Miguel de Allende?" Crocker asked.

"Most likely. And TX as in Texas."

The danger posed by Unit 5000 operatives entering the States struck Crocker like a kick to the head. "Holy fuck," he said out loud.

"Yeah, holy fuck."

Melkasian pointed to the speakerphone and gave a thumbs-up. Rappaport looked at Crocker and said, "Let's see if Sue and Sy Blanc agree."

The consensus among the CIA analysts was that Unit 5000 had activated a plan that involved smuggling the three Iranians with Venezuelan passports into the United States. Their purpose for doing so wasn't clear, although the NSA had picked up some chatter on Hezbollah and Hamas websites and blogs about a possible terrorist attack on the upcoming Mardi Gras parade in New Orleans.

Everyone agreed that the Iranians had to be stopped. Sue reported that Mexican PFM had tracked them to the city of Chihuahua. They were driving a silver 2009 Corolla registered to a Venezuelan businessman living in Mexico City, and seemed to be heading to Ciudad Juárez, across from the Texas border.

Donaldson and Anders were brought into the discussion, and it was decided that the FBI and Homeland Security would be alerted immediately. Also, Crocker, Tré, and Mancini would leave for Ciudad Juárez as soon as possible. There they would coordinate with the CIA case officer on the scene named Jim Randal.

After the phone conference ended, Melkasian got on his cell and arranged for a private CIA-owned carrier to fly the three men directly to Ciudad Juárez.

"You need to be at the airport at six a.m.," Melkasian reported.

"We'll be there."

Crocker didn't know whether it was the seriousness of the threat or all the caffeinated sodas he'd consumed in the conference room, but either way, he was fired up. Back at the safe house, he briefed his men on the upcoming mission. Then the three of them went to a local Italian joint for dinner—fried calamari, pasta, grilled fish, salad, dessert, and bottled water.

Later that night, after packing his gear, he called Holly, who was watching a rerun of *Suits*, which Crocker didn't care for but was one of Holly's favorite shows. She said, "Tom, my therapist has diagnosed me with PTSD and mild depression."

The PTSD didn't surprise him, given what she'd gone through in Libya, but the depression was troubling. "You trust her?" he asked.

"I have no reason not to. I told you I haven't been feeling well."

"But isn't it normal that you would feel down for a while after what happened?"

"She put me on Prozac."

Crocker wasn't a big fan of prescription medication. To his mind, doctors often used it to deal with one set of symptoms without taking into consideration how it might affect the patient's overall health. "How much?"

"Forty milligrams daily," Holly answered.

"That sounds like a lot."

"Well, you're not here. And I don't know what else to do, Tom."

She was right. Changing his tactics, he said, "When I get back, I want to take you on a vacation."

"I'd really like that," Holly responded. "What do you have in mind?"

They had climbed Mount Kilimanjaro together, gone cave-diving in the Yucatán, trekked in Patagonia. A love of outdoor adventure was something they shared. "I thought we could go mountain biking and camping in Monument Valley," Crocker said. The Navajo Tribal Park in Utah was not only breathtakingly beautiful, it also seemed to replenish his soul every time he visited.

"I think I'd prefer something a little more luxurious this time," Holly replied. "Like skiing in Park City, or a beach somewhere."

The vacation he had in mind was far from other people, in a place where he could clear his head. But he said, "Sure. Skiing could be fun."

"Could be, Tom? You don't sound enthusiastic."

"I am."

She asked, "You want me to start making plans now?"

"Not yet."

"Not yet?" She sounded disappointed.

"Soon."

He slept soundly and woke in the morning refreshed. Melkasian filled them in on the latest intel as he drove them to the airport. The Iranians had spent the night at a motel in Chihuahua, about a five-hour drive south of the U.S. border.

The pilot of the Learjet 60XR had long gray hair that he wore in a ponytail. Mancini knew him from a mission they'd been on in Iraq, soon after the fall of Baghdad.

"A lot of shit has gone down since then," the pilot reminded them.

Events moved quickly in the war against terror. Sometimes it seemed they were grappling with an octopus. You chopped off one tentacle and another sprung into action. Which made sense, given the fact that there were numerous Sunni and Shiite terrorist groups. Sunni groups included al-Qaeda, al-

Qaeda Magreb operating in Northern Africa, and al-Qaeda in the Arabian Peninsula; Abu Sayyaf Group in the Philippines and Malaysia; Ansar al-Islam in Iraq; the GIA in Algeria; Asbat al-Ansar in Lebanon; Jundallah, Harakat ul-Mujahidin, Jaish-e-Mohammed, Lashkar-e-Tayyiba, and Lashkar-e-Jhangvi, all operating in Pakistan.

Shiite terrorist groups included the al-Aqsa Martyrs Brigade in the West Bank and Gaza, Hamas, Hezbollah, Palestinian Islamic Jihad, Palestine Liberation Front, and others.

Some of them cooperated with one another. Others were rivals. Loyalties and leadership shifted.

It wasn't Crocker's job to keep track of the various Islamic terrorist organizations and their activities. Experts and analysts at CIA, NSA, NSC, Pentagon, Homeland Security, and FBI did that. Once they identified operatives and targets, Crocker and his men in Black Cell acted as the sharp end of the spear.

Outside the window of the Learjet, Crocker watched thin white clouds drift past like childhood dreams. He had spent many days and weeks as a boy playing good guys and bad guys in the woods behind his house in New England with sticks fashioned into rifles. The fact that he was now doing that for a living seemed preordained.

Looking at the sky and feeling the tight vibration of the plane as it cut through the atmosphere at 550 miles an hour, he experienced a moment of perfection, realizing that fate had put him in the right place, in a role he was suited for, and had surrounded him with men like himself whom he trusted and admired.

He knew exactly what they had to do: stop three Iranian

men before they crossed into the States and disappeared, possibly only to be heard of again after they carried out their sinister mission, whatever that was. Only then would the Iranians have actual names and faces—like the al-Qaeda terrorists who killed more than three thousand innocent people on 9/11. Then their backgrounds would be discussed and their motivations speculated on in newspaper articles and on blogs.

Sitting back, he sipped from the plastic cup filled with ice water and listened to Tré beside him talk about Bushido—the ancient code of the samurai—which he said he had been studying and applying to his life. Tré named the eight virtues: rectitude or justice, courage, benevolence or mercy, politeness, honesty and sincerity, honor, loyalty, character and self-control.

Across the aisle, Mancini put down the book on naval warfare he was reading and asked, "According to Bushido, how does one determine the right course of action in a particular situation?"

"It teaches that a true samurai should behave according to an absolute moral standard, one that transcends logic," Tré answered. "What is right is right, and what's wrong is wrong."

"So the difference between good and bad and right and wrong are givens, not concepts subject to discussion or justification," Crocker said.

"Correct."

"Then how does one determine what's right and wrong?" Mancini asked, playing devil's advocate, which he liked to do.

"There are no set rules to determine that. A warrior should know the difference."

Crocker could get on board with that.

CHAPTER SEVENTEEN

*For everyone who asks, receives; he who seeks, finds; and
to him who knocks, the door will be opened.*

—Luke 11:10

THEY LANDED at an airstrip on the governor of Chihuahua's
ranch a few miles south of Ciudad Juárez. Jim Randal, a
young man with a bland, round face, met them wearing a
Teflon vest under his tan safari shirt and surrounded by four
armed guards. "Welcome to the most violent city in the
world," he said.

Crocker had heard horror stories about mass decapitations
and the hundreds of women who went missing only to turn up
dead and mutilated. Randal explained that since 2006 something like eleven thousand people had been killed in the city
of a million as rival drug gangs fought for control of one of
the most lucrative routes, a direct line to the U.S. black market for marijuana, cocaine, and meth.

Crocker's own brother had once been a cocaine addict, and
Crocker had seen drugs ravage the lives of countless friends
and other members of his family. He'd also participated in the

so-called War on Drugs in countries like Colombia, Panama, and Bolivia, destroying coke labs in the jungle and helping arrest financiers and traffickers. To him it wasn't a war but an epidemic. The cure, he thought, lay in helping stem the desire for drugs, educating young people about the dangers of addiction, and providing treatment to users.

Their black SUV stopped at a house with a high white metal gate. Two of the armed Mexican guards got out and rang the buzzer. "Why are we stopping here?" Crocker asked.

"My boss wants to brief you," Randal answered.

"Who's your boss?"

"Lyle Nesmith. A brilliant analyst and tactician."

"We didn't come here to meet people."

A maid wearing a white apron ushered them through a cool stucco house to a patio with flowering plants and a fountain. A buffet of enchiladas, fajitas, and tamales had been laid out on a long tiled table. A waiter asked what they wanted to drink.

Crocker was losing patience. "Where's Nesmith?"

"He's upstairs on a call," Randal answered with a confident grin. "He's coming."

Twenty minutes later the agent-in-charge greeted them, a short, fit, bald man with a graying goatee and round rimless glasses. "You missed them," Nesmith said as he and Crocker sat down across from one another at one of the round metal tables.

"Missed who?" Crocker asked, almost spitting out the food in his mouth.

"The Iranians. I just learned that the Toyota Corolla they were driving tried to cross the border at the Ysleta International Bridge."

"What?" Crocker rose to his feet.

"Don't worry, they were turned away by U.S. immigration agents who noticed that none of their names matched the name on the car's registration."

"Why weren't they detained?" Crocker asked.

Nesmith calmly adjusted his glasses. "There was some sort of miscommunication between D.C. and here," he said. "The ICE agents had the Iranian names on their detention list, not the Venezuelan names on their new passports."

Crocker wanted to punch something. "What?"

"Calm down. I've got people out looking for them now. We'll find them."

"How long ago did this happen?" Crocker asked. "I mean, exactly when did they try to cross the border?"

Nesmith looked at his silver Rolex. "Roughly an hour ago."

"Fuck!" Crocker crossed to the far corner of the yard. Looking up at the broken glass on top of the high wall, he wondered what to do now and whom to call.

He was joined by Mancini and Tré. The latter said, "A samurai master once said: True patience means bearing the unbearable. If that helps."

Mancini added, "And abused patience turns into fury."

Crocker spent the time playing fetch with Nesmith's two black German shepherds—strong, sure-footed, beautiful dogs. An hour passed, during which the table on the patio was cleared and the blue sky clouded over.

Crocker saw Nesmith emerge from the house and walk toward him with Randal by his side. "See what they want," he said, turning to Mancini.

Mancini crossed the yard, spoke to Nesmith, and returned.

With his arms crossed against his chest, he said, "They found the silver Corolla."

"Where?"

"Parked outside a motel in the southeast part of town."

Crocker: "Are the three Iranians registered there?"

"Nesmith says they are."

"Let's go."

He wanted no part of Nesmith, Randal, or the four armed guards, except that he and his men needed weapons, hats, fake beards and mustaches. He also needed Randal to serve as their driver, since they didn't know their way around.

Nesmith argued that a raid like the one they were about to launch required clearances from the local police and backup, but Crocker insisted on keeping the circle small.

They set out midafternoon in a taxi they had rented for the day with Randal at the wheel, talking a mile a minute, informing them that they were entering an extremely dangerous part of town that was run by a branch of the powerful Mexican drug cartel Los Zetas.

"I don't give a fuck about any drug cartel," Crocker retorted. "Press on."

"You don't understand how pervasive their influence is," Randal explained. "I'm talking everyone from beggars on the street to the Presidential Palace and everything in between. You see that old lady out there selling tortillas? She's probably one of their informers. As soon as we pass, she'll report on us. We're going to get stopped and questioned. You'll see."

"Shut up and drive."

Los Anillos Motel was an L-shaped dive at the end of a

block lined with small assembly plants and warehouses. It looked like the kind of place where people came to hide or slit their wrists. There were a half dozen vehicles parked in the lot out front. One was a silver Corolla.

"That's it," Mancini said.

Crocker, with his mustache dyed black and the brim of a straw hat pulled low over his forehead, got out with a 9mm Glock tucked under his black T-shirt. He looked around, stretched, then walked to the end of the motel, strolled past a little Pemex gas station, and circled around back.

On his return he leaned in the driver's window and spoke to Randal in a low voice. "Go to the desk and find out what room they're in. Call me on the radio. I want you to stay in the office and make sure the person there doesn't warn whoever might be in the room. As soon as you see us crash through the front door, hurry back to the car and start the engine."

"Okay. I got it. I understand. What are you guys gonna do?"

"Go. Now!"

"First I've got to call Nesmith."

"You do and I'll beat your head in," Crocker said matter-of-factly.

Randal nodded, got out, and walked stiffly to the motel office. A few minutes later his voice came over the walkie-talkie held by Mancini in the backseat. "Room eleven."

"Let's deploy," Crocker said.

Mancini, wearing a New York Mets cap pulled down so low that only his dark eyes and thickly bearded face showed, waited for Crocker to again circle to the back. He counted three minutes on his watch, then rapped hard on the red door. No one answered. Ten seconds later he heard Crocker crash through the rear window.

Mancini kicked in the door and hurried in with Tré behind him. The only person they found was Crocker, holding his Glock and vigorously shaking his head. He mouthed the words "No one's here."

The three men moved fast, checking the closets, bathroom, under the unmade double beds. They found no suitcases, only dirty towels, and a discarded newspaper and two empty water bottles in the trash. Crocker thought he saw an impression on the cover of a Spanish-language magazine on a night table near the phone. He stuck it in his back pocket and said, "Let's get out of here."

They were back on the *carretera* in minutes. Randal thought they were being followed by a white van. Crocker watched it through the dust-covered side mirror and saw a woman at the wheel and a baby in a child seat behind her.

"We're clear," he said. "Keep driving."

Randal steered them to a six-story apartment building on a street behind the U.S. Consulate, pulled into the underground garage, and closed the iron gate.

"That was close," he said, getting out.

Crocker: "No it wasn't."

Upstairs, in the third-floor apartment that was their temporary base, Crocker used the old pencil-and-white-paper trick to lift an impression off the magazine cover. It was a name, "Cucho Valdez," and a number, "7862."

Randal didn't know what the number meant, but said the name belonged to a smuggler associated with the drug cartels who ran a silver and curio stall in the Mercado Juárez, on Avenida 16 de Septiembre in the center of town.

"Let's go talk to him."

They piled back into the taxi and slowly nosed through rush hour traffic to the city center.

"What's the significance of the sixteenth of September?" Crocker asked.

"It's the day Mexico celebrates its independence from Spain," Randal answered.

Mancini, who seemed knowledgeable about practically anything having to do with history, geography, weapons, foreign cultures, and technology, added, "It's actually the day Father Miguel Hidalgo rallied people to march on Mexico City. Kind of like our Fourth of July, which was the day the Declaration of Independence was signed, even though United States sovereignty wasn't formally recognized until the Treaty of Paris, ratified after the Revolutionary War."

"Then what's up with Cinco de Mayo, May fifth?" Tré asked.

"Cinco de Mayo commemorates the day in 1862 when Mexico defeated the French Army in the Battle of Pueblo," Mancini answered.

"What were the French doing here in the first place?" Tré wanted to know.

"Ostensibly to collect on debts owed to France, but really they used that as an excuse to try to establish a pro-French government that would extend France's interests through Central America."

They parked in a lot across from a large two-story cement structure with a big red Coca-Cola sign on top. Randal handed a beggar kid a twenty-peso note to watch the car. Then he led the way into the building and a phantasmagoria of colors and smells—wildly colored blankets, wrestlers' masks, ceramic dolls, saints, red chilies, cheeses, silver trays. Rag-clad kids and cripples crowded around them and pleaded for dollars.

Randal shooed the beggars away and pushed through narrow aisles jammed with tourists and Mexicans. Crocker and his men followed.

"You want beautiful earrings for your señorita?" a young woman asked.

"You want the best Mexican sombrero decorated with real silver for good luck?" asked a boy with two missing front teeth.

"No, gracias."

"You want a statue of Quetzalcoatl to put in your house?" asked an old lady with long gray braids.

"What would I want that for?" Tré asked back.

"To keep out evil spirits."

Randal turned left into a stall that offered ponchos, jackets, and sweaters out front. A teenage girl with a large mole above her lip asked in English how she could be of help.

"We're looking for Cucho Valdez," Randal said.

"Cucho is inside eating lunch."

They had to lower their heads to get past vividly colored papier-mâché gourds, piñatas, and leather saddles. The walls were lined with display cases filled with silver coffee services, cups, trays, and jewelry. Cucho sat behind a glass counter that held carved silver lighters and antique pistols, chewing on a chicken leg.

He was a man of about thirty with dark skin, high cheek-bones, and black hair that hung to his shoulders. Almost pretty in a rough-hewn way with sad, hangdog eyes. Seeing the four strangers, he said, "I love doing business with Americans."

Randal asked, "Is there somewhere we can talk to you in private?"

"Why? You guys looking for something special?"

Crocker leaned forward and said, "We're real estate investors from Canada hoping to do a deal with three Venezuelans. They told us that you could tell us where to find them."

Cucho didn't even blink. He wiped his mouth with the back of his hand and asked, "You dudes with the DEA?"

"No. Not at all," Randal answered.

"Sorry. I don't know any Venezuelans. Valdez is a common name here, and a lot of people are called Cucho. People call me that because they think I look depressed. But I'm not depressed, it's just the way my eyes are formed. I can't help it. I'm actually a very happy person. You've probably got me confused with someone else." He wiped his hands on a piece of newspaper, picked up a lime-colored cell phone from the glass counter, and punched some numbers.

Randal said, "We're friends of the governor."

Cucho didn't seem to care.

"Who are you calling?" Crocker asked.

"Randy Simmons. He works with the DEA," Cucho answered.

"Why?"

"Maybe he can help you."

Tré, without any prompting, removed a Glock from his

waistband, pressed the barrel against Cucho's forehead, and said, "Put the phone away."

Cucho stuck the phone in his shirt pocket and started to stand.

"Where do you think you're going?" said Tré. "Hold it right there."

"Okay," Cucho said, stopping in midcrouch with his hands raised over his head. "What's the problem here? I told you before, you got the wrong man."

Tré, grinning: "There isn't a problem, except that you're acting weird."

When Cucho stepped back, Crocker swung around behind the counter and grabbed him in a headlock. Tré vaulted the counter, gun still drawn. The three men stood in the crowded dark space.

Tré: "What do we do now?"

Crocker saw Randal on the other side of the counter, blocking the girl with the mole above her lip, who was trying to push past him. Pointing to a roll of tape on a shelf behind the counter, he said to Tré, "Wrap some of that over his mouth, then use it to secure his wrists and ankles."

That accomplished, the two of them wrapped Cucho in a Mexican blanket that covered his entire body head to toes. "Toss me the keys to the vehicle," Crocker said to Randal.

"Why? What are you going to do with him?" was his nervous response.

"You and Manny stay with the girl and keep her quiet. Offer her money if you think that'll work, then meet us at the car in three minutes."

"But—"

Crocker and Tré hoisted Cucho onto their shoulders and exited out the back of the stall to a loading dock, down eight stairs to an area filled with assorted-sized trucks, to the street. They walked to the end of the block, turned left, and entered the parking lot.

Crocker used a key to open the car, loaded Cucho into the trunk, got in, and started the engine. The kid they had paid to watch the car was nowhere in sight.

Two minutes later Crocker spotted Randal and Mancini leaving the market. As Mancini climbed in back, Crocker started the engine.

Randal, halfway in and sweating profusely, shouted, "We can't do this!"

Crocker: "Why not?"

Randal: "Taking a man like this is illegal."

"Either get in or stay out," Crocker barked.

Randal got in, shut the door, and asked, "What are you planning to do with him?"

"Take him somewhere where we can beat the living shit out of him and find out what he knows about those Iranians," Crocker said, steering out of the lot.

Randal leaned over the backseat and shouted, "No! I won't allow it! You're not authorized!"

Crocker reached back with his left arm, grabbed Randal's jaw, and shoved him back so hard his head slammed against the rear seat. "Shut up and listen!"

He turned the car onto a main avenue and wove through traffic with no idea which direction he was headed. "Which way is out of town?" he asked.

"Keep going straight ahead, but—"

Off to his right he saw a stadium-like structure surrounded by a large parking lot. "What's that?" he asked.

Mancini: "Looks like a bullring."

The structure was completely dark except for a few lights at the front. Crocker turned into the deserted lot, drove to the rear of the bullring, and cut the engine.

"Help me get him out," he said, stepping out into the building's shadow.

"You can't treat an innocent man like this," Randal protested. "It's completely unacceptable."

"Are you kidding, man? No way he's innocent," Tré shot back.

The sky was turning dark blue, and the stench of animals and death hung around them. Crocker got in Randal's face and said, "Stay in the car if you don't want to be a part of this. Walk away and a hail a cab!"

Randal shook his head but said nothing. He stood with his hands on his hips and watched Crocker and Tré pull Cucho out of the trunk, unwrap the blanket, and stand him up against the brick wall of the bullring. Mancini grabbed a six-inch hunting knife from a nylon sheath strapped to his ankle and held it up to Cucho's throat. He said, "Drug and people traffickers are the scum of the earth."

"Mr. Valdez, this is what we're gonna do," Crocker offered calmly. "After we remove the tape from your mouth, I'm going to ask you a question. If you don't answer to my satisfaction, I'm going to tell my friend here to cut off one of your fingers. Then, since I'm a nice guy, I'm going to give you one more chance. You'll be writhing in pain then and about to pass out. I'll ask you the same question. If you don't answer fully and truthfully that time, I'm going to tell him to slice your balls off. You're going to be in an unimaginable amount of hurt then. So I'll take mercy on you and cut your throat."

Terror filled Cucho's eyes. The clouds behind them had turned dark red.

Mancini sliced through the tape around Cucho's ankles, grabbed one of his hands, and held the knife ready. Then he nodded to Tré, who ripped the tape off Cucho's mouth and covered it with his hand.

"Ready?" Crocker asked.

Cucho nodded. Tears were already welling in his eyes.

"Three men who claimed to be Venezuelan contacted you today. What did they want?" Crocker asked.

Cucho moved his head as if he was ready to talk. Crocker pointed to Tré, who removed his hand from Cucho's mouth.

Tré said, "Boss, I don't think Cucho is a guy."

"What?"

"Check the neck. No Adam's apple."

Tré was right. The loose clothes, the insolent attitude, the rough but pretty face. They all pointed to the same conclusion.

Crocker said, "I don't care what the fuck you are, I'll still tear you apart."

Cucho took a deep breath, coughed, and said, "Okay. . . . Three men did contact me. I didn't ask where they were from. They had money, cash, and said they were looking for a way to cross into the U.S."

"They wanted to be smuggled in illegally?" Crocker asked.

"Yes."

"What did you tell them?"

"I told them I couldn't help them."

Crocker looked at her and said, "You're a stubborn bitch, aren't you?" He didn't expect an answer. Turning to Tré, he instructed, "I'll hold her hand against the wall, you tie something over her mouth." Then, to Mancini: "Ready?"

Cucho thrashed her head from side to side: "No, don't cut me! I told them—I told them I couldn't do it myself, but I sent them to someone I know. A man who has a tunnel."

"Who is this man, and where can we find him?" Crocker asked urgently.

"His name is Ruiz. I'll draw you a map."

"Fuck the map. You're taking us to him. Now."

An off-kilter half moon shone like a cruel smile in the sky. Cucho sat in back, between Mancini and Tré, with Randal next to Crocker up front. Her desperation seemed to grow as they wound through residential streets to a wider industrial road lined with warehouses and businesses.

Mancini said, "Two cannibals are talking. One says to the other, 'I don't like my mother-in-law.' The other one says, 'Then try the noodles.'"

Tré chuckled. "Where do you come up with this stuff?"

Mancini had more. "What's gray and comes in quarts?"

"What?"

"An elephant."

Tré laughed hard, then, turning to Cucho, said, "It ain't funny. I can't help laughing, but it really ain't funny at all. You into men or women?"

Cucho: "None of your business."

"Focus," Crocker said from the front seat.

"Not to worry, chief. I'm sharp as a razor blade."

Cucho directed them off the road to a decaying parking lot with several stores at one end. She pointed to the building on the far left. "That's it."

"That's what?"

"The tunnel I told you about is located inside that building."

In the dim yellow streetlights Crocker saw a one-story tan-colored cement building with green trim. The white neon sign overhead read "Mercado Ruiz." As he watched, a big girl with braids chained a row of battered shopping carts together out front. The place looked like it was closed for the night.

Tré said with a sigh, "Fucking dead end, if you ask me. Let's kick her ass."

Cucho pointed to the rugged landscape behind the building and said, "I'm telling the truth. You see the U.S. is over there, past those hills."

"What time were the Venezuelans planning to cross?" Crocker asked.

"Probably after the market is closed for business. After dark."

Crocker looked at his watch. It was a few minutes past 1900. He asked, "Where does the tunnel start?"

"Inside the market."

"Where?"

Tré, like an echo: "Yeah, where? Be specific!"

"I can't be specific. I've never been inside. I don't shop there."

Crocker started the engine. Without turning on the headlights, they slowly circled around the building. Parked behind the Mercado Ruiz was a panel truck. Men were moving bags from the truck to inside the market.

Turning to Mancini, he said, "Take a radio with you and watch the front. Alert us if anyone enters."

"Roger, boss."

"Tré, you wait here. I'm going to check the dock."

He got out, stretched, and walked casually past the truck, where he saw two men in dirty T-shirts hauling bags of what looked like flour or maize into the market. He proceeded to the end of the building and stopped. Just as he was about to circle around to the front, he saw the taxi headlights flash twice.

He hurried back to the car and asked, "What's up?"

Tré reported, "Manny said four dudes just got out of an SUV and entered."

"Tell him to stay out front until he hears from us."

"Sure thing."

Looking at Cucho sitting in the back, Crocker asked Tré, "You bring the tape with you?"

"Affirmative, chief."

"Tape her mouth, wrists, and ankles, then leave her on the floor."

"My pleasure."

Randal elected to stay behind. Crocker figured he'd probably call Nesmith and tell him what was going on. Not that it mattered. They didn't have time to stop him now.

He led the way purposefully across the rear lot, past the truck to the loading dock where the two workers were stacking bags against a wall. Crocker hoisted one of the sacks on his shoulder and climbed a set of concrete steps to a storage area with rows of cardboard boxes. Behind him, Tré carried another sack.

Crocker's senses were on high alert. To his right he saw an office. Light spilled out the open door onto the stained concrete floor, and he heard men talking inside.

He motioned to Tré to wait behind the boxes, then took three steps toward the office door. A mustached guard holding a submachine gun stepped out. He waved the gun in front of Crocker's face. "Quién es?"

"Paco," Crocker grunted.

"No aquí. Afuera!" (Not here. Outside!)

Crocker nodded and stumbled, pretending to be drunk.

Two men leaned out of the office and looked his way. One appeared to be Middle Eastern. The other held two Doberman pinschers on metal chain leashes. The dogs bared their teeth and growled at him. The stocky man holding them pulled the dogs back, and the two men walked down a hallway and out of sight. Crocker felt a chill shoot up his spine.

He wanted to go after the two men, but the guard with the Uzi stood in his way. Instead of searching him, the guard called over his shoulder, turned, and hurried after the others. Crocker was about to drop his sack and follow when a fourth man, shorter, older, and wearing a blue apron, emerged from inside. Seeing Crocker, he waved his arms and cursed in Spanish.

Crocker didn't understand everything, but knew he was being called an idiot and a drunk, and was being told to leave the bag at the loading dock. When he didn't move, the man took a walkie-talkie from his apron and started to lift it to his mouth.

Crocker had just decided to drop the bag and charge when he saw Tré spring from behind the man and grab him in a headlock. The walkie-talkie clattered across the concrete floor. Tré covered the man's mouth with his free hand.

"Drag him into the office," Crocker whispered, picking up the walkie-talkie and hearing men speaking urgently in Spanish. Inside, in one of the desk drawers, he found twine and a rag, which they used to gag him, bind his wrists and ankles, and tie him to a chair.

"Ready?" Crocker whispered.

"I'm cool."

"Follow me."

He led the way down the dark hallway and entered a large storage room stacked with boxes. At the far end was another door that he opened carefully to reveal a room filled with white fluorescent light. Some sort of generator or large refrigeration unit occupied the left side of the room. The rest of it was filled with mops, brooms, buckets, ladders, and other supplies.

From his vantage point, Crocker couldn't see past the generator. But he heard a door creak open, then two men laughing. He and Tré crouched behind the generator, and Crocker flashed hand signals to indicate that he'd take out the first man.

The dogs picked up their scent and started barking. One of the Dobermans poked his sleek head around the side of the big machine and lunged, snapping at Crocker's wrist and missing, but locking its jaw around the pistol in his hand. Still, Crocker managed to squeeze off two rounds, one of which tore into the lead man's thigh.

As the man's screams reverberated in the small room, Crocker sprung into his midsection and slammed his body against the opposite wall. The man went down, and the dogs attacked the back of Crocker's legs. The pain was immediate and intense, causing his muscles to clench.

He tried kicking them off, and to his left, glimpsed Tré wrestling a submachine gun away from the mustached guard, who was bleeding from his nose. Crocker reached around, grabbed hold of one of the dogs by the head, ripped it away from his thigh, and flung the dog into the wall. He heard ribs snap and the thud the animal made when it hit the floor.

It stopped moving, but all kinds of alarms were screaming in his head because the second Doberman had its teeth deep into the flesh around his left ankle. He tried to pivot to his right, but the leash was wrapped around his right foot, which was partially pinned by the fallen man. Crocker lost his balance and fell, and the Doberman was immediately on top of him, lunging for his throat.

Teeth in his face, hot dog saliva dripping onto him, he grabbed its ear with his right hand and pulled back. The dog squealed and snapped its teeth at Crocker's wrist.

He quickly pulled his hand away, then tried to get hold of the dog's neck, but the dog sunk its incisors into his forearm and hit a nerve, causing massive pain that he felt all the way up his arm into his neck.

Crocker was losing the battle and trying to feel for his fallen pistol with his left hand. All he found on the floor was blood, teeth, a leash. Lunging, he grabbed hold of the dog's right paw and yanked it back violently until he heard the bone snap. The Doberman yelped and bore down harder. Then two shots popped, and rounds passed through the dog's chest with a spray of blood.

He pushed the muscular body to one side. Tré helped him up.

"Fuck."

"Can you walk, chief?"

His hands were covered with blood and shaking. The back of both legs screamed in agony. "I'll do my best."

He hobbled over to the guard's submachine gun and the Glock he'd lost, which were lying together on the floor. Cordite burned his nostrils. Blood dripped down the back of his leg into his sneakers. The pain was horrible, but he'd been through worse.

Tré ran ahead as he limped to keep up, past the guard's body that still twitched on the floor, through the door, down four steps to a room with a cot in it. On the other side of the bed, near a door to a little bathroom, Crocker saw a square hole in the floor and a metal cover that was open and leaning against the wall.

"We need to find a light before we go down," Tré said.

"No time!"

"Dark places freak me out."

Crocker felt his way down the rough concrete steps that descended about twenty feet. He couldn't see shit until he reached the bottom. Starting about six feet in front of him, he saw a string of bare bulbs that partially lit the tunnel. The bulbs were connected to an orange cord and spaced roughly ten feet apart.

"Ask and you shall receive," he whispered to Tré.

"This is better."

The tunnel was about five feet high and four feet wide, reinforced in some places with wooden planks and cinder blocks. Two steel rails had been spiked into the compressed dirt floor. The air was stale and smelled of salt and sulfur.

"You see anyone?" Tré whispered behind him.

"Not yet."

He moved as fast as he could, given that he had to crouch and the muscles in his legs were knotted up and damaged. Seeing a dark shape ahead, he stopped and focused. The shape turned and moved closer. He saw the flash of a weapon discharging in the distance and hit the ground. Rounds sailed over their heads and embedded themselves in the dirt.

As both men readied their guns to return fire, the lights went out.

"Sorry, Tré," Crocker whispered.

"Bum luck."

The two SEALs felt along the side walls, being careful not to trip over the rails. Crocker pushed himself as hard as he could, despite the warnings in his head to slow down.

Dirt got into his eye, and he stopped. Wiping it away with his wrist, he saw a white light wash the tunnel ahead. Tré grabbed his shoulder. Kneeling on the dirt floor, Crocker aimed the Uzi and squeezed off a long salvo. A yelp of pain echoed back.

"I think you got one," Tré whispered.

Crocker: "You run ahead. You're faster!"

Tré bolted. Crocker used every ounce of energy and focus he had left in him to follow. More shots whizzed past. He stumbled, fell, got up, and resumed limping. Tré returned fire. He heard muffled shouting.

The light source was now only a few feet ahead, creating ghoulish shadows that shifted and danced against the walls. Men were grappling on the floor, and then a large shadow rose and hurried down the tunnel. Crocker pushed himself to catch up and saw a dead man lying on his side still holding a flashlight, his dark eyes staring into space.

Stepping over a pool of blood that was seeping into the earth, he felt his way along the wall. Each gunshot ahead produced another little rush of adrenaline. His hearing was hypersensitive and he was running on fumes, growing weaker from the pain and loss of blood.

He heard men grunting in English and Farsi, and recognized Tré's voice exclaiming "Motherfucker!" Then came the sound of a knife slicing into flesh and cartilage. A groan. Someone rose slowly in the dark. He saw the glint of a knife in one hand, a pistol in the other. Stopping, he held his breath as his heart beat a tight pattern in his chest.

"Chief?"

"Tré."

"Two of 'em down. One more to go."

As Tré continued forward, Crocker wanted to utter some congratulation or encouragement, but the words wouldn't come out. He leaned against the wall and tried to will his body forward. More gunshots echoed. Then he saw a white flash and heard the thud of something louder. The walls shook; wooden planks and dirt fell from the ceiling.

He covered his head with his hands as debris showered over him. Just when he thought he was going to be buried, it stopped. But he was trapped, cut off, blinded, and having trouble breathing. Dirt and dust clogged his mouth and nostrils.

He pulled off his shirt and tied it over his nose and mouth. Then he got up onto his hands and knees and clawed his way up a mound of dirt. A plank fell and hit his back. He pushed it aside, then felt for an opening. Finding a fist-sized hole, he burrowed his hand through, then dug around it furiously until the ends of his fingers were starting to bleed.

When the hole was three feet wide, he managed to get his left shoulder through, and pushed and squirmed until he got stuck. So he took a deep breath, pulled out, and dug some more. This time he paused a moment to gather his strength, inserted his head and shoulder, then wiggled through to the other side and rolled down the pile of rocks and dirt to the floor of the tunnel.

Crocker still had trouble breathing because the air was clogged with dust, and he was covered with scratches and dirt. Through the mist he saw a diffused light and heard a groan.

He wasn't aware that he was moving until he stumbled over something and caught himself before he fell.

Then suddenly he was wrestling with a man who was quick and wiry, and had hot pungent breath. The man dug his nails into Crocker's biceps while reaching for something with his other hand. On the ground Crocker saw the outline of a knife in the murk. The shape reminded him of the KA-BAR he'd been given on graduation from BUD/S, with a seven-inch blade made of 1095 steel. But that one had a SEAL trident engraved on one side and the name of a SEAL who had died in combat on the other. The one he saw now had an aluminum grip instead of a leather one.

He heard Tré moaning and caught a glimpse of him beyond the man, holding his right shoulder.

He saw a gleam in his adversary's eye as his fingers tightened around the hunting knife. His face was covered with thick black whiskers. His bared teeth were long and uneven.

Crocker thrust his head forward and bit into the man's neck. He responded by smashing Crocker on the side of the head with his fist. His other hand still held the knife, which now flashed in the tight space. Before he had a chance to thrust it into Crocker's flesh, Crocker drove the heel of his hand into the man's Adam's apple once, twice, a third time, until he crushed the man's windpipe. His assailant emitted a last cry before going limp.

"I think we did it, Tré. I think we stopped them."

He repeated the words in his head like a mantra as he dragged Tré forward another hundred yards, then slung him onto his shoulder and climbed a set of concrete steps. His head hit something metal that stunned him briefly. It felt like a door. He pushed, swung it open, stuck his head through. Breathing hard and blinking, he saw what looked like an office with two metal desks and a potted ficus tree by the window.

He lifted Tré through the opening, sat him down in one of the brown leather chairs, and flipped on a halogen desk lamp. The room seemed to contain nothing personal, not even a calendar or a framed photo, just a travel poster for Vail, Colorado, on the wall. In the top drawer of one of the desks he found a manila envelope. Inside the envelope he found nine credit cards, four driver's licenses, a map, and a set of keys.

Crocker used the little energy he had left to pick up one of the phones and dial the number he had committed to memory. A woman's voice answered. "Yes?"

"This is 34266. I need an immediate ERS."

"Hold on while I trace your location."

"Okay," she said thirty seconds later. "Hang up."

Minutes later, tires screeched outside and car doors slammed. He unlocked the door to admit two big men with short hair, drawn pistols, and bulletproof vests under their suit jackets. One of them had a marine corps logo and "Semper fidelis" tattooed on his neck.

"34266?" the man asked.

"Yeah. Nice tat."

Crocker noted his reflection in the window and was reminded of a rescued miner, covered from head to toe with dirt, bleeding from his hands and one shoulder.

The men carried Tré. He felt fresh air on his face and saw yellow streetlights and the outlines of glass buildings.

"Where the hell are we?" he asked as he was being helped into a black SUV.

"You're in an office park, sir, in El Paso, Texas."

CHAPTER EIGHTEEN

The beast in me is caged by frail and fragile bars.
—Johnny Cash

HE SAT next to Holly with a bucket of popcorn in his lap. On the screen in front of them the villain in the metal mask sneered at the hero, causing spit to fly out of his mouth. The visceral hatred behind his words made Crocker clench his fists.

Then bullets started to fly, the chase started, and the volume in the theater grew until it hurt his head so much he felt like screaming. The sound of tires screeching, the grinding of metal against metal, bullets firing, ricocheting—it was too real.

He became the man in the black cape running, sweating, dodging bullets. His blood pressure and heartbeat shot up.

Crocker, feeling pain emanating from his hands and realizing what was happening, craned to look back at the exit and, turning to Holly, whispered, "I'll be right back."

He hurried up the aisle, through the double doors, and

found the men's room, which was cold and smelled of ammonia. He scanned beneath the stalls, the urinals, and sinks to check whether anyone was there. When the door swung open, he turned and instinctively scanned the heavy man's face and body. He wore a plaid shirt and looked soft and unarmed. Crocker knew that if he had to, he could take him easily.

Their eyes met. He balled his fist and waited for the man to reach for a weapon. Instead, the man turned abruptly and left.

Crocker zipped down his fly, did his business, and exited. In the lobby he paused for a moment, trying to decide whether to buy a bottle of water from the concession stand and rejoin Holly or wait. He decided to step into the mall, where there was more space.

He sat on a bench listening to Elton John's "Circle of Life" play over the mall's PA system, considering the actual warfare and havoc he'd witnessed in places like Afghanistan, Somalia, and Iraq, and thinking about how experiences burn into your brain and are hard to expunge.

Images of fallen and maimed teammates flashed in his head. As he tried to remember their names, he looked up and saw Holly walking toward him with a confused expression on her face. She'd gained weight while he was out of the country, which made her look softer. She was as beautiful as ever, but older.

"You okay?" Holly asked, her dark hair glistening in the light.

"I'm fine. The noise started to bother my ears."

"But you missed the ending."

He took her arm in his. "Let's get something to drink."

She cuddled next to him as if they were teenagers, and they walked past Banana Republic, American Eagle, Victoria's Secret, and all the other so-called high-end stores—each in its own way offering some kind of escape from the ordinary. It seemed to Crocker that they only underlined the banality of their customers' lives.

"Why can't they just sell shit and leave it at that?" Crocker mused as they sat down across from each other in the food court, sipping their cold drinks—a Dos Equis in his case, a Diet Coke for her.

There was a vagueness in her eyes that he attributed to the Prozac she was taking.

"What's really bothering you, Tom?" Holly asked.

"Nothing."

He wanted to tell her about what had happened on the tarmac in Foz do Iguaçu, the underground prison in Barinas, and the tunnel under Ciudad Juárez, but knowing that she was struggling with her own PTSD issues, he stopped.

Recently his mood had been vacillating between defensiveness, anger, and aggression. After a harrowing mission like the one he'd just been on, his return to civilian life often followed the same pattern: Initially there was excitement about being home and deep appreciation of the simple pleasures of being alive. But after a week or two that hyperawareness would start to morph into a critical view of the world around him and a sense of unease. The pretty female reporter on the sidelines of a football game who he'd considered fun and sexy turned into someone vain, self-important, and predatory. The commentators became vile and greedy manipulators.

He saw the worst in people, and even put thoughts in their heads. He was sure they didn't appreciate the freedoms they enjoyed. They even made fun of people like him who were fighting to protect them, and this put him on edge. It made him long to escape the artificial world and return to the reality of battle, carnage, and aggression, which is how he felt now.

Trouble was, his CO had given the men of Black Cell six weeks of R&R, and only three had elapsed. So Crocker did what he usually did when he was filled with excess energy—he trained. Even though his legs and back hadn't fully healed, he started every morning with a ten-mile run through the woods with Brando, then drove to ST-6 headquarters, ran the obstacle course a couple of times, and took target practice for an hour. After dinner he went to the gym and lifted weights.

Still feeling unsettled, he went to see his CO, Captain Sutter, and told him he was ready to deploy.

"Come back in three weeks and we'll talk," Sutter said bluntly.

"I'm ready now, sir," Crocker insisted.

"No, you're not."

Sutter ordered him to see the team psychologist, Dr. Petrovian, a jovial guy with a pink face and round wire-rimmed glasses.

"What's on your mind?" Petrovian asked.

Crocker didn't want to talk about himself but knew Sutter would be on him if he didn't. "So," he said, "I've been a little on edge. The last mission we went on was intense. A number of my guys got hurt."

"I heard you were interrogated and tortured. How do you feel about that?"

"Angry."

"How did the loss of control affect you?"

"I wanted it back."

"Are you afraid of being captured again?"

"It's the third time it's happened. I'm getting used to it. Not really."

"Are you worried that you won't be sent on more missions?"

"No. But I'm dying to finish this one!"

Petrovian nodded, then cleaned his glasses on the front of his button-down shirt. "You say you're on edge. Does that mean you're having trouble sleeping?"

"I'm having trouble sitting still."

Petrovian was aware of Crocker's aversion to medication, so he administered the same psych evaluation Crocker had taken before, with the usual stupid questions, then recommended meditation. So three times a day—after his morning run, after he returned from shooting at the range, and just before going to bed—Crocker sat alone in a dark room with a candle burning and listened to the flow of thoughts in his head. He didn't try to stop or control them, he just listened.

What he learned was: One, he had a burning desire to find Alizadeh and kill the son of a bitch. Two, he was disappointed in Holly. Even though he loved her deeply, she wasn't as available to him as before, and he needed her, which bothered him. And three, he spent a lot of time fantasizing about Mercedes, who had e-mailed him a picture of herself standing with her back to the camera on a beach at sunset, wearing a bikini. Under the photo was the message: "Happy New Year! XOXO, M."

The meditation helped him focus. It also got him out of his own head.

He called his sister, who had been leaving messages for him at the house telling him she was worried about their dad. When he called his father, he sounded good. They talked about the Redskins making the NFL playoffs and the benefit his dad was organizing for the VFW.

"You still friends with that woman?" Crocker asked.

"You mean Carla?"

"Yeah, Carla. How did things work out with her landlord?"

"She moved into another apartment."

"How does she like the new one?"

"She likes it a lot. Why?"

He didn't feel right about grilling his father or asking if he was giving Carla money—which is what his sister was worried about—so he let it go.

Next he went to visit Ritchie, who'd just returned from three weeks at Johns Hopkins Medical Center in Baltimore, where he'd had reconstructive surgery on his face and jaw. Ritchie was excited that in another two days he'd be able to eat solid food.

"I'm dying to sink my new teeth into a burger and fries," he said. "I think about it, even more than sex."

Crocker was glad to see that Ritchie's outlook was positive and his face had almost healed. Except for some discoloration in the skin they had grafted from his ass and tightness under his jaw, he looked the same.

"Is it okay if I call you butt-face from now on?" Crocker joked as he left.

"You can call me whatever you want. Just call."

Cal was in Sacramento visiting his sister. Akil was snorkeling somewhere in the Caribbean with his German girlfriend. Tré was convalescing at his parents' home in D.C. Mancini was busy replacing the roof on his garage.

When Davis's very pregnant wife saw Crocker standing at the door of their blue and white split-level, concern quickly crossed her face. "You taking him away again?" she asked.

"No, it's a social visit," Crocker answered, shivering in the cold.

The two SEALs bundled up Davis's one-year-old son, took him to a nearby playground, and loaded him into a swing.

"How's it going?" Crocker asked.

"Better," Davis said as he pushed his son, who screamed with delight every time the swing ascended. "I had a hard time...back there."

"Barinas?"

"Yeah." His blue eyes seemed even bluer than before.

"It's perfectly natural in our line of work to get scared shitless sometimes," Crocker said.

"You ever think about the people you kill?" Davis asked.

Crocker didn't like to admit it, and he never mentioned it to other members of his team, but sometimes he felt a kind of kinship and almost a little sympathy for the men he battled. Not sick bastards like Alizadeh, who terrorized, maimed, and murdered innocents, but common soldiers and guards like the two he and Tré had killed in the store in Juárez.

"Yeah," Crocker said.

"Me, too."

*   *   *

Alex Rinehart's grandmother descended the basement steps of her brick colonial house and found her grandson seated at a desk in front of the window. His brow deeply furrowed in concentration, he studied an open book and scribbled something into a spiral notebook.

She set the tray with a glass of nonfat milk and a plate of freshly baked Toll House cookies beside him and read the title of the book—*Advanced Quantum Physics Workbook*.

"My," she gushed. "Is this something you're studying for school?"

Alex looked up at her and smiled with a look of pure love that touched her heart.

"Oh, Alex!" she exclaimed, ruffling his unruly dark hair and hugging him to her chest.

He squirmed free because he didn't like to be touched, grabbed a cookie off the plate, then quickly looked up at his grandmother to see if she was okay.

She was. She'd grown used to his strange behavior, and understood that despite his unease around others, he had strong feelings and real affection for people. But she was worried. Recently his teachers and therapists had observed that he was withdrawing further. The drugs Dr. Struthers had prescribed hadn't seemed to stem this process or even help. This was ominous, the doctor had warned, and could lead to Alex completely retreating into a world of his own.

He devoured a second cookie, gulped down half the milk, and returned to the book with an intensity that startled her.

"Alex, darling, is that something you're studying at school?" his grandmother asked again.

Instead of answering, he turned to a clean page of the notebook and started writing furiously, covering the paper with notations and equations.

"Alex, can you hear me?"

He kept writing as though she wasn't there, stopped, rubbed the top of his head vigorously, ripped the page out of the notebook, crumpled it, tossed it onto the floor, then resumed writing on a new sheet.

"Alex..." she whispered, picking up the balled paper and depositing it in the wire basket.

If he heard her, he didn't stop or acknowledge her in any way. She literally felt heat rising from his head.

"I love you, Alex. I want you to know that. There are a lot of good people in the world. I'm sure there are some nice boys at your school who'd like to be your friends."

His concentration was so intense that his grandmother couldn't tell whether he was enjoying himself or in agony. The pace of his writing seemed to pick up. Alex was working himself into such a frenzy that his grandmother found it disturbing to watch.

Choking back a tear, she said, "I'll be in the kitchen making dinner if you need me. Join me if you want to." Then she quickly kissed him on the head and left.

CHAPTER NINETEEN

The person with big dreams is more powerful than one with all the facts.

—Albert Einstein

CROCKER WAS following the trail of water dripping from Mercedes's body. She wore the red bathing suit he'd seen her in before. The hallways in the house were a labyrinth of circles. He was starting to feel dizzy. The only light came from candles in sconces on the walls.

He entered a big room and stopped. Vivaldi's *Four Seasons* was booming from speakers hung high in the corners. Wearing the wet red bikini was a little man seated at a long high table, hunched over a bucket of KFC chicken. Crocker thought he resembled Farhed Alizadeh, but he couldn't see the man's face.

A phone rang. He woke up.

"Crocker?" a familiar Kentucky voice asked. "It's Captain Sutter. Stop by my office this afternoon at two."

The clock by the phone read 7:46. It took him a second to get his bearings and answer, "Yes, sir."

It was Wednesday, February 20. Holly had left him a note on the kitchen table. "I've got an appointment, then I'm going to the gym. I'll meet you at home for dinner. Have a nice day."

At HQ Captain Sutter reminded Crocker that he and his team had another week and a half of leave.

"I know that, sir."

Sutter showed him a clipping from the *Charlottesville Daily Progress* with a picture of a horse his brother was training that he said might be running in the Kentucky Derby.

"What's the horse's name?"

"What's It 2 Ya."

"Cool name."

"How you feeling, Crocker? Sit down."

"Fine."

"You talk to Dr. Petrovian?"

"I did."

"He help you get your head screwed on straight?"

"He tried. Said some of the threads have worn out, which is why it wobbles a little when I walk."

"Sounds like you're okay," Sutter said. "Either that, or you've lost your mind."

Crocker felt better just sitting in the CO's office. Being called in usually meant he had an upcoming mission. This time it might mean he was being put out to pasture like one of Sutter's brother's racehorses.

Sutter said, "I wanted to tell you what I know about the three men you encountered in the tunnel."

Crocker sipped from the bottle of water he'd brought with him. He hadn't given the men a lot of thought since he'd been home. In fact, he couldn't remember their faces. But he did vividly recall the tunnel ceiling falling and the feeling of suffocation. He had decided a long time ago that if he had to die, he'd rather catch a bullet and go quickly than suffocate or drown.

Sutter continued, "Although they were carrying Venezuelan passports with new names, they were really Iranian members of Unit 5000."

"I believe I knew that already, sir."

"The FBI used contact information recovered in El Paso to find and arrest two more individuals living in New Orleans," Sutter said, referring to a document on his desk. "They were also Iranian undercover operatives. They had magnetic bombs in their possession like the ones used in Thailand and Athens, and plans for detonating a number of explosive devices during the Mardi Gras parade and celebration. They also had sarin."

Sarin is a colorless, odorless nerve agent that is extremely lethal when inhaled or absorbed through the skin—five hundred times more deadly than cyanide. Back in 1988, Saddam Hussein had bombarded the Kurdish city of Halabja in northern Iraq with bombs containing sarin that killed five thousand people within a matter of minutes.

Crocker leaned forward. "The FBI has been able to confirm that?" He had assumed that the Iranians were infiltrating the U.S. in order to carry out some long-term plan. He never thought they would be called on to act so soon.

"Yes."

"Were they planning to carry out other attacks beyond New Orleans?"

"I heard that the attack on the parade was going to be used as a diversion for a larger and potentially more lethal attack on the Waterford 3 nuclear plant, which is roughly fifty miles northwest of the city."

Crocker sat speechless as he considered the possible ramifications.

Sutter removed his glasses and folded his hands in front of him. He said, "The FBI and CIA believe there are more coming."

"More attacks?"

Sutter nodded. "The president is furious. Donaldson thinks this is retaliation for some of the things the president has recently authorized in Iran," he said, referring to the actions made by the CIA's head of operations.

Crocker knew about the Stuxnet worm, a computer virus that had temporarily shut down Iran's nuclear program. And he'd heard a rumor, which he hoped was true, that the virus had hit other targets in Iran, including IRGC headquarters.

"Donaldson is planning a response," Sutter said.

"Good." The United States and Iran had been waging a secret war for years now, and Crocker and his team had played a part in it, starting a year ago off the coast of Somalia and most recently in the tunnel under Ciudad Juárez.

"What's the status of Black Cell?" Sutter asked, leaning back in his chair.

"Ritchie, Cal, and Tré are still healing. The rest of us are good to go."

Sutter lowered his voice. "I want to warn you, Crocker, this op is likely to be highly dangerous. It's unlike anything we've attempted before. I'd go so far as to classify it as a suicide mission—but I'm not sure Donaldson will tell you that."

Crocker was on the edge of his seat. "Where, sir?"

"I can't disclose that now. I want you to take a couple of days and think about it. You and your men have been through a number of bad shit storms already."

"If this has to do with responding to Unit 5000, or if it involves confronting Alizadeh in any way," Crocker said without hesitation, "I'm all in."

Sutter shook his head like a concerned father. "I want you to sleep on this."

"Sir, there's no doubt in my mind that we're ready."

Sutter sighed. "Don't say I didn't warn you. Be here at 6 a.m. tomorrow. We're flying up to Langley. Plan to spend the night."

He sprung out of bed at 0430, jogged through the woods, showered, shaved, and dressed in his only black suit. Three hours later he saw the spires of the Capitol building and the Washington Monument piercing the morning fog, which filled him with pride. Great men had lived, fulfilled their dreams, and died in this city. He didn't pretend to be as wise or as important as they were, but he considered it an honor to be part of the tradition of service to a great ideal.

Outside the Dulles terminal, he and his CO in a khaki uniform climbed into the waiting black sedan. At CIA headquarters, they walked over the great white-and-gray marble seal in the lobby and past the Wall of Honor, which listed the names of CIA agents killed in action. Crocker had known some of them, including Mike Spann, who had died fighting off Taliban prisoners in northern Afghanistan in late 2001.

Their footsteps echoed through the glass-enclosed atrium where one-sixth-scale models of the U-2, A-12, and D-21 spy planes were suspended overhead. An aide in a dark blue suit waited at the elevator to escort them up to a fourth-floor conference room.

Lou Donaldson, Jim Anders, Sy Blanc, and Leslie Walker welcomed the two men. Crocker thought Ms. Walker looked even more attractive than the last time he'd seen her, with her long brown hair pulled back, wearing a tight charcoal gray pantsuit and white blouse. He was introduced to a half dozen other analysts from CIA, a man and a woman from the National Security Agency, two agents from FBI, a woman from Homeland Security. When the deputy director of the National Security Council arrived with a young African American aide, they all took their seats.

Donaldson opened the meeting by saying that no one in the room was authorized to discuss any of the information that would be covered with anyone except those present. Then he introduced General Brad Nathans, deputy director of the NSC.

Crocker had never met Nathans but had heard a lot about him. He knew he was a former marine general who had served in the First Gulf War and the invasion of Iraq, and had subsequently lost his right arm in a terrorist bombing in Kuwait. Nathans was reputed to be a brilliant strategist, a military historian, and a tireless worker. More important, he was part of the president's trusted inner circle.

Nathans cleared his throat and, speaking from notes, repeated what Sutter had told Crocker about the arrest of the Unit 5000 operatives in New Orleans and the seizure of weapons, sarin, and explosives. Then he went further, explaining that three more people had been arrested in the New Orleans area. Two had recently entered the country on student visas. The other was a U.S. citizen.

The man from FBI pointed out that the investigation was ongoing and more arrests were expected. "This was a complex and wide-ranging conspiracy," he warned. "It could have been devastating. Thank God those men were stopped in El Paso, because they were primarily responsible for carrying out the attacks in New Orleans. The other people we've arrested, with the exception maybe of one of the students, were playing support roles—moving money, renting rooms and vehicles, storing supplies. We're almost one hundred percent sure this operation was baked in Iran."

An eerie hush filled the room. Even though all the people there were tough professionals, they seemed deeply affected by what they had just heard.

The general cleared his throat and deepened his voice. "Nothing I say from this point on can leave this room. Nothing. Understood?"

Everyone nodded.

"One of the individuals we're holding has told us that the Quds Force, and Unit 5000 in particular, is planning more attacks against the U.S."

Crocker knew that despite increased patrols and updated technology, the long borders the United States shares with Mexico and Canada were still relatively porous. The fact that an organization as devious and capable as the Quds Force had launched a program to infiltrate terrorists and bombers into the States scared him.

"When and where are these attacks likely to occur?" Sy Blanc asked.

"The man we're holding claims he doesn't know," Donaldson answered. "But the president has decided to take the gloves off. He's had enough."

Crocker liked the tone of his remarks so far, but wondered where this was going.

Nathans said, "Some of you here have heard of Scimitar."

Crocker looked at Sutter, sitting beside him, who shook his head. He didn't know about it either.

"Scimitar," Nathans explained, "is a top-secret group of anti-regime Iranian operatives that the CIA has organized, supplied, funded, and supported inside Iran. It's Lou's baby, so I'll let him tell you about it."

Donaldson sat up and adjusted his collar. Crocker didn't like his arrogant manner but had to admit that he seemed to have grown bolder and less risk averse the higher he'd climbed the bureaucratic ladder.

Donaldson said, "What I can tell you about Scimitar is that it was authorized three years ago by presidential finding and approved by the congressional oversight committee. It consists of about a dozen highly trained individuals who live in and near Tehran. They have supplies, resources, and safe houses, and they've developed sources internally. So far we've only used them to collect intel.

"Because of the aggressive nature of what has just transpired, with the Iranians going so far as to infiltrate their operatives onto American territory to initiate an attack, the president has made the decision to activate them further," Donaldson continued. "In other words, their role will soon expand from collecting intel to going operational. The problem is that they don't have the expertise or combat capability to carry out the operation we have in mind."

Now Crocker understood why he was present. The prospect of a direct attack on Iran excited him. He watched Donaldson turn his long, serious face to him, then heard him say, "That's why we invited Chief Warrant Officer Crocker. All of you, I believe, are familiar with Black Cell."

People turned to him and nodded. He saw the excitement in Leslie Walker's warm brown eyes and felt proud.

The next morning Crocker, Sutter, Anders, Blanc, and Walker sat in Lou Donaldson's office, drank coffee, chewed on bagels, and started to sketch out a plan. They began with the presumption that Crocker and his team would be dropped into Iran with gear and weapons. Members of Scimitar would meet them and provide logistical support. Black Cell would attack targets inside the country, then retreat to a remote location from which they could be extracted at night. The list of possible targets included nuclear sites, military bases, and the homes and offices of high-ranking Iranian officials. According to Donaldson, the president had made clear that any mission he authorized had to meet three criteria: One, it had to be targeted specifically to respond to the thwarted Unit 5000 strike on New Orleans. Two, it had to have a reasonable chance of success. And three, it had to have enough of an impact to discourage the Iranians from launching future terrorist attacks.

For the most part, Crocker stayed out of the discussion.

But he did point out that criterion number one seemed to eliminate most of the CIA's list of targets, namely the nuclear facilities and military bases.

"Not necessarily," Donaldson said.

Sy Blanc: "I agree with Crocker. How does our hitting a military base in Iran qualify as a pointed response to Unit 5000's recent activities and its plan to hit New Orleans? And how does it serve as a warning to Quds Force not to launch future attacks?"

Anders: "They're two tentacles of the same rogue state."

Walker: "That's a stretch."

Donaldson asked, "Then what do you propose we hit?"

Crocker spoke up. "Since we know that this was planned by the Quds Force, and specifically Farhed Alizadeh, it seems logical to target him. Correct?"

Blanc: "Yes, but—"

Donaldson cut him off. "Nice idea, Crocker. But I don't think Alizadeh is a big enough target. Besides, I'm not sure we know where he is."

Anders: "We don't."

"Why isn't he big enough?" Blanc asked.

Anders: "First of all, no one's ever heard of him. And second, is taking him out really worth risking Scimitar and the lives of your men?"

Everyone in the room with the exception of Crocker seemed to agree. He spoke up. "Let's not forget what this guy has done—the hijacking of the nuclear material off the coast of Somalia, his operations in Libya and the attempt to steal WMDs, his drug smuggling operation out of Ciudad del Este, building a base in Venezuela, and this attempt on New

Orleans. I say we take him out, then broadcast his crimes to the media."

"And make him a martyred hero in Iran?" Donaldson asked. "I don't think the president will appreciate that recommendation."

Talk then shifted to assassinating a higher-profile official, including the minister of intelligence and security, Heidar Moslehi; the Supreme Leader, Ayatollah Ali Khamenei; the chief commander of the Revolutionary Guards, Mohammed Ali Jafari; and the commander of the Quds Force, Major General Qassem Suleimani.

Crocker's mind started to wander. He imagined Alizadeh sitting somewhere, talking about how the United States was bloated and soft.

Anders argued that any U.S. attack on the president of Iran or the Supreme Leader would be seen as an act of war and would probably provoke a furious response from the world's Shiite community. He didn't think the president was willing to risk that.

Crocker imagined Alizadeh throwing his head back and laughing.

The discussion then focused on Ali Jafari and General Suleimani. Donaldson looked at his watch and suggested they break for lunch while he sat in on a video conference with the White House.

Crocker wasn't hungry. He said, "I recommend that we strike back at the people who are planning these attacks and hit their headquarters."

"Whose headquarters?" Donaldson asked back.

"Quds Force headquarters," Crocker answered.

"I think Chief Crocker has raised an interesting scenario," Sy Blanc offered.

"Where is it?" Donaldson said, gathering the papers he'd spread out on the table.

Anders: "Where's what?"

Donaldson: "Quds Force HQ."

Walker cleared her throat. "They have an office in Tehran that is actually located in the compound of our former embassy," she said. "But their national headquarters is in the city of Ahvaz, in the southwest. They moved it there several years ago to be closer to Iraq."

"That's the office General Suleimani and Farhed Alizadeh operate out of, and where they've been planning and launching the attacks against us?" Donaldson asked as he stood.

"As far as we know, yes," she responded.

Donaldson: "I want you to confirm that."

"I will, sir."

Crocker and Sutter sat with Sy Blanc in a corner of the CIA cafeteria. Blanc looked out the window at the snowflakes starting to fall on the patio and said, "Why are we always so slow to respond?"

"Remember the USS *Cole* bombing in 2000 by al-Qaeda?" Sutter asked. "I hope we don't make the same mistake again."

Blanc tasted a forkful of his tuna salad, then pushed it away and drowned the taste with coffee. "The Quds Force has been a huge, ugly thorn in our side for years, especially in Iraq, where they have hundreds of agents who've been actively arming and running the Shiite militia since 2003. In my opinion they're directly or indirectly responsible for hundreds of U.S. coalition casualties." Blanc looked as though he had swallowed something bitter.

Sutter: "How do you know this?"

"NSA managed to eavesdrop on a meeting in Tehran in 2008, shortly after the Green Zone was pummeled by rockets. Iraq's vice president at the time, Adel Abdul Mahdi, asked General Suleimani if the Quds Force was behind the attacks. Suleimani joked, and I quote, 'If the fire was accurate, it was ours.' "

"We should have punished him for that," Sutter commented.

Blanc had more to get off his chest. "In Afghanistan, they run something called the Ansar Corps, headed by another religious zealot named General Gholamreza Baghbani, who has organized a network of drug traffickers to ship opium and heroin into Iran and supply the Taliban with weapons. They've got another unit, Unit 400, which is currently fighting alongside President Assad's forces in Syria. And now there's Unit 5000. These fuckers are evil. And to a real extent, Suleimani, Alizadeh, and others have more authority than the president, because they report directly to the ayatollah."

"Alarming," Sutter said.

"The fact is, the Quds Force has been working against us and attacking us for years, and we've done nothing about it. I suppose it's because so many of their activities have occurred far away, making the threat they pose somewhat abstract to many of us here in Washington."

Crocker saw Leslie Walker coming toward them, weaving around the tables. Judging from her expression, Crocker surmised she was carrying an important message. Turning to Sy

Blanc, he said, "Quds Force officers and their proxies have tortured me and my men and kidnapped my wife, and we have the physical and psychological scars to prove it. So Alizadeh and his terrorists aren't abstract to me, and I couldn't be more motivated to get them. I want that chance, and I hope to God I get it."

"Me, too," Anders said. "Me, too."

CHAPTER TWENTY

If I had no sense of humor, I would long ago have committed suicide.

—Mahatma Gandhi

THEY FLEW back that night in the same Gulfstream jet. As Sutter sat across the aisle pecking on his laptop, Crocker studied the satellite photos Leslie Walker had given him of Quds Force headquarters in Ahvaz, Iran—a six-story concrete structure with little porthole-like windows, antennas and satellite dishes on the flat roof. It was located in a densely built-up urban area, with a bank on one side, a modern movie theater on the corner. He used a red pen to circle military checkpoints at both ends of the block, and was already considering how he and his men might enter the area undetected.

Crocker had been to Tehran but had never set foot in Ahvaz, which he now learned is a city of approximately 1.5 million on the banks of the Karun River. Located in the Khuzestan desert and surrounded by sandstone hills, Ahvaz, according to the Weather Channel website, is one of the hottest cities on the planet, with the average high temperature in July a toasty 115.2 degrees and peaks regularly hitting 120. The city also had the distinction of being the world's most polluted, according to the World Health Organization, with an annual average of 372 micrograms of airborne particles per cubic meter of air. Washington, D.C., by contrast, had a level of 18 micrograms, and Tokyo 23. The WHO study cited sulfur dioxide and nitrogen exhaust from nearby power plants, burn-off from oil wells, and vehicle exhaust as the main pollutants.

Not a great place to live, Crocker thought. Neighboring Iraq had attempted to annex the city in 1980 during the Iran-Iraq War. Reading further, he learned that a minority of the area's residents are Arabs rather than Persians, which might have explained Saddam Hussein's ambitions—either that, or it was further evidence that the man had been insane.

They landed just before midnight. Driving home with Elvis crooning "Something" over the radio, his brain jumped ahead, calculating where his team would insert, what they'd need in terms of equipment and support, and how they'd move within Ahvaz. He couldn't help himself, even though he was tired and a final decision regarding the scope and target of the mission hadn't been reached. Outside it was cold and windy. As a kid in Massachusetts, he liked to sleep in front of the fireplace on nights like this.

The grandfather clock on the second floor chimed the quarter hour as he entered, patted Brando on the head, and started upstairs. He was looking forward to the warm bed he shared with Holly, but the door to the master bedroom was locked. Wondering why, and realizing this had never happened before, he tried the door again. He considered opening the couch in his office and sleeping there so as not to wake her, but he was worried, and decided to knock instead. "Holly?" he called. "Holly, are you okay?"

Half a minute later she opened the door. Wearing a long cotton nightgown, she looked disheveled and tired, with a bandage on her chin. "You're home," she said, half asleep and heading back to the bed.

"Is anything wrong?" he asked. "How come you locked the door?"

"I thought I heard something downstairs."

"It's windy outside. Could've been a tree branch." He saw her 9mm automatic on the nightstand next to her side of the bed. "What happened to your chin?"

"I went downstairs to check on the noise. I wasn't completely awake. I slipped on the stairs and tripped. Silly me."

He took her by the hand, sat her on the edge of the bed, and cleaned and rebandaged the cut on her chin. Then he checked her teeth and found no damage. "You hurt anything else?" he asked.

"Not really, except for my pride," she answered, looking embarrassed. Staring at the carpet, she shook her head and asked, "What's wrong with me, Tom?" with sad resignation in her voice.

He put his arms around her and said, "Nothing that a little time, rest, and tender loving care won't fix."

"Oh, Tom." They kissed. She felt delicate and tender in his arms. He wanted to make her better, and protect her, and wash away all the guilt and anguish that clouded her soul.

Gently, he pushed her back onto the bed, lay down beside

her, and held her hand. Another hungry part of him wanted to make love to her, but he knew the time wasn't right.

In the morning when Crocker got out of the shower, Holly was gone. Lying on a chair by the bed he saw a book called *Healing after Loss*. The subtitle read: *Daily Meditations for Working Through Grief.*

Twenty minutes later he arrived at ST-6 headquarters and found Sutter sitting in the same uniform he'd worn the day before, his stockinged feet on the desk, reading a document as he sipped from a mug of coffee with a trident on it.

"Captain?"

He looked up and set the mug down on his desk. "Sit down, Crocker. How many times have you seen the movie *Lawrence of Arabia*?" he asked in his backcountry drawl.

"I don't know. Half a dozen. Why?"

"Fascinating story, on so many levels. I couldn't fall asleep last night, so I streamed it twice on my computer. The different tribes, the desert, a hero wrestling with his own internal demons. Kind of reminded me of you."

"Thank you, sir."

"Inspired me, too. One highly motivated man can make a difference, especially if he understands the culture of the people he's dealing with," Sutter said as he tossed the document he was holding at him. "Read this."

Crocker caught it and quickly scanned the two-page report on Scimitar, which had nothing to do with tribes or the desert, but briefly described a group of twelve young Iranians who had been working clandestinely with the CIA to help sabotage the Iranian government. The report didn't mention what they had managed to accomplish so far or their capabilities. Their leader was a man named Ramin.

Sutter asked, "What do you think?"

"Interesting. But what did you mean about me wrestling with my personal demons?"

"Oh, that." Sutter smiled, scratched his jaw, took a long drink of coffee, and picked up another document from his desk. "Remember the psych evaluation I told Doc Petrovian to administer to you? Well, he concluded that you're a combination of an aggressive PT and an introverted intuitive."

"What do you mean by PT?" Crocker asked.

"It stands for personality type," Sutter answered. "Don't get all worked up. What he's saying is that you display the characteristics of an ideal leader, but you're also conflicted."

"Conflicted how?" Crocker asked, starting to feel defensive.

"It means you like being able to dominate and command others and exercise power, but you also like to stay in the background until you feel the need to take over. So you like being part of a traditional power structure, but you're also someone who primarily trusts his intuition, which makes you a loner and a rebel. You're active and adventurous, but you also need time alone to sit back and observe the world and make associations."

"Petrovian said that?" Crocker asked.

"Sound like you?" Sutter asked back.

"Kind of."

Sutter got up and refilled his mug from a stainless-steel urn behind his desk. "Forget about the psychological profile for the time being."

"Sir—"

"I need you to do two things. One, select three men to go with you into Iran."

"Only three, sir?" Crocker asked.

"Yes, three. Don't fight me on this. I want you to consider carefully what you're going to need in terms of operational specialties, personal characteristics, and language skills."

"I still don't know the specific mission."

Sutter leaned back and yawned. "I won't be able to tell you that until it's approved by the president."

"When's that likely to happen?"

"Today. Tomorrow. Figure another four hours after that, we'll want you to deploy."

Crocker stood at attention. "That soon, sir?"

"Yes, that soon." Sutter rose and handed him a blue notecard with a name written on it. "Here's the second thing I need you to do."

Crocker read the name and asked, "Who's John Smith?"

"Some deep, deep black-ops guy Donaldson says you need to coordinate with."

"When and where, sir?'

"Turn over the card."

On the other side Crocker read "Williamsburg Lodge in Williamsburg, Virginia," and "Twelve thirty p.m." He'd attended a wedding reception there once.

"Today, sir?"

Sutter nodded. "By the way, Doc Petrovian told me some of the other people with your combination of personality traits include Al Capone, Fidel Castro, and Jeffrey Dahmer."

"Thanks."

"I'm thinking of sending someone over to your house to see what you store in your freezer."

"I hope that's a joke, sir."

Sutter laughed.

He entered the spacious white lobby of the Williamsburg Lodge—a sprawling two-story colonial-style inn a block or so from the historic center. At the front desk he asked for Mr. Smith.

"Is Mr. Smith a guest here?" the thin male clerk with stiff brown hair asked.

"I don't know. But he asked me to meet him here."

"Your name, sir?"

"Mansfield."

The clerk turned, consulted a computer screen, whispered to an older clerk, then returned and said, "Mr. Smith is waiting for you in the Golden Horseshoe Grill."

"Where's that?"

"Take that hallway straight back, past the big fireplace. You'll see the entrance on the left."

"Thanks."

Entering the room, he waited for his eyes to adjust to the low light. The walls were paneled with walnut. Old wagon wheel fixtures hung from the ceiling. A man with a white apron stretched across his big belly polished glasses with a white towel behind the bar.

"John Smith?" Crocker asked.

The bartender shrugged and nodded toward a big man in the darkness at the end of the bar as if to say, try him.

The man he indicated had gray hair to his shoulders and was speaking on a cell phone.

"John?" Crocker asked.

The big man nodded and pointed a finger at the lounge, which was empty except for three elderly couples, two of whom were seated together. Crocker selected a table in the far corner by a window that overlooked the golf course. It was overcast outside. Two men passed in a golf cart, one wearing a pink sweater and green pants.

"What are we doing here?" Crocker heard a deep voice ask.

He looked up and saw the big man standing behind a chair on the other side of the table.

"John Smith?" No way that was his real name.

The man sat. He had huge shoulders, no neck, and a very strong and unusual face—large hooked nose, high cheekbones, a prominent forehead with thick black eyebrows. He looked like a Bedouin chieftain, despite the straight gray hair, which Crocker realized was a wig, and the mustard-tinted glasses that hid his eyes.

"You play?" Smith asked, setting his BlackBerry on the table and nodding toward the course.

"Never."

"I didn't think so."

"You?"

Smith smiled without showing any teeth. "I do a little of everything. You want me to play golf, I play golf. You want to play tennis, I play tennis. You like to dance the mambo, I learn to do that, too."

Crocker said, "Lou Donaldson asked me to meet you."

"Louie the doughnut, yeah. I let him think he's my boss."

Smith twisted his mouth and lifted his eyebrows, a set of facial contortions that seemed to express the complex feelings he had about him. "You want to hear about Scimitar?"

"Yeah."

The young waitress arrived. Crocker ordered a steak sandwich with fries. Smith told the waitress he was fasting and only wanted a glass of water with a twist of lemon. Then he leaned over the table and said in a low voice, "Whatever you've heard about Scimitar, I'm afraid to say, is probably an exaggeration. I'm the only one who has actually met and worked with these people. They're real, and they have provided us with some good intel. But they're not much."

The cold water left a metallic taste in Crocker's mouth. "Not much in what sense?"

"Operationally, I'd say, they're useless. They can help you get around, show you places, hide you, feed you, et cetera. But with the exception of maybe two individuals, I'm not sure they can even fire a gun."

"Tell me about the composition of the group," Crocker said.

"There are about ten core members. Four of them are women. All of them are college educated, modern people. They hate the religious repression and long for a more open, tolerant, European-style representative government. The leader is a man called Ramin Kian, who was a former engineer in the army. He's the oldest; I'd say late thirties, maybe forty. Ramin's an emotional guy, passionate, but something of a flake."

"A flake in what sense?"

"What I mean is, when he gets excited about something,

he can be highly engaged and effective. But he loses interest quickly. He's also a coward."

"Does he know anything about this operation?" Crocker asked.

"I communicated with him last night—I can't reveal how. But I can tell you, he's very pumped about it, which is a positive."

"What did you tell him?"

"I told him the U.S. was interested in launching an attack against Quds Force headquarters or possibly some of its leaders. He said an attack on Quds Force HQ is impossible."

"Did he explain why?"

"Why? Because the building is heavily fortified and the streets around it are barricaded and monitored twenty-four/seven."

"There's always a way," Crocker said.

"I'm repeating what he told me. In his opinion, any assault on their HQ would require helicopters and at least two dozen heavily armed troops, so it's out of the question."

"In his opinion."

"We're relying on the intel he provides, so his opinion counts a ton, especially in the minds of Donaldson and other decision makers," Smith said.

Crocker nodded. "I get it."

Smith's eyes followed a female golfer who was passing by the window. "Ramin had another suggestion," he said.

The waitress arrived with Crocker's food. As he bit into the sandwich, Smith asked, "You ever hear of Futsal?"

"Futsal. No."

"It's a variation of soccer that's played indoors on a hard

surface. Two teams of five players each, one of whom is the goalkeeper."

"Yeah?"

"Apparently it's a big sport in Iran, with professional leagues. It happens to be very popular in Ahvaz. Ramin has a close friend who owns a team and an arena. He says Farhed Alizadeh and General Suleimani are big fans of a team called Farsh Sari, in division two of the super league. They regularly attend games at this guy's arena and sit together in specially reserved seats."

Crocker stopped chewing and said, "Sounds promising."

"I think so, too. Ramin thinks he can enlist his friend's help, and maybe your team can ambush them as they're arriving at or leaving a game."

"What's the name of Ramin's friend?" Crocker asked.

"Adab Mashhad."

"What do you know about him?"

"Not much. I've confirmed that he's the owner of the Shohada Gaz Arena in Ahvaz. He also holds a prominent position in the national drilling company. Ramin says the two of them studied engineering together."

"When is this Farsh Sari team playing next?" Crocker asked.

"Ramin's looking into that now. I'm speaking to him again tonight."

By ten that night Crocker had sketched out a plan and selected Akil, Mancini, and Ritchie to go with him. He had spoken to each man and told them they were going to be dropped inside Iran with orders to attack several high-priority targets.

The likelihood of them being either captured or killed was high. All three volunteered.

If and when the op was approved by the president, the four men would travel with John Smith via CIA jet to Al Taqaddum Air Base outside Baghdad. From there they'd be ferried south by helicopter to Basrah, which was roughly a two-hour drive or twenty-minute helicopter ride to Ahvaz, just over the border in Iran. The details of their insertion were still being worked out by the CIA.

Crocker sat in Sutter's office with Mancini and Sutter's second in command, going over the PLO—patrol leader's order—that was standard practice in all ST-6 missions. They discussed insertion, extraction, infiltration, actions at the objective, movement, emergency medical evacuation, communications, loss-of-comms plan, hand signals, concealment, covers, weather, clothing, supplies, specialized equipment, weapons, medical supplies, first-, second-, and third-line gear, and contingencies.

A few minutes before midnight, Sutter's phone rang. It was Donaldson with the news that the president had okayed the mission. Crocker's team was going in deep black, which meant they couldn't carry anything that identified them in any way—no IDs, photos, dog tags, U.S. military weapons.

"What's the timing?" Sutter asked into the speakerphone.

"The team Farsh Sari is playing in Ahvaz the night after tomorrow, so they have to launch now," Donaldson answered.

"That's the twenty-fifth, correct?"

"Affirmative."

Sutter looked at Crocker, who nodded, barely able to contain his excitement. "You can tell the president they're ready to go."

CHAPTER TWENTY-ONE

You armed me with strength for battle; you humbled my adversaries before me.

—Psalm 18:39

HIS TEAM was waiting at the airport, but Crocker couldn't leave without explaining to Holly what he was about to do, even though his orders forbade him from discussing his missions with anyone. He'd never broken that pledge in almost ten years of working with ST-6 and Black Cell. But tonight he was making an exception.

She was asleep when he got home. He woke her, sat facing her, and holding both her hands said, "I want you to know that I'm leaving tonight on a mission to go after Farhed Alizadeh in Iran. And I couldn't be more excited."

She looked at him and trembled, and in that moment seemed to fully understand the gravity of what he was telling her. "I can't say I'm not pleased," she said, "but I'm also scared. Thank you for telling me. And please, please, come back."

"Don't tell Jenny about the mission, but I want both of you

to know that if something happens, I'm still the luckiest man alive. I've been blessed with a beautiful, intelligent daughter that I don't deserve, and the most wonderful wife I could have ever imagined."

"Tom, I love you so much . . ."

He kissed her, pulled away, and took one last glance at the room, Holly on the bed and on the wall their framed wedding picture in which a look of absolute joy showed on her face. He wanted to take those images with him, even to the other side of death.

Starting down the stairs, he realized there was one other thing he wanted to take with him. Stepping lightly and carefully, he entered Jenny's room and planted a kiss on her sleeping head, taking a moment to record her delicate profile, which always gave him joy and reminded him of his first wife.

With both images stored deep inside, he descended the stairs to the office, where he grabbed one of the prepacked bags for undercover summer ops, with a couple of black T-shirts and pants, toothbrush, hunting knife, and black Nikes. He stopped in the kitchen, pulled two energy bars and a bottle of water out of the cabinet, then patted Brando's head and told him to look after the girls until he got back before exiting into the night.

Time now passed as if in a dream, and every moment seemed significant. Half an hour later he boarded the Gulfstream, where he was greeted with a thumbs-up from John Smith, who was talking on his BlackBerry. The long gray wig had been replaced by a black skullcap that covered his bald head.

Akil, Ritchie, and Mancini arrived silently and threw their

gear into the baggage compartment under the wing. The Gulfstream took off. Approximately seven hours later, they landed at Naval Air Station Sigonella in Sicily to refuel and stretch their legs. Around six hours later they arrived at Al Taqaddum Air Base outside Baghdad.

Except for the sounds of the wind buffeting metal hangars and the whine of engines, the night was silent. Stars sparkled brilliantly with light from a distant time. Crocker stood near the jet waiting for the thud of distant explosions but heard none.

Two CIA officials in T-shirts and mirrored sunglasses greeted them and led them to a canteen, where they washed up, then ate scrambled eggs, hash browns, and fresh fruit, and drank coffee. Then they boarded an unmarked Black-hawk helicopter for the trip to Basrah International Airport.

Everyone they encountered—pilots, officials—seemed to understand the gravity of the mission. Crocker and his men felt it, too; there was none of their usual banter. Each man was occupied with his own thoughts. Each of them knew there was a good probability he might not come back. Nevertheless, Crocker didn't waste time worrying about that or the difficulties they might encounter. He focused on how privileged he felt about finally getting the chance to take the fight directly to the Falcon on his turf.

In Basrah they waited on the tarmac while John Smith communicated with Ramin Kian via satellite phone. Smith returned an hour later and barked, "You're good to go."

"When?" Crocker asked.

"Ninety minutes. The helicopter is going to drop you by a scrap metal yard southwest of the city near the steel plant and the Imam Khomeini Freeway. Ramin will meet you there with two of his people. He'll signal with a green laser marker."

"Good," Crocker said, gazing up at the three-quarters moon and canopy of stars. He was reminded of a camping trip with Holly deep inside Yosemite park and a night they'd spent in their sleeping bag holding each other and naming constellations. He cut off the memory and forced himself to focus.

Smith said, "The op will take place tomorrow night. Ramin's got the details all worked out. We're planning to extract you from the same site near the scrap yard at midnight. So be there."

"We plan to." The desert air had already dried out his nostrils and mouth.

Smith said, "If you encounter a problem, call me on the sat phone. I'll be waiting across the border in the town of Nahairat. I can get to you quickly if there's an emergency. But I have strict orders not to enter Iran."

"Fine." Crocker thought of asking why but decided not to. Washington always came up with strange restrictions, even at critical times like these. They couldn't resist the urge to try to micromanage dangerous ops from halfway around the world, despite the fact that at this point there wasn't a whole lot they could control. Nor could Crocker, for that matter—which he was well aware of. He'd never met Ramin, had no idea how competent he was, and had no details about the other people they'd be working with.

John Smith led them to an empty hangar, where they changed into black T-shirts and pants, and donned night-vision goggles. They did a final check on their black backpacks and weapons. Each man carried one Russian- or

Chinese-made submachine gun and automatic pistol, extra ammo, two grenades, and an SOP knife. Crocker's submachine gun was a Russian AEK-919K Kashtan with suppressor and folded buttstock, which resembled an Uzi and weighed less than five pounds. His choice of handgun was a Chinese-made TU-90 semiautomatic, which looked a lot like a U.S. M1911.

He also packed the emergency medical kit; Akil was responsible for the sat phone and radio; Ritchie carried explosives, detonators, and wire; Mancini toted extra ammo and other supplies.

As they walked back to the Blackhawk, Smith said, "The pilot is going to swing over the Persian Gulf and approach from the south. He'll have to fly low, because the Iranians have pretty robust border security and a strong military presence in Ahvaz."

Now you tell me, Crocker thought. He asked, "Is there a particular reason why? Didn't the Iranians recently shoot down one of our drones near there?"

Smith had to shout over the helicopter engines, which were starting up. "The heightened security has to do with the unrest in 2006."

"What unrest?" Crocker asked.

"Arab separatists blew up some banks, government buildings, a shopping center. Thirty or so people died."

"Sounds serious."

"There were some demonstrations and stone throwing, until the Iranians moved in and quashed it brutally. Naturally, they blamed us. Claimed the terrorists had been trained and armed by the CIA."

"Were they?" Crocker asked.

Smith shrugged, which Crocker interpreted as an admission. That explained a couple of things, including why Smith wasn't cleared to go into Iran. He was probably a marked man because of his participation in earlier operations.

He had one last question before he boarded the helicopter. "By any chance did this Ramin guy work with the Arabs who set off the bombs in 2006?"

"No," Smith said. "Don't worry. He's a hundred percent Persian through and through."

Persians are difficult people, Crocker said to himself as he strapped in and the bird lifted off. He'd worked with Iranians before, with mixed results. The ones he had dealt with were prideful in the extreme, suspicious of foreigners, and arrogant.

Their pilot was a Hispanic guy from San Antonio with a big smile and a bum right leg injured during a crash landing in southern Afghanistan. He warned them to expect turbulence due to warm wind blowing in from the east.

"Throw it at us," Ritchie said. "We're used to bumps."

The copter skimmed in low over the desert. Outside all Crocker saw were hills of sand and rock. Banking slightly left, they passed over a patch of green and a small house with camels tied up to a post.

"Five minutes!" the pilot shouted over his shoulder.

They flew over more shacks, then a four-lane highway with a few headlights. Crocker felt adrenaline pumping into his bloodstream. He grabbed his pack and his Kashtan, held up two fingers, then slid the helicopter door open. Across from him Mancini and Akil nodded to signal their understanding.

Through the doorway he saw two tall smokestacks ahead. Below was a field of shipping containers, parked trucks, and piles of metal. The helicopter banked sharply right.

"Where the hell are you going?" Crocker shouted at the pilot.

"I'm trying to locate the green laser."

The helo circled once, but they saw no green laser. The pilot shouted, "I'm going to circle one more time, then I've got to pull out."

"Fuck that!" Crocker shouted back. "Let us out."

"Here?"

"Here is fine. Hover so we can drop a rope."

"But my orders say—"

"Fuck the orders. We're getting out. You can blame it on me."

Crocker threw out the rope. Ritchie slid down first, followed by Mancini, Akil, and himself. As he touched the ground he went into a crouch, his weapon cocked and ready. Seeing a large shipping container twenty feet away, he signaled to his men to seek cover behind it.

By the time he reached it, the helicopter had become a fading dark blot in the sky. He wiped the dust off his face, cleared his nostrils of sand.

"What now?" Ritchie asked.

"We wait for this Ramin guy."

They hadn't even started, and already things were wrong. Twenty minutes passed. Then Akil saw a pair of headlights flash twice in a parking lot near the back of the big steel plant.

"What's that mean?" Ritchie asked.

"Don't know," Crocker answered. "You and Manny wait here. Akil, come with me."

They ran in a wide circle around the edge of the yard to the side of the plant, then hugged the dirty brick wall to the back of an old BMW.

"The motor's running," Akil whispered. "I see three people inside. The driver's-side window is open."

"Stay here and cover me," Crocker whispered back. With the Kashtan in his right hand, he ran to the dark garagelike building in front of them, went into a crouch, and scurried to the driver's window.

Crocker heard Middle Eastern music and someone singing along to the bouncy melody. He took a quick breath, came up, and pressed the barrel of the Kashtan against the side of the driver's head.

The man lurched forward so hard his chest hit the steering wheel.

Crocker said, "Shut your mouths and put your hands over your heads!"

The man in front and the man and woman in the backseat complied immediately. He saw what he thought was a high-powered military pointer pen on the brown leather passenger seat.

"Is one of you named Ramin Kian?" he asked.

"That's me," the driver said. His hair was short and gray. He had a square, bony face and looked older than Crocker had expected.

"I'm Mansfield," Crocker said. "Behind me is my colleague Jerid. What happened to the green laser?"

"It worked yesterday when I tested it, but not tonight."

"Kill the engine and get out. I want all of you to follow me."

"Where?" the young woman who had been smoking a clove cigarette in the backseat asked.

"Put out the cigarette and do as I say."

She frowned but complied. Crocker got his first good look at her and the third passenger as they exited the vehicle. She was an attractive young woman, about five nine, with dark, almond-shaped eyes, wearing tight jeans, her shoulder-length black hair covered with a black scarf. The male was very thin and young looking, with amber-colored eyes.

Ramin, last one out, had pissed his pants. Crocker watched him reach under the front seat and pull out a dark sweatshirt, which he tied around his waist.

They walked quickly and in silence. The Iranians looked scared when they saw the two other armed SEALs waiting behind the shipping container.

"I'm sorry if we frightened you, but it couldn't be helped," Crocker said.

"Okay. Y-y-yes," Ramin stammered. "We're glad you're here, but this is very dangerous for us."

Crocker: "Your English is good."

"I studied two years at the University of Maryland."

"College Park?" Ritchie asked.

"Yes. The Terrapins."

Ritchie: "I used to live on Adelphi Road, not far from the campus."

"Adelphi Road. Of course."

"Are you a football fan?" Mancini asked.

"No, basketball. Steve Blake, Chris Wilcox, Juan Dixon."

"Awesome team."

"We won the national championship in 2002 under coach Gary Williams," Ramin said proudly.

Ritchie: "I remember."

Ramin seemed like a personable guy, even if he wasn't a trained soldier. He pulled Crocker aside. "John told me he was going to get me and my family out of the country and find me a job in the U.S. Did he say anything to you about that?"

"No, he didn't. But if he told you he was working on it, I'm sure he is. I'll talk to him next time I see him."

Ramin looked confused. "My mother is very sick."

"I'll talk to him. I'll tell him that. John told me you have a plan."

"I do." The wind picked up, throwing sand in their faces. Ramin walked over to his shorter colleague and placed a hand on his shoulder. "This is my friend Danush," he said. "He's going to pick you up from here tomorrow at 6 p.m. and take you to the arena."

"My name is Anahita," the girl said in British-accented English, looking annoyed that Ramin hadn't introduced her.

Crocker took her hand. "Nice to meet you, Anahita."

She lowered her eyes to the ground. "I'll be with Danush."

"Tomorrow night?" Crocker asked.

"Yes."

"We'll all fit in the car?"

She nodded.

"The arena is near here?" Crocker asked.

"Thirty kilometers," Danush said.

"So it's relatively close."

"Yes, about a twenty-minute drive. Twenty-five at most," Ramin said. "Danush's brother will meet you there. He manages the sports arena."

Crocker turned to Danush. "Your brother," he repeated. "What's his name?"

"Shah."

He saw the smirk on Ritchie's face and knew what he was thinking.

"Shah what?" Crocker asked.

"Just Shah."

He looked at Danush and nodded. "Okay. You take us to the arena, then what happens?"

"You'll meet with his brother and he'll show you where to hide."

"John Smith told me you had a plan. What's the plan?"

"We do have a plan," Ramin answered defensively.

"That's it? We meet Danush's brother and he shows us where to hide?"

Ramin looked at his watch. "You want me to show you everything now?"

"Yes, please do."

Ramin said something to Anahita, who turned, reached under her blouse, and removed a piece of white paper. She unfolded it and handed it to Ramin. On it was a bird's-eye-view sketch of the arena, entrances, and parking lot. It matched the satellite photo Crocker had in his backpack.

Pointing to a spot on the paper, Ramin said, "This is the sports arena. The customers enter in the front, but special dignitaries arrive in the back. Here. That is where Alizadeh and Suleimani always enter. They come together in one car with a bodyguard and driver. Another vehicle with more bodyguards will follow them."

Crocker pointed to the curb in the drawing. "This is where the vehicles stop and the two men get out?" he asked.

"Correct. The bodyguards always get out first. They look

around to make sure they haven't been followed, then one of them opens the back door."

"I see," Crocker said. "Do the bodyguards wear body armor?"

"I don't know."

"Will Suleimani and Alizadeh be armed?"

"I don't know that, either."

"We'll assume they will be." Pointing at the sketch, Crocker asked, "Are there usually other vehicles parked back here?"

"Yes."

"And people?"

"Sometimes people, too, yes."

Danush said something to Ramin in Farsi, then turned to Crocker and said, "You don't need to worry about other people. My brother will clear them. He'll show you where to hide."

Crocker had dozens more questions, having to do with disguises, uniforms, other guards and policemen at the arena, and their escape. Ramin and Danush answered some of them. When it was time for them to leave, they led the SEALs a hundred yards past a chain-link fence to an old shipping container. This one had a lock on it, which Ramin opened with a key.

It stunk inside, and old mattresses covered the metal floor. "You can sleep here tonight," Ramin said.

"I give this place half a star," Ritchie cracked.

Akil: "Don't you have something with a view of the swimming pool?"

Ramin frowned.

"What happens next?" Crocker asked.

"We lock you in for the night," Ramin answered. "Then we come back tomorrow morning and bring some food and beverages."

"We brought food and water with us."

"Then Danush will return about 6 p.m. to drive you to the arena. The game doesn't start until seven."

Akil turned to Crocker and raised an eyebrow.

"Two things," Crocker said. "Number one, you're not going to lock us in this shipping container, so forget about that. Number two: What's likely to happen at the steel plant tomorrow? Are we going to wake up and find this area overrun with people?"

"Mr. Mansfield," Ramin answered, "I must say I find some of your questions insulting. We're intelligent people who are risking our lives to help you. We've thought about all of these matters. The plant is closed for the rest of the week as people get ready to celebrate the birthday of the Prophet."

The breeze threw sand in Crocker's eyes. "I'm sorry. I didn't mean to insult you," he said. "But I need to know what to expect."

"You can expect peace and quiet here. Nobody visits the plant when it's closed."

"Okay."

"Any more questions?" Ramin asked.

Crocker shook his head. "Is there any way for us to reach you?"

"No. It's too dangerous, and I don't have a secure phone. We'll be back tomorrow."

"Until tomorrow morning then."

"Until tomorrow."

Ramin turned and walked away with his two associates, leaving Crocker with a bad taste in his mouth.

"There goes the mighty Scimitar," Ritchie said as he watched them climb into the BMW and drive off.

Akil turned to Crocker. "What do you think?"

"If they do what they say they're gonna do, we'll be fine."

"What do you think are the odds that's going to happen?" Akil asked.

"Fifty-fifty."

"I don't know if they can be trusted," Ritchie said, picking sand out of his teeth.

"We'll find out."

The men chose to sleep on the flat roof of the container, where they could breathe fresh air and keep an eye on their immediate surroundings. To pass the time, Mancini, who had recently seen the movie *Lincoln*, talked about the strange coincidences between the sixteenth president and the thirty-fifth, John F. Kennedy. Both were shot by a bullet to the head on a Friday. Lincoln was elected to Congress in 1846, Kennedy in 1946. Lincoln's successor (named Johnson) was born in 1808. Kennedy's successor, also named Johnson, was born in 1908. Lincoln's assassin had three names and was born in 1838. Kennedy's assassin also went by three names and was born in 1939.

"So?" Ritchie asked. "What's it mean?"

"It's interesting, that's all. Did you know that a week before his death, Lincoln dreamt that he heard crying in a room in the White House? He found the room and saw a coffin and someone crying. When he asked who was in the coffin, the person responded, 'It's the president.' Then he looked in the coffin and saw himself."

"Was that in the movie?" Akil asked.

"No. They left out a whole lot of interesting stuff."

"Do us a favor," Ritchie said. "Don't tell us what you dream tonight."

"Why? You don't want to know what's coming?"

"I'd rather be surprised."

Crocker tried to push away the doubts he had about Ramin and Scimitar, and focus on the positive—they were in Iran and within striking distance of Alizadeh and Suleimani. If they did manage to get as close as Ramin said they could, they'd kill the Quds Force leaders. The more difficult task, and one they hadn't discussed with Ramin, was exiting the arena unharmed, then escaping across the border.

One thing at a time, he told himself, acknowledging that they were operating in the gray area of guts, instincts, and faith.

In an attempt to give his restless mind a break, he looked up and tried to find the constellation Orion. Through the hazy, cloud-swept sky, he located its brightest stars, blue-white Rigel, and reddish Betelgeuse, then traced the rest. In Greek mythology Orion was a hunter and usually depicted holding a club in one hand and a lion's head in the other.

He considered it a good omen.

In the morning the SEALs ate MREs and took turns washing in water from a spigot at the rear of the plant. Then they huddled and went over responsibilities. What they wanted to do was position themselves at the back of the arena and fire at the officials and their bodyguards from two directions, thus reducing any chance of escape.

Crocker and Akil would fire from Position 1, along the back wall of the arena. Mancini and Ritchie would situate themselves at a forty-five-degree angle from them somewhere in the rear parking lot (Position 2). One shooter from each position—Crocker at 1, Ritchie at 2—would focus on taking out the bodyguards and disabling the vehicles. The other two shooters, Akil and Mancini, would aim at the targets—Alizadeh and Suleimani.

Ramin didn't return in the morning like he said he would, so the SEALs spent the day cleaning and checking their weapons, reviewing positions, fire vectors, and signals, and going over various contingencies. By five everything was locked and loaded. The men were ready.

"Where the hell is he?" Ritchie asked.

"Fuck Ramin," Akil said. "All we need is the kid to drive us to the arena."

An hour passed and no one arrived. By 1815 hours Crocker started to worry. Ramin had said the game would start at 1900, and the arena was approximately twenty miles away.

Security around the city of Ahvaz was tight, and the Iranians were known to use electronic surveillance. With no way to communicate with Ramin, they waited.

At 1830, as the sun started to set, Crocker considered calling John Smith on the sat phone and telling him to pull them out. Ten minutes later a vehicle entered the back lot of the steel plant and flashed its headlights twice.

He and Akil approached through a mist of yellow-orange

dust. The vehicle wasn't a BMW, but a white Toyota sedan. Danush sat behind the wheel with Anahita in the seat beside him.

"What happened?" Crocker asked through the driver's-side window, trying not to lose his cool. "Ramin said he'd be back this morning. He never came."

Anahita leaned over and said, "There's been a problem."

"What does that mean?"

"The problem is that the arena is closed and the game was canceled."

"Why?" Crocker asked, checking their eyes for signs of betrayal, and alert to the sound of approaching people or vehicles.

"A pipe broke," she answered.

"A sewer pipe," Danush added.

"A sewer pipe broke inside the arena?" Crocker asked. "When is it likely to be fixed?"

Danush shrugged and looked at Anahita for help. "We don't know," she answered. "It's a big mess, as you can imagine."

"Where's Ramin?" Crocker asked, still superalert to the emotions that played on their faces and in their eyes.

"He asked us to come. He thinks he's being followed."

"Is he?"

The two Iranians looked at each other. Danush shrugged and answered, "We don't know. He gets nervous when things go wrong."

Crocker leaned his hand on the roof of the car. Everything they had told him sounded reasonable so far. Anahita got out, lit a cigarette, and gazed at him intently with her dark eyes. She looked disappointed.

She blew smoke over her shoulder. A small plane passed overhead.

He took note of it, then turned to her and asked, "Do you have another idea?"

She leaned her head back, exhaled smoke into the sky, then shook her head. "I don't know."

"Then you and Danush should go."

She looked at her colleague still sitting in the car and said, "We're both very angry about this, because you're here. It's a big opportunity."

"Maybe we will never have another chance," Danush added.

"I feel the same," Crocker said. "Do you know where Alizadeh and Suleimani live?"

"We do," Anahita answered, "but the streets are heavily guarded."

"What about their office?"

"The headquarters?" Danush asked. "No, that's impossible."

"Lots of things were impossible before someone did them," Crocker said, gazing up at the sky, very aware that the window of time in which they had to launch an op was closing.

As she smoked her cigarette Anahita explained that John Smith had asked the same question about attacking Quds Force headquarters a week ago, and as a result, Ramin had done a study of the security of the building and its accessibility from adjoining structures. There was a bank to the right of it if you looked at the building from the front, and a movie theater on the left. The walls between them had been bombproofed with steel plates. The prospect of drilling or blasting through the walls in Quds Force HQ undetected were almost zero.

She explained that they had developed a source inside the movie theater, and the person had confirmed this.

"What about the roof?" Crocker asked.

"What roof?"

"The roof of Quds Force headquarters."

Danush: "You would need a helicopter to get there, and the guards would see and hear it."

"There's a guard station up there, too," Anahita added. "It's manned day and night. But there's an old passageway between the buildings that was blocked up when the theater was renovated three years ago."

"What kind of passageway?" Crocker asked.

"A doorway, I think. Some kind of emergency exit on the third floor that's blocked."

"Blocked, in what way?"

Danush shrugged. "With steel plates, I think."

Crocker was in no mood to accept defeat. "You said you knew someone who worked in the movie theater. Can he get us inside?"

"When?" Anahita asked.

"Tonight."

She grinned, covered her mouth with her hand, then conferred with Danush in Farsi.

Akil, who stood behind Crocker, followed their discussion.

"What do you think?" Crocker asked.

"We have to arrange some things first," Anahita said, "but we can try."

CHAPTER TWENTY-TWO

Some people never go crazy. What truly horrible lives they must lead.

                              —Charles Bukowski

APPROXIMATELY TWO hours later, the two Iranians returned in the same car. The engine continued running as Anahita stepped out and red dust swirled in front of the headlights.

"What happens now?" Crocker asked, shielding his eyes with his hand.

Her figure cast a huge black shadow over the plant. "Danush is going to take you to a place five minutes from here. When you get there, our friend will transport you in a truck."

"Let me make sure I understand. You're saying your friend is going to drive us to the movie theater?" Crocker asked.

The veins on her forehead shone in the car's lights. "It's extremely dangerous," she replied, "but he's going to try."

"Good. Thanks. What's this man's name?"

"You can call him Rahman."

"You know him and think you can trust him?"

She nodded and retied the scarf around her head. "Yes."

"Are you coming?" Crocker asked her.

"No, I'll wait here and worry. Maybe I should pray."

"Pray, but don't worry," Crocker replied. "This is what we do."

Akil sat in the passenger seat next to Danush. Crocker, Ritchie, and Mancini tried to look inconspicuous in back. The car rumbled past the steel plant and turned onto a paved four-lane road with little traffic. The gas flares from oil wells danced against the night sky ahead.

In an attempt to break the tension, Ritchie asked Danush if he'd ever been to the United States.

"No, but I would like to some day." His English seemed to improve the more he spoke.

"If you go, what's the first place you want to visit?"

"Miami," Akil suggested. "I'd recommend Miami. South Beach, hot chicks, great clubs."

"No, the Big Apple. New York City."

"Why?" Ritchie asked.

"To see all the millions of people from all over the world living together in tall, tall buildings, riding in subways underground. And I want to go to Madison Square Garden to see the Knicks. They're my favorite basketball team. I watch them on live streaming on my computer."

Danush turned the Toyota onto a dirt road and wound past a hill to a place that smelled like rotten eggs. Crocker saw three trucks parked at odd angles fifty feet ahead. Danush stopped, shut off the engine, and got out.

"Where are we now?" Crocker asked.

"This is a garbage dump. I have to talk to Rahman."

"Is it okay if Akil goes with you?"

Danush considered for a moment and nodded. Akil left his submachine gun on the floor in front.

Crocker watched them disappear behind the trucks. Fifteen long minutes stretched by, according to his watch.

"Wasn't Rahman the name of that blind cleric who helped plan the first World Trade Center attack?" Ritchie asked.

"Sheikh Omar Abdel-Rahman," Mancini answered. "He was an Egyptian cleric who ended up preaching at some mosque in Brooklyn. In his sermons he told fellow Muslims it was okay to rob banks and kill Jews. He said Americans were descendants of apes and pigs who had been feeding off the scraps from the tables of Zionists."

"I had a feeling you'd know that," Ritchie said. "Where's that blind camel-fucker now?"

"Living in Ahvaz, Iran," Mancini answered.

"Very funny."

Mancini: "Last I heard he was serving a life sentence for conspiracy at some federal pen in the U.S."

"Nice."

Crocker saw the dark outline of a man climb into one of the trucks. The engine started. Then he noticed Akil waving from the back. When the headlights came on he saw that it was a Scania garbage truck for industrial bins, with a front loader arm and hydraulic lift that rested on top of the cab.

Crocker turned to Ritchie and said, "Go see what Akil wants."

Ritchie ran back two minutes later. The pupils of his dark eyes were drawn tight. "The truck is going to take us. Bring the gear!" he shouted through the window.

Rahman was a short, squat, thick-armed man with thick black hair, a mustache and goatee. He looked like a wrestler, and wiped sweat and dust off his face with a blue bandana as he conversed with Akil.

Akil: "He wants us to ride in the back, and he wants to cover us with garbage."

"Garbage?"

"To hide us," Akil explained.

"Tell him to make sure it's dry," Ritchie commented. "I don't want any liquids or toxic chemicals dripping on me and burning into my skin."

"Since when did you grow a pussy and become a Kardashian?" Akil asked.

"What the fuck does that mean?"

"Guys. Guys," Crocker said, cutting them off and aware that they were all getting revved up. "Okay, Rahman's driving us to the theater. Does he think he can get past the guards on the street?"

Akil nodded. "He believes so. Yeah."

"Then he's the man. Load in!"

One after the other, the SEALs climbed up the tall sides into the hopper and hid between the hydraulically powered moving metal wall and the rear panel of the truck. Rahman and another man covered them with stacks of cardboard boxes.

When Rahman said something in Farsi, Akil laughed.

"What's funny?" Crocker asked.

"He told me a joke. He asked me, What do you call a Persian woman who knows where her husband is all the time?"

"What?"

"A widow."

"Fuck, that's bad."

"Iranians aren't known for their sense of humor."

"Let's hope this isn't his idea of a sick joke," Ritchie said.

There was nothing in the hopper to hold on to, so each time the truck hit a bump, they flew into the air, and each time it turned, they rolled into one another. The experience reminded Crocker of a ride at an amusement park, minus the sodas and cotton candy. Half an hour of jostling and bouncing later, the truck stopped and Ritchie threw up.

"Hold your breath," Crocker whispered when he heard someone climb the metal steps, then poke into the boxes overhead. Tense seconds passed with fingers on triggers and safeties open. Any moment Crocker was expecting something sharp to slice into him.

The four SEALs exhaled together as the footsteps descended. Ritchie stunk to high heaven.

The truck lurched forward, turned right twice, then started backing up. It stopped abruptly. Ten minutes passed before someone slapped the side of the hopper twice. Akil climbed out to look. He slapped the side three more times, and Crocker and the other two SEALs pushed off the boxes and got out.

Each man took some welcome breaths of fresh air as they squeezed past green dumpsters and entered the dark rear of the theater. Crocker, Mancini, and Ritchie climbed up to the third-floor landing where they waited for Akil and Rahman.

When Rahman arrived, he opened a metal door with a key on his belt and led them through a dark lobby that smelled of butter and popcorn. They followed him into a dark movie theater. Using a flashlight he borrowed from Akil, Rahman found the place on the wall where the connecting door to the neighboring building had once been.

Akil turned to Ritchie and whispered, "That's it."

Ritchie felt along the wall, tapped on it, and put his ear up to it. He whispered, "No way I can blast through that without causing a big commotion."

"How big?" Crocker whispered back.

"Real big," Ritchie answered. "Anahita told us the whole wall had been reinforced with metal. I think there's metal plates behind here, too."

Akil carried a rough sketch of Quds Force HQ that Danush had given him, and he now unfolded it. He said, "Our main targets are on the fourth floor," referring to Alizadeh and Suleimani.

"This isn't going to work," Crocker said.

Ritchie: "What do you mean, boss?"

"Not this way, it isn't."

"But—"

"Quiet," Crocker said, as anxious looks were exchanged. Turning to Akil, he said, "Ask Rahman to show us to the roof."

Akil translated. A game-looking Rahman nodded. They climbed quickly behind him, holding their weapons and seventy-five-pound packs on their backs.

Breathing hard in the tight space, Akil said, "Rahman is going to turn off the building's alarm system, so if we want to hide on the roof, we should do it now."

"Why?"

"Because he's got about thirty seconds to re-engage it."

Crocker asked, "How long will it take him to get to it?"

"A few seconds."

"Tell him to go now."

Rahman waved his arm and muttered something. Akil translated: "First, he wants to know how we're going to get out."

"Tell him we'll manage. And thanks."

Rahman grunted a sound of disapproval.

"What'd he say?"

"He says he'll drive one of his trucks to the back of the theater in the morning."

Crocker: "Tell him that's not necessary."

Rahman grabbed Crocker's wrist and pointed to his watch.

Akil: "He wants to know what time."

"Tell him ten fifteen."

Mancini whispered to Crocker. "Chief, I need Akil to record something for me first."

"Make it quick."

The two SEALs went off into a corner while Crocker removed his pack, knelt, then gave Rahman the signal to go. The second he left, Crocker started to count the seconds in his head. At sixteen he pushed through the door and did a quick recon of the roof, which was flat and covered with thick black tar. To the right of the door sat a seven-foot-high metal cooling unit painted white.

Crocker got on his belly and crawled ten feet from the back of the unit to the edge of the building. He guesstimated a four-foot gap and a six-foot fall-off between the roof of the movie theater and that of Quds Force headquarters. Sticking out from the HQ roof near the front of that building was a rectangular cement structure that looked as if it housed a stairway, cooling unit, and guardhouse. Two soldiers with automatic weapons stood outside it.

His recon completed, Crocker turned, crawled back quickly, and waved the men through the door. They made it just in time.

The SEALs sat with their backs against the cooling unit and waited. As the sun started to light up the sky, Crocker heard a man from a nearby mosque call out the morning prayer known as Fajr over a microphone. His high, pleading voice echoed through the streets.

"What's he saying?" Ritchie asked in a low voice.

"God hears those who call upon him. Our Lord, praise be to You," Akil answered. "Glory be to my Lord, the Most High."

Richie nodded. "I'm cool with that. It's only when Allah starts telling them they've got to kill other people that I have a problem."

Akil: "Allah never tells us that."

"Why?" Ritchie asked. "Because he doesn't exist, or people deliberately misinterpret what he's saying?"

"Quiet!" Crocker whispered.

A warm breeze blew in a cover of low gray clouds. A cool light rain started to fall.

"How much longer are we gonna wait?" Ritchie asked, wiping the precipitation off his forehead.

"Yeah, boss, what's the plan?" Akil echoed.

Crocker looked at his watch: 0732. "I figure by 1000 hours

whoever is coming to work today will be in the building," he whispered. "That's when we're going to launch. Akil, you and I will go first. We'll take out the guards. Mancini, you and Ritchie take the stairway and head down one flight to four. Look for Alizadeh and Suleimani. They're our primary targets."

"Then what?"

"We grab whatever hard drives, thumb drives, or CDs we can find and fight our way back to the stairway."

"Then?"

"Then...we get the fuck out of Dodge."

"Everybody's gonna need to wear earplugs and a gas mask when we get inside," Mancini said.

"Why?"

"I got something planned."

The whole scenario seemed damn unlikely as Crocker articulated it and played it back in his head.

Maybe it would have been better to wait for another opportunity to hit them at the arena.

It was too late to second-guess himself, so he stopped, looked up at the sky, and let the little drops of water pelt his face, which felt like some sort of cleansing.

He'd been challenging himself since he was a teenager, doing crazy stunts on motorcycles and trying to outrun the police. He'd broken practically every bone in his body during one scrap or another but had always managed to escape.

Crocker said a silent prayer asking God to look after Holly, Jenny, his father, sister, and other relatives and friends and keep them safe. "If you find it in your heart to deliver me from this, too," he added, "I promise to always be your faithful servant, never back away from danger, and do what I believe is right."

At 0955, he screwed the silencers on the ends of both of his weapons, then saw a flash of light illuminate the sky. Thirteen seconds later thunder rumbled overhead, and he slapped Akil on the shoulder and pointed to Quds Force headquarters.

Crocker went first, on his belly, until he got within four feet of the edge. From that angle he could see three Iranian soldiers with their backs toward them and automatic weapons slung over their shoulders. They stood under the front lip of the guardhouse, smoking cigarettes and looking down at the street.

Lightning flashed again, and just as his uncle had taught him to do when he was six years old, he counted the seconds on his watch until the thunder came. Ten seconds. It was moving closer.

"Next time there's lightning, I'm gonna jump," Crocker whispered into Akil's ear. "If the soldiers don't notice me, give me a couple of seconds to start around the other side of that structure, then start taking them out."

Akil nodded.

With the next flash, Crocker got his feet under him, cradled his weapon across his chest, ran to the lip of the roof, and jumped. He hit the Quds Force HQ roof, flexed his knees, slid on the gravel, and somersaulted over his right shoulder as lightning cracked overhead. Springing back up onto his toes, he knelt behind the base of a satellite dish on his left.

When no shouting or gunfire ensued, he continued to the back of the sand-colored cement structure. As he reached the back left corner, he heard the *phewt-phewt-phewt* of suppressed automatic fire.

Crocker spun and continued to the front corner, knelt, aimed, and fired. A stream of nine-millimeter bullets cut down an Iranian standing with his back to him. Another bent over his wounded compatriot beyond the opposite corner. Crocker squeezed the trigger and took him down, too.

Then he hurried to the wounded soldier, who was holding his chest. The man started to shout a warning that was cut off by the two bullets Crocker pumped into his head.

Seeing another flash of lightning, he entered the structure and located the door that led to a metal stairway. Akil limped up behind him holding his ankle and wearing a gas mask.

Crocker pointed to the steps. Akil slapped his arm and pointed to his ears.

Crocker had forgotten his earplugs and mask. He quickly fished them out of his pack, along with another thirty-round magazine for the Kashtan that he stuck in the back pocket of his pants. Ritchie and Mancini ran up behind him with masks in place and guns ready, pushed past, and entered the dark stairway.

Their footsteps echoed off the metal steps down to the fourth floor. At the landing Crocker squeezed past them and entered a hallway with Akil at his elbow. About fifteen yards away he saw an older man in dark pants and a white shirt who was holding a brown folder. Mancini rolled a grenade across the carpeted floor that exploded and obscured everything with thick purple smoke. They were in.

Crocker felt his way along the wall in the direction of the office in the far corner—the one that, according to the diagram, belonged to General Suleimani. Another grenade went off. Even with the mask in place, he caught a whiff of a sickening smell, then passed a kitchen of some sort where he saw a woman doubled over, puking against the wall.

A siren blasted so loud it literally stopped him in his tracks and hurt his chest. He heard what he thought was Akil's voice announcing in Farsi that there was an emergency that required everyone to evacuate the building immediately.

Someone stumbled into Crocker, who bashed him in the face with the butt of his weapon as the siren produced by a black fourteen-by-fourteen-inch device Mancini had brought continued to screech in ungodly 150-decibel short blasts.

Crocker continued toward the target office and felt his skin burning, thanks to another device Mancini had deployed— a compact NLW microwave emitter that penetrated clothing and caused water molecules to vibrate at high speed under human skin.

Crocker took a more old-fashioned approach, kicking in the door to Suleimani's office and firing at the two men hiding behind the big wooden desk. Their bodies flew back. Blood splattered against the window and the wall and started to seep into the sepia-colored carpet.

Crocker rushed forward to see whether he could identify Suleimani when something hit the back of his head. Since he wasn't wearing a helmet, he staggered for a second, then wheeled and released a stream of bullets that tore apart a bald man's neck and chest and sent the metal lamp he was holding flipping in the air and crashing to the floor.

Crocker felt a lump on the back of his head and a trickle

of blood. Stepping over the writhing body, he hurried down another hallway to the front of the building. Gunshots ricocheted and echoed. He practically smashed into Ritchie, who was running the other way. Ritchie said through his mask, "The floor has been neutralized. We're grabbing shit and heading for the stairway."

"You find Alizadeh?"

"We killed everyone we could find. It's hard as hell to see."

"Go ahead! Don't wait for me."

He entered the square office that faced the avenue below, saw a big photo of Ayatollah Khomeini on one wall, a large blue-and-white Army of the Guardians of the Islamic Revolution flag on the other. On the desk sat a framed photo of a girl kneeling beside a German shepherd that looked like Brando's little brother. Behind him stood tall shelves filled with books in Farsi.

The edge of one of the stacks of shelves stood out farther than the others. He pushed on it, and it clicked into place. Looking for a button or lever, he found one under a nearby shelf. He pulled it and the stack sprung open. Inside the wall was a little dark room, at the end of which he found a circular stairway filled with smoke.

Crocker took a deep breath through the mask and climbed down one flight to another dark space. Here the stairway ended. Sweating profusely, he felt along the wall, found a door, and pushed it open a crack. A helmeted man stood with his back to it. Another uniformed man was talking excitedly. A third man out of view was saying something, too.

Crocker reached into the side pocket of his backpack, grabbed a grenade, pulled the pin, counted five seconds, then opened the door, rolled it forward, and quickly closed the door. The explosion shook the walls and hurt his head.

Readying the Kashtan, he plowed through the doorway into the smoke-filled, red-misted room, where men were moaning and screaming for help. He saw one figure on the floor holding his mangled leg. A chunk of plaster from the ceiling fell on Crocker, and he slipped and fell, hitting his chin and ripping off the mask.

Part of the ceiling crashed onto a metal table, and someone opened fire. Gas burning his eyes, Crocker rolled left past the legs of a chair and under the table. Bullets ricocheted throughout the room. Seeing a man's booted foot, he grabbed hold of it and pulled.

The man hit the floor, and Crocker scrambled clear of the table with his Chinese handgun ready, smoke and dust obscuring his view. He could see enough to tell this was a conference room, with a rectangular table in the middle, charts and maps, and speckles of fresh blood on the walls.

He fired two bullets in the head of the man he'd pulled down. On the floor he saw two other bodies. None of the dead men looked familiar.

Hearing people shouting in the hall, he dusted debris off his head and exited the room. Approximately twenty feet away he saw the backs of two soldiers who were running behind a shorter man of the same approximate shape as Alizadeh. He tore after them, steadied the TU-90, and fired. One of the soldiers spun and slid into the wall, leaving a wide ribbon of red. The other returned fire with an automatic weapon.

Crocker dove into an open doorway, waited several seconds, then poked his head out. The second soldier and the man who was with him turned right at the end of the hallway and out of sight. He'd lost the Kashtan somewhere, so he took the automatic weapon dropped by the soldier against the wall. It was an Iranian variant of a M5, called an MPT-9 Tondar—short, with a pistol grip and long curved magazine that Crocker hoped was mostly full. He ran to the end of the hall and hung a right.

He wanted Alizadeh so bad he could almost taste it. But this hallway turned out to be empty, except for discarded papers and shoes. He realized he was headed toward the back of the building. Two-thirds of the way, he saw gray smoke drifting out a doorway, then spotted a trail of fresh blood leading to a stairway.

The angry voices of men shouting in Farsi echoed from below. Out of breath and eyes watering, he hurried down. When he reached the landing and turned left, he saw another flight of steps, and past them Alizadeh and a soldier resting in the corner next to the door to floor two. Alizadeh's foot was bleeding. The soldier was bent over him. Looking up and seeing Crocker, he reached for the weapon slung across his chest.

Crocker launched himself, firing the MPT-9 at the same time. Bullets tore into the soldier's torso, but still he managed to squeeze off a few shots. One struck Crocker in the right forearm, causing him to land awkwardly on the second step from the second-floor landing, twist his right ankle, and crash into the soldier, whose body helped break his fall.

As he struggled to get his bearings, he felt something slice into the skin on his right shoulder. His eyes coming into focus, he saw the triumphant look on Alizadeh's face, eyes glowing with hatred and the shining silver Swiss military watch on his wrist—the same one he'd seen in the underground prison in Barinas.

"Crocker?" the Iranian spat out as he pulled the knife out of Crocker's shoulder and got ready to thrust the blood-covered blade into his heart.

"Yeah. Fuck you," Crocker hissed, twisting his body to the right and pounding Alizadeh in the neck with his left elbow. He spun back and smacked the stunned Iranian in the arm hard enough to dislodge the knife, which hit the metal door with a clang.

Crocker heard men shouting from below. Their footsteps grew closer.

Alizadeh groaned and reached for the knife with short hairy fingers. Crocker grabbed the thick black-and-silver hair at the back of his head and, despite the intense pain in his forearm, smashed the Iranian's face into the wall, shattering his nose and sending blood spraying against the wall and door.

The footsteps came closer. Crocker wanted to see his rival's bloody face one last time. He spun him around, trapped Alizadeh's head between his knees, and growled, "This is for all the other people you've hurt, you son of a bitch!" Then he pulled Alizadeh's head forward and twisted it sharply until his spine cracked and the hatred drained out of his eyes.

On impulse, he took Alizadeh's watch and stuffed it in his pocket as the soldiers drew closer. He saw the tips of their boots on the landing below, and for a second he thought his time was up.

But then a stubborn burst of energy lifted him to his feet and helped him limp out the door to the second floor. His body moved on automatic to the back corner office, where he kicked out the window glass, jumped down onto the hood of a parked car, and rolled off.

Crocker pulled himself to his knees and took a deep breath as the gentle raindrops cooled his face. Remembering Rahman's promise, he limped around the back of the movie theater, where the green garbage truck was just pulling out. Rahman at the wheel saw him and stopped long enough for Crocker to grab hold of the ladder on the side of the hopper with his left hand. That's when the exhaustion and the loss of blood overcame him. The last thing he remembered was hitting the mess of papers and trash inside and seeing Ritchie's surprised face.

CHAPTER TWENTY-THREE

Don't let yesterday use up too much of today.
— Will Rogers

HE WAS sitting with his back against a metal shipping container, listening to Mancini explain how he had paid Rahman a thousand dollars for the old van they had driven from the garbage dump to the scrap metal yard where they were now, and how it was the sweetest thousand he had ever spent.

Someone had applied a blowout patch to Crocker's forearm, bandaged the wound near his shoulder, wrapped his ankle, and given him some painkillers. His body felt numb. The sky above his head was deep black. A steady, cool rain fell.

He watched Akil fifty feet away using gasoline and a lighter to set a pile of wooden loading pallets on fire. He was about to scream at him to stop when he heard a roar in the sky.

Thunder? No. A Blackhawk helicopter with its lights out.

Ritchie and another man helped him in the door. And as the bird lifted off, he felt his heart ease in his chest.

"We're going home," Akil said.

Ritchie: "We did it, man. We did it."

Mancini: "Fuck, yeah. Now what's for dinner?"

By the time the SEALs landed at Naval Air Station Oceana in Virginia Beach twenty-three hours later, Crocker was running a 102-degree fever. He was transported to the Portsmouth Naval Hospital, where doctors cleaned the infected wound near his shoulder and shot him up with painkillers and antibiotics.

When he woke the next morning, the first things he saw, like a beautiful dream, were the faces of Holly and Jenny. He blinked and looked again to make sure he wasn't imagining them, then realized the constriction he felt from the tubes in his arms and the machines he was hooked up to was real. So were the shouts of surprise from Jenny, the kisses, the joy on their faces, and the relief in Holly's eyes.

Crocker hugged and kissed them back, and quietly thanked God. Then he wiped the tears from his eyes and said, "I want both of you to know that everything I've been through, every injury I've sustained at Alizadeh's expense, every worry I've experienced, every doubt, pain, sacrifice, and sleepless night feels worth it right now, being here with you and seeing your faces."

Nine days later, a more somber, healthier Crocker sat in the backseat of the silver sedan, watching the sights along Wisconsin Avenue pass by. At Chevy Chase Circle, they left the District of Columbia and entered Maryland. He remembered that he had once dated a Swiss au pair who worked near here and lived in a room over a garage. She had frizzy hair and a beautiful mouth, and had dumped him for a law school student from Georgetown U.

The driver eased the car up in front of a redbrick house and stopped.

"Here we are, sir."

Crocker climbed out, adjusted the jacket of his blue dress uniform around the bandages on his forearm, shoulder, and chest, and walked slowly to the front door, trying not to limp. An older woman with a handsome face and curly white hair answered the bell.

"Chief Crocker?" she asked.

"Yes, ma'am."

"Welcome," she said. "Please come in."

She and a tall older man thanked Crocker profusely, then she showed him to the basement and knocked on a brown door. Half a minute later a tall boy with a mop of thick brown hair and sad brown eyes opened it.

The boy's grandmother said, "Alex, this is Chief Crocker. He's the Navy SEAL who hunted down the man who killed your parents."

Alex nodded slightly, then lowered his eyes.

As Crocker reached into his pocket, Alex's grandmother whispered in his ear, "That's the biggest response I've seen from him in weeks. He hasn't spoken a word since the incident."

Crocker held out the silver Swiss military watch and said, "Alex, this watch belonged to the man who took your mother's and father's lives. I brought it back from Iran with me, and I want you to have it."

As he slipped it on the boy's wrist, the boy looked up.

"Did you get him?" Alex asked in a voice that was barely audible.

His grandmother gasped and squeezed Crocker's bad arm, reminding him once again of the raid in Ahvaz.

"What did you say?" Crocker asked, leaning closer to Alex.

"Did you get him?" Alex asked, louder this time.

"Yes. He's dead."

Alex's lips trembled as he looked up at Crocker and said, "Thank you."

"You're welcome," responded Crocker.

"Did you know them?" Alex asked, looking at the watch, then at his grandmother who had a hand over her mouth and was sobbing.

"You mean your parents?"

Alex nodded.

"I met your father in Afghanistan. We went running together one night. I liked him a lot."

Alex smiled as tears spilled from his eyes.

"Alex, both your mom and your dad were brave Americans. They weren't soldiers like me, but in a way they were braver, because they were unarmed civilians who served their country overseas even though they understood the dangers."

The boy swallowed hard and nodded. "I know."

"Be proud of them always."

The boy wrapped his arms around Crocker and said, "I will."

ACKNOWLEDGMENTS

We'd like to thank all the highly talented professionals at Mulholland Books / Little, Brown who made this book possible, including John Parsley, Wes Miller, Ruth Tross, Pamela Brown, Theresa Giacopasi, Ben Allen, Chris Jerome, and Kapo Ng. We also want to express our appreciation to our agent, Heather Miller, and our families for their love and support: Don's wife, Dawn, and his daughter, Dawn; and Ralph's wife, Jessica, and his children, John, Michael, Francesca, and Alessandra.

ABOUT THE AUTHORS

DON MANN (CWO3, USN) has for the past thirty years been associated with the U.S. Navy SEALs as a platoon member, assault team member, boat crew leader, and advanced training officer, and more recently as program director preparing civilians to go to BUD/S (SEAL Training). Until 1998 he was on active duty with SEAL Team Six. Since then, he has deployed to the Middle East on numerous occasions in support of the war against terrorism. Many of today's active-duty SEALs on Team Six are the same guys he taught how to shoot, conduct ship and aircraft takedowns, and operate in urban, arctic, desert, river, and jungle warfare, as well as close-quarters battle and military operations in urban terrain. He has suffered two cases of high-altitude pulmonary edema, frostbite, a broken back, and multiple other broken bones in training or service. He has been captured twice during operations and lived to talk about it.

RALPH PEZZULLO is a *New York Times* bestselling author and an award-winning playwright and screenwriter. His books include *Jawbreaker* and *The Walk-In* (with CIA operative Gary Berntsen), *Plunging into Haiti* (winner of the Douglas Dillon Award for Distinguished Writing on American Diplomacy), *At the Fall of Somoza*, *Most Evil* (with Steve Hodel), *Eve Missing*, *Blood of My Blood*, and the upcoming novel *Saigon*.

You've turned the last page.

But it doesn't have to end there . . .

If you're looking for more first-class, action-packed, nail-biting suspense, join us at **Facebook.com/ MulhollandUncovered** for news, competitions, and behind-the-scenes access to Mulholland Books.

For regular updates about our books and authors as well as what's going on in the world of crime and thrillers, follow us on **Twitter@MulhollandUK**.

There are many more twists to come.

MULHOLLAND:
You never know what's coming around the curve.

HODDER